THE KEEPER

A Novel

April Nunn Coker

Book Cover Design: Beti Bup
www.thebookcoverdesigner.com
Formatted by Enterprise Book Services, LLC

The Keeper is a work of fiction. Names, characters, places, and incidents are either the product of the author's imagination or are used fictitiously. Any resemblance to actual persons, living or dead, or events is entirely incidental.

The Keeper/April Nunn Coker
Thriller – Fiction
First Printing
Manufactured in the U.S.A.

DEDICATION

To Jimmy,

my knight in shining armor.

Thank you for your love and support

through the years.

I love you forever.

"Thanks be unto God for His unspeakable gift."

2 Corinthians 9:15 KJV

To Jami —
Thanks!
Buckle up!
Enjoy Jill Coker ♥

Chapter One

JOLIE SOWELL DREW one long, last drag from her cigarette before mashing it into the ashtray of her decade-old, slightly rusted, red Ford Taurus. She looked down at her fingernails and frowned. Had they turned yellow from her having smoked for years? Or had they turned yellow from the bleach she used every day cleaning water troughs and moats?

I'll quit soon, she told herself for the millionth time. My fingernails don't look as bad as others I've seen. I would polish them, but it wouldn't last more than a day or two. Besides, smoking calms my nerves. Oh well. Who am I trying to impress, anyway? The animals don't care.

Jolie worked the night shift and was glad that as of six o'clock every evening, she would not have to deal with the multitude of visitors who daily trekked through the zoo with unruly children. From the steady stream of visitors walking toward the entrance, she decided it would be a good day for the zoo. She sighed, glad she and the other members of the night crew would only have to deal with each other and the animals.

As she slowly drove through the gate, the bright yellow coreopsis and the pink and white periwinkles provided a cheerful greeting. As she waved at the parking attendant, she spotted her parking place high above the entrance to the zoo. It was 3:30 and at 96 degrees, near the peak of the afternoon's heat. Even the trees surrounding the employee's parking lot drooped. Yellowed leaves already floated to the ground. Jolie felt sorry for them. No matter how much the grounds keepers watered them, the trees and flowers stayed thirsty.

Jolie eased her car into her assigned parking space. Before turning off the engine, she leaned forward and took a deep breath of the cold air swirling from the car's air conditioner. I do believe air conditioning must be man's greatest invention, she said to herself. She recalled last year's summer when she sweltered for almost three months before saving up enough money to have it fixed. That had been a lean summer with her working extra shifts and buying no extras whatsoever. As a zookeeper she would never make a lot of money, but the perks outweighed the wages. Who else got to bottle-feed and play with tiger cubs on the job?

The blast of heat almost took her breath away as she climbed out of her still dependable Ford Taurus. It had been her parents' gift to her when she graduated from high school almost three years ago. It wasn't new then, but it was the newest thing she had ever had or would for a while, so she had taken very good care of it, except for smoking in it. Her parents hated that she had smelled up their old car with what they called her "nasty habit" but at least the car was hers, registered in her own name. It had served her well her one year of college and now hauled her baby girl to daycare and then herself to work every day with barely any problems, even though the odometer had turned over 150,000 miles several months ago now. She prayed often that it would just keep on running, especially if she happened to hear an unusual noise. She couldn't afford to have it fixed on her salary, much less with daycare taken out of it.

It was a long walk to the keepers' lounge and her reddish-blonde curly hair frizzed as it stuck to her neck, but that walk was practically the only exercise Jolie got, except for walking to and from exhibit areas feeding and cleaning, and then chasing her toddler during the day before work. Jolie never had to worry about her weight anyway. She was still the same size she had been in college, if not smaller. Being a single parent of a toddler allowed little time for eating, and she had never gained the weight she lost from The Divorce. From directly behind her she heard someone call her name.

"Hey, Jolie, hold up! What's the big hurry to start hauling poop?" It was Kaycie Harlan, one of the other night shift keepers and the only one who was around Jolie's age. The only big difference between them was that Kaycie already had three children and had never gone to college. What bothered Jolie sometimes was that Kaycie made the same salary she did. She supposed college hours didn't matter when all they did was shovel poop, and one pair of hands was as good as another, but it still rankled a bit.

"Kaycie!" Jolie scolded, giggling. "Visitors will hear you!"

"I don't care!" Kaycie was huffing and puffing when she caught up with Jolie.

"Not a good way to impress the boss," Jolie remarked, glancing around to see if Jay was anywhere in sight. Evaluation reviews were coming up soon, and she knew that Kaycie wanted to move up to Keeper III. But offending visitors would not be a good way to do that. Actually, Jolie felt she had a better chance of moving up than Kaycie did, because Kaycie seemed to have a difficult time realizing the possible impact of her words before blurting them out, which often offended people, including her boss.

"Eh, he's not anywhere around. Got any plans for your days off?"

"Just the usual."

Thank goodness today was the last day of Jolie's work week. It had been a long, hot one, and she was looking forward to a couple of days off to enjoy her little girl and get some things done around the house. At the zoo nobody got a full weekend off, and only the supervisors and curators got Friday and Saturday or Sunday and Monday off, so she had to be content with Wednesday and Thursday. At least the stores weren't crowded, and her parents got a break during the week from keeping Ellie.

"You never do anything fun, do you? Not that you can on a Wednesday or Thursday. Tim and I are going to the club Saturday night after I get off work, if you want to go," Kaycie suggested.

"You know I can't do that with Ellie home."

"I thought Ellie stayed all night with your mom and dad on Saturdays and Sundays so you could work."

She had a point. She usually didn't pick Ellie up until at least 11:00 on Sunday mornings anyway. She actually could go out on Saturday night without affecting Ellie or her parents. But it had been a long time since she had gone out. Or even wanted to, after Sean. Still, it had been almost a year. Plenty of time to get over him and get on with her life. Maybe a night out would be good for her.

"She does, but I would hate to be a third wheel on your date."

"Not to worry, girlfriend. Tim has a really sweet and good-looking friend who just went through a bad divorce and he needs a distraction. You'll be perfect!"

"Oh, great," Jolie muttered. "Two lonely old broken hearts. Sounds like fun."

"You'll like him, I promise. Trust me, you'll see." Kaycie threw a slender arm around Jolie's slim shoulders and squeezed. Kaycie was a good head taller than Jolie, but they were equally as thin.

In the keeper's lounge they stuffed their purses and lunch bags into their lockers and clocked in. At least the lounge was cool. It would give Jolie something to look forward to while she sweated through her duties. As she quickly tied her unruly tresses into a pony tail, she wondered as she did every summer why she remained in Texas when there were 49 other states she could live in. But moving would cost money she couldn't spare, and she depended too much on her parents to help with Ellie. Summers were terribly hot but easily forgotten when the other seasons were so mild and comfortable. Still, autumn seemed pretty far off right now.

Supervisor Jay Latimer and coworker Lucas Slade soon joined them. Jay was a strong man, just a little past his prime, in his mid-forties. After working his way up in the past fifteen years from Keeper I to Keeper III, and then becoming supervisor of the second shift, he knew the zoo like the back of his hand. He enjoyed working with the animals, but keeping good employees was always a challenge. As long as he had been on the second shift he had probably seen 50 employees come and go. It seemed he spent the majority of his time training workers, and when he finally got a really good one, they would move on to another position in the zoo or leave the zoo altogether. He couldn't blame them because night shifts were difficult, especially for young people who wanted social lives or had families. He hated losing good workers. They were getting harder and harder to come by.

His nose wrinkled involuntarily as he caught a whiff of the lingering cigarette smoke that had accompanied Jolie inside the building. He couldn't stand cigarettes and didn't understand the attraction they held for young people. But as long as they didn't smoke while on duty, he would have to tolerate the smell of smoke on them. After Jay hooked his radio on his belt, pocketed his zoo-issued cell phone, and greeted his workers, he gave them their assignments for the first half of the shift.

As usual, everyone paired up to drop off animal diets and run animals into their holding areas for the night. When Kaycie and Jolie worked together, Jay nearly always let them pair up while he worked with Lucas or alone. Unlike most supervisors, he did exactly the same work he expected them to do, and they respected him for it. Kaycie and Jolie headed to the big cats area, while Jay and Lucas drove off in a mule truck to run in the hoof stock.

As Jay drove off with Lucas he heard the rumble of thunder in the distance. Great, he thought. Thunder always made the deer and other hoof stock nervous, sometimes making getting them into the barns difficult.

"Did you hear that?" Lucas was on top of things, as usual. He was a newlywed, fresh out of college, eager for a zoo career, but Jay knew that he had his sights on a leadership position in a larger, more well-known zoo. He had mentioned visiting the San Diego Zoo, the National Zoo, and the Denver Zoo, his eyes lighting up and taking on a certain wistfulness. Jay realized that Lucas would move on as soon as the opportunity presented itself. His wife was a schoolteacher, so she could find a job anywhere. Too bad, because he was a good worker, although since she was about to deliver their first child, they might want to stay a while. "Maybe if we divide up, we can get them in faster."

"Good idea," Jay agreed. He pulled the mule to a stop and they both hopped out, heading in opposite directions. I hope this is easy, he thought, raking a hand through his graying sandy hair and then mopping his brow. His knit polo-style zoo shirt was already soaked with sweat from the humidity. Rain wouldn't bother him at all, but he didn't like the prospect of getting struck by lightning, risking his life trying to get a dumb animal to go into its own shelter. He had lectured his crew about the necessity of getting animals inside during bad weather, but avoiding injury while doing so. The last thing Timber City Zoo needed was a lawsuit by a bereaved spouse or parent.

To their surprise, most of the animals hurried into their respective stalls without detouring around trees, bushes, and ponds. Jay and Lucas were closing the door on the barn, each animal in its own stall feeding happily on his dinner, when the skies opened up. Only the deer remained in the yard, scattering almost spitefully when it was time to come in. Jay muttered a mild oath under his breath. Maybe they would come on in before he got drenched. "Wait here by the gate," he ordered Lucas as he trotted back into the yard.

Across the zoo, Jolie and Kaycie sprayed down the floors of the cat house and placed the diets in the bins before opening the doors to let the cats in. It was one of Jolie's favorite areas. She loved to talk to one of the cougars, which had been hand-raised from a cub. She never went inside the cage with Zoe, but the cat would rub against the bars, allowing keepers to place a flattened palm against the bars to feel her coarse fur. Moments like these made the poop-scooping worth it.

But something was wrong with Zoe this evening. She was not interested in her food. She didn't even come over to rub her side against the bars so that Jolie and Kaycie could pet her. She lagged behind the

7

other two cougars, then came in to her stall slowly and lay down on the concrete floor, her tail twitching. Jolie noticed her eyelids even drooped. It had to be the heat and humidity. It made everyone sluggish.

"Come here, Zoe! What's the matter, baby? Aren't you hungry?" She turned to Kaycie, who was pulling the doors to the exhibit back down with their rope and pulley. "I guess she must have grabbed someone's turkey leg again."

"I don't see how that is possible anymore." Kaycie tested the doors to make sure they were secure. "Not since they replaced the wire with glass and planted those thorny bushes in front of the exhibit."

"Oh yeah, I forgot about that." Several years ago a visitor who had been teasing the cat with a turkey leg was surprised when Zoe snatched it from their hands deftly and lightning fast through the thinly spaced piano wire that surrounded their exhibit. It was a wonder the visitor hadn't lost his hand along with the turkey leg. "I wonder why she isn't hungry then?"

"Maybe she isn't feeling well today. Or maybe it's just too hot."

"Maybe." Jolie heard the same rumble of thunder that had alerted Jay. Just as she and Kaycie exited the cat house to head to the monkey exhibit, the clouds erupted. By the time they entered the holding area, they were soaked to the skin. The rain was so loud they could barely hear themselves speak, but the lightning bolts were deafening.

The first crashing bolt drew a scream from Jolie, who still hadn't gotten over her childhood fear of thunderstorms. She had possessed a deathly fear of being struck by lightning as long as she could remember, which made being an outdoor zookeeper scary sometimes. In spite of the earsplitting thunderbolt and torrential rain, Jolie could sense Kaycie laughing at her. Even as she shivered her face grew hot with embarrassment. This one would be hard to live down.

"You okay?" Kaycie laughed. Now it was Jolie's turn to giggle. Kaycie's fine almost black hair plastered itself to her head; her knit uniform shirt clung to her. Her porcelain skin looked even whiter in the dripping water. "What are you laughing at?" Kaycie's expression darkened.

Jolie grabbed some paper towels from a nearby dispenser and handed some to Kaycie. She didn't want to know what the rain had done to her. Neither one of them wore makeup to work because it just slipped off in the sweat and humidity anyway, but at least their hair was usually combed and pulled back into a ponytail or hair band. Jolie's hair had a tendency to grow kinky in the humidity, but the rain would make it resemble a circus clown's. She sighed in resignation. Nothing she could do about it now.

"Okay, okay," Kaycie muttered from behind the paper towels on her face. "Well, at least we're not going out after work." She laughed as she threw the paper towels in the trash. "The monkeys don't care how we look!"

Luckily, all of the zoo's twelve squirrel monkeys had scampered indoors well before the deluge. They eagerly grabbed the chunks of fruit that Kaycie and Jolie had dumped into their feeding bowls, but one cowered in the corner, shivering and wide-eyed, visibly jumping at every thunderbolt. He ignored the food, staring at the girls as if wanting to be rescued.

Jolie pointed to him. "Look at that little guy. He's scared to death. Come on, sweetie, come and get your dinner." She beckoned from the other side of the cage bars. The tiny little monkey's face had furrowed in distress but he stopped shaking and turned her way. Just as Jolie was positive he was about to move toward her, a lightning bolt and its ensuing thunder flashed and sounded at the same time, plunging the entire area into darkness. Jolie's heart leapt into her throat as Kaycie threw her arms around her so hard that Jolie almost fell. Squealing, the monkeys scurried into a corner where they huddled together in the pitch blackness.

"Good gravy!" Kaycie exclaimed with her usual eloquence. "That hit somewhere close."

Jolie and Kaycie glanced at each other, their faces only inches apart. Jolie's arms were pinned under Kaycie's, who relaxed a little, allowing Jolie to take a deep breath.

"Jay and Lucas," they said at the same time, their eyes wide.

Across the zoo, Lucas stuck an index finger inside his ear and jiggled it, hoping to clear the awful noise from his head. That last bolt of lightning had struck close. Too close. And it had knocked out the electricity, too. Luckily he had been inside the hoof stock barn when it hit. But where was Jay? He had been outside trying to run the deer into the barn, difficult with the threatening thunderstorm spooking them. Jay had instructed Lucas to stay in the barn and be ready to shut the gates when the deer were in, which left Jay out in the weather and Lucas safely inside.

Worried that his boss might be injured or even worse, Lucas braved the downpour and ventured out of the barn to search for Jay. It was already dark, but he could see the four deer Jay had been trying to get inside hauling whitetail toward the gates, so he ducked back inside and slammed the gates shut as they barreled into their stalls. "Now you decide to come in," Lucas shouted above the din of the rain on the tin roof of the cavernous barn.

Already soaked, Lucas unhooked the flashlight he and the others routinely carried on their belts and again left the safety of the dry barn to look for Jay. For all he knew, Jay could have been struck by lightning.

The hoof stock yard lay on about three acres of gently rolling grassy land. It was dotted with oak and sassafras trees, which made searching for animals or humans a challenge, much less in the pouring rain and encroaching darkness. Lucas called Jay's name several times but doubted that anyone could hear anything in the pelting rain. With not a dry place anywhere on his powerfully built body, he now shivered with cold even though he had been sweating in the summer heat only minutes before. He feared another close call with lightning, but since that last awful bolt he hadn't heard any more thunder. Maybe the storm was moving on.

The thought came too soon because just then the yard and skies lit up as bright as noontime. He braced for the deafening thunder, but it was a few seconds this time before it sounded, this time a bit less nerve-wracking. He scanned the yard with his flashlight, hoping for a glimpse of Jay. He thought he saw something moving in the distance a few yards away. Squinting, he could see with the dim light of the flashlight and random flashes of distant lightning that a tree had split in the middle of the yard. That accounted for the deafening crash and loss of power. The falling tree must have downed a power line. Thank goodness all the hoof stock were in. Wait. Was that something moving under the tree?

"Jay!" Lucas called again, sloshing through the saturated grass toward the downed tree.

Someone or something lay under one of the broken branches of the tree. Then he detected the faint call of his own name. It was Jay, his stocky body pinned underneath.

Tearing at the branches so he could kneel at Jay's side, Lucas surveyed his boss with his flashlight and steeled himself for the worst. He couldn't see any blood but that didn't mean that Jay had not been impaled by a branch. The water was coming down so fast that blood flow could be washing away. "Hey, boss, it's Lucas. Let me help you."

Jay's normally tanned face was pale but he was lucid. "Did the deer go in?"

Lucas smiled in spite of the possible danger Jay was in. That was his boss, always worried about everyone else above himself, including the animals.

"Yeah, they're in. Let's get you outta here." As he began to lift a thick branch which lay over Jay, his boss winced in pain.

"My leg," Jay panted.

Lucas panned the light down to Jay's legs, seeing that one of them was lying in an unusually awkward position under the tree. He carefully moved a smaller branch to get a better look. A sharp white edge poked through Jay's jeans. His left femur was broken and pushing through to the outside of his pants. He needed medical attention, pronto. Lucas remembered that he had a radio, then immediately offered up a prayer that it was still working in this weather. The rain ran down his face into his eyes, which made it difficult to see, but Jay seemed about to drown from it. Jay's eyes remained closed, his lips pursed in pain. He seemed not to notice the huge raindrops hammering his face.

Jolie's radio buzzed in the quiet darkness, causing both her and Kaycie to jump. They were still trying to get their bearings in the blackness of the squirrel monkey house. "Jolie here."

"Jolie, call 9-1-1. Jay's hurt. We're in the hoof stock yard."

Kaycie's eyes widened along with Jolie's. Jolie watched Kaycie fumble through her cargo jeans pockets for her personal cell phone. Like many zoo employees, she ignored zoo policy and carried her own phone anyway. Finding a zoo phone in this darkness, even with their flashlights, would have been difficult. Jolie wasn't even sure if there was a zoo phone in the monkey house.

Kaycie seemed to remain calm as she dialed 911 while Jolie shivered, not so much from the cooler temperatures as from fear of how badly Jay might be hurt. Someone would need to call his wife. As Jolie listened to Kaycie's instructions to the 911 dispatcher, she wondered what Jay's wife would do. She didn't hear the faint cry of a wounded animal across the zoo as it lay dying from a slit throat.

Chapter Two

MOLLY LATIMER LAY the baby down in her crib, smoothing the silky blonde wisps across the tiny forehead. Little Liza was oblivious to the storm outside. Molly breathed a prayer of gratitude for the sturdy brick home that insulated them from the lightning and booming thunder. She jumped when the lightning hit especially close and mouthed a prayer for her husband's safety. Hopefully he had taken refuge inside, but she knew that animals were sometimes stubborn and spooked easily, and Jay would unwittingly put his life on the line to get them inside during the storm. As always, she hastily put such worrisome thoughts out of her mind, having found that doing so made the nights a little easier.

A whimper brought her gaze from her sleeping infant to the doorway of the nursery, where four-year-old Laci stood, her thumb in her mouth, clutching a tattered pink baby blanket. Laci blinked and whimpered again, her blonde curls tousled from sleep.

"It's okay, sweetie." Molly scooped up her older daughter. "You can sleep with Mommy."

They had snuggled under the covers when the phone startled Molly out of her drowsy on-the-brink-of-blissful-sleep state. Laci stirred but didn't wake up. Molly shuddered with an ominous chill as she grabbed her cell phone from the nightstand.

"Hello." Speaking barely above a whisper, she hoped not to disturb Laci.

Then came the words she had dreaded hearing since Jay had begun working nights at the zoo. Her heart seemed to stop, barely allowing her to take the next breath. She slipped out of bed, mechanically pulling on the jeans she had worn all day, the ones with Liza's spit-up and residue from Laci's after-playschool popsicle. An ambulance had taken Jay to the hospital.

She had gathered her purse and shoes when she realized with a start what she was about to do. Had she lost her mind? She was about to walk out of her house and leave her two babies alone!

She dropped the purse and shoes, pulled her cell phone from her back pocket, and punched her best friend's phone number. She would have called her mother or sister or another family member, but Jay had taken this job two hundred miles away from her hometown. She had always wondered what she might do in a crisis. Now she knew. She hoped the few she called friends would come through for them.

A sleepy voice interrupted a voicemail greeting.

"Toni!" Tears threatened as soon as Molly heard her friend's voice. "You have to help me! Jay's been in an accident and I need to get to the hospital, but I need someone to watch my girls!"

Toni must have heard the desperation and panic in Molly's voice because she cut her off. "Stay there. I'm coming right over."

Molly collapsed in a chair, tears spilling down her cheeks. Then she sat up and wiped her face with her hands. She would not break down. Not yet. She had to be strong for Jay. For the girls.

In less than ten minutes, which to Molly seemed an eternity, Toni was banging on the front door. Molly leapt up and flung the door open, her purse and keys in hand. With Toni was her husband Kent. "Kent will stay with the girls while I drive you to the hospital."

A sob escaped her as Molly realized she hadn't thought about someone needing to drive her to the hospital. She couldn't drive in this state. Thank you, Lord, she breathed.

She followed Toni to her car, oblivious to the rain that pelted her face. All she could think about was Jay. Jolie hadn't said how bad his injuries were, probably because she didn't know much herself. Or was it because they were too bad to tell her over the phone? Fear shook her as Toni drove. What would he be like when she got there? Would he be conscious? Would he know her?

When they arrived at the hospital, Molly clung to Toni's arm as they made their way to the emergency room desk. A nurse led them to a curtained area at the far side of the ER and as they rounded the edge of the curtain, Molly gasped as her knees started to give way. At her side with her arm around her waist, Toni helped her stay up. Jay lay still, his face pale, tubes coming out of his nose and arm, his left leg wrapped and lying on top of the covers. His eyes were closed, his breathing slight. The only sounds were the noises of the machines monitoring his vitals and the background ER noise, but Molly was aware of nothing but Jay.

"Oh, God," she whispered. "Please let him be okay." Wrapping her fingers around his, she bent to kiss his forehead, damp and cold with rain and perspiration. Jay's familiar taste and scent overwhelmed her for a second, sending tears spilling from her eyes. She bit her lip, willing them to stop. She didn't want Jay to see her crying. He lay so still, the only movement the rise and fall of his chest, the same chest she had leaned against and rested her head upon countless times since she had known him.

A LARGE FEMALE emergency room nurse bustled past her, bumping her into Toni. All business, the nurse did not offer any information, so Toni blurted, "Can you tell us what happened? How was he injured? Is he going to be okay?" Still clutching Jay's fingers, Molly leaned weakly against Toni, thanking God for a friend who would speak when she couldn't. She wasn't sure she could trust her own voice or emotions.

"The doctor will be in soon to explain his condition. I'm just here to check his vitals."

"Wait," Molly heard herself saying as the nurse turned to leave. "I'm his wife. Can't you tell me anything?"

At that point, Lucas entered the small curtained area, joining Toni and Molly. The nurse bristled. "I can tell you that there are too many people here now for us to do our jobs. You all need to go sit in the waiting area and wait for the doctor."

This time Molly bristled. "I'm not leaving. And I want to know what happened to my husband!" Hot tears threatened.

Lucas and Toni gently tugged her away from the bed, but her gaze never left Jay. She tried to stand her ground, but Lucas was too strong and before she knew it she was outside the treatment room and in the chair area.

She turned to Lucas, choking back angry tears. "Somebody better tell me what happened!"

Lucas cleared his throat as he coaxed her into a chair. Toni sat on her opposite side, still holding her arm. "Molly, Jay's leg was broken by a tree limb during the storm."

There was more. She could tell. There had to be more he wasn't telling her. "He lost a lot of blood."

"Shouldn't they be giving him blood?" Then she remembered. Jay had the rarest of blood types, Type AB-. Did they not have blood to give him?

Lucas shook his head. "No, he didn't lose enough to need a transfusion. But they are keeping him sedated because of the bad break."

"Bad break?" Molly whispered.

"Left femur. The thigh bone. Broken smooth in half. Sticking out of the skin." Lucas exhaled and slumped, his eyes on the floor. He had done it again. He had meant to break it to her gently. Fail.

Molly paled. Troubling thoughts bubbled to the surface. Just a broken bone? Then he would be fine. But how in the world would he work? She might have to go back to work. But she wouldn't think about that now. She could not think about that now.

A diminutive middle-aged woman in blue scrubs approached them. "Which one of you is Mrs. Latimer?"

Molly sat straight up in her chair, wiping her face with the back of one hand. "I'm Mrs. Latimer."

"Hello, I am Dr. Packer." She bent and patted Molly's hand. "Your husband is resting now but I want to get him into surgery as soon as possible to reset his femur before any infection sets in." She continued as Molly took a sharp breath. "We may have to insert a pin to hold it straight. We will need you to give us permission."

If Jay needed surgery, why hadn't they already begun? She shuddered to think of the awful pain he must have suffered before being sedated. She wished she could be with him in surgery.

"You have my permission." She scribbled her name on the forms on a clipboard that appeared before her.

She was allowed to spend a moment alone with Jay before they wheeled him into the operating room. He looked so vulnerable lying on that gurney. More tears slipped down her cheeks. "I'll be here when you wake up, sweetheart," she murmured as she took his hand in hers. With the other hand she smoothed back his hair and then bent to kiss his pale lips just as the orderlies came to wheel him away. Usually strong and rugged, this man lying on the gurney didn't bear much resemblance to her beloved husband. She steeled herself before returning to Toni and Lucas. She wondered if Kent would be able to dress her girls and fix their breakfast.

Toni seemed to read her thoughts. "I'm going to call Kent and tell him that we may be here a few more hours," she said as she, Lucas, and Molly followed the gurney. One of the orderlies motioned for them to stop before Jay and his entourage disappeared behind double doors.

Molly nodded and followed Lucas and Molly to the waiting area where she sank into a comfortably upholstered chair. She barely noticed Lucas whispering something to Toni before Toni left to use her phone. Lucas sank down in the chair next to her, putting his arm around her and drawing her close. She held back tears, resting her head on his shoulder as she breathed a silent prayer for a successful surgery for Jay.

She had always harbored misgivings about Jay working nights at a zoo, but it was what he wanted. She had never believed that he would be able to find a zoo job that would pay enough to support them, but when he was offered the job of night supervisor at Timber City Zoo, he jumped at the chance even though it meant moving two hundred miles away from their hometown. With the new job came a new fear of danger that always lurked at the back of Molly's consciousness. Any time Jay was late getting home, or if he commented that another zookeeper had left a lock undone, she would worry herself sick, imagining lions, wolverines, or elephants attacking her husband. Like all zookeepers, he had to be cognizant at all times of gate locks and animal location in order to prevent mishaps, and there had to be a certain level of trust among coworkers, many of whom seemed to value animal life above human life.

Still, she was grateful that Jay had a job he loved, and that his supervisor's salary allowed her to stay home with her babies. They did have to adhere to a strict budget and live in a modest home, but they were happy together. Money could not buy everything, but she had everything she needed, and she was grateful for their little home and family. All she wanted was a healthy, happy family, but now something had happened to Jay. How would this impact their family? Would she have to return to work? She could always get a substitute teaching job at the elementary school, but how would they ever afford daycare for two children? She would not think about that now. She could not think about that now.

The sound of approaching footsteps helped to distract her from her troubling thoughts. Two young women hurried down the hallway toward them, their hair and clothing a wet, drippy mess. Lucas glanced their way but remained seated with Molly's tearful face still buried in his shirt.

"Lucas! How is Jay?" One of the girls spoke, her voice seeming loud in the quiet waiting area. It was the one with the frizzy strawberry blonde hair. Must be Jolie, Molly mused as she looked up. Red hair. Yes,

it must be Jolie. Jay always said he could spot her anywhere because of her frizzy red hair.

"Hi, I'm Kaycie. You must be Molly," the other girl said. Kaycie. Of course. The outspoken one. The one Jay was afraid was going to open her mouth at the wrong time and end up losing her job.

Molly nodded dully, then remembered her manners. "Yes, and thank you for calling me," she said. The girls were suddenly speaking at once and it was hard to focus on what they were saying. Lucas stood and motioned for them to come with him, so they followed him down the hallway a few yards, leaving Molly alone with her thoughts. Tears threatened again, and this time she didn't try to stop them. When Toni returned, she found Molly crying softly, her face resting in her hands.

"Everything's going to be okay, Molly," Toni whispered as she sank into the chair next to Molly and put her arm around her.

Molly looked up at her, her red-rimmed blue eyes shining. A tiny smile tugged at the corners of her mouth. "I don't know what is wrong with me. I know he is going to be okay. He is in good hands, and I thank God that Lucas got to him early enough. I guess I am just tired." She rested her head against Toni's shoulder. "I am so grateful that you are here with me, and that Kent is with the girls."

"Don't be silly. This is a lot to deal with, and don't you worry about me and Kent. That is what friends are for." After a moment, she asked, "Want something to drink?" Toni patted her shoulder.

Molly realized how parched she was after all the tears. "Yes, I could use a drink of water."

"I'll be right back," Toni promised as she rose from her chair, gently easing Molly over. "There has to be a water fountain around here somewhere."

Molly dried her eyes. Jay would be okay. He had to. He had two beautiful little girls waiting for him at home. Two little girls that he wanted to see grow up. Two little girls whose lives he wanted to share with her. She closed her swollen eyelids. "God, please make Jay better. We need him," she whispered.

Chapter Three

JOLIE RETURNED TO the mirror one last time before heading out the door with Ellie. She was going on a date, an actual date! She wished she weren't quite so thin, but at least she didn't have circles under her eyes, and her cheeks were not drawn. During The Divorce and pregnancy, her mother had constantly told her to eat something. Sean had taken away her appetite, and then the pregnancy had. The only thing that kept her going during those long months was the fact that a tiny life was depending upon her. She certainly had not felt like living for herself. Even now Ellie was the only reason she got up in the morning. But it was getting better. There were things she actually looked forward to now, like this date.

She had donned her favorite outfit, one that usually drew compliments. At least she felt good in it and it was comfortable. It consisted of a flowy tunic, black leggings, and a pair of black stiletto sandals. She had decided to leave her hair loose about her shoulders like a red cottony halo, revealing a flash of silver earrings whenever she turned her head. She looped a long necklace around her neck and studied herself in the mirror. The effect was charming, if she did say so herself.

"Come on, Pumpkin, let's get your bag and go," she called to Ellie, ignoring the butterflies that tickled her stomach. Where is she? It had been quiet the last few minutes, which couldn't be a good sign in a household with a toddler. Jolie left the bathroom in search of her little girl, whom she found sitting on the kitchen floor grabbing at the cat's tail as it tried to eat. At least she wasn't eating the cat food this time.

Ellie turned as Jolie entered the kitchen. "Kitty," she grinned, pleased with herself.

"Ellie! You just had a bath!" Jolie lifted her up to her hip where she brushed cat hair from her daughter's damp fingers and from around her mouth. Ellie always wanted to taste everything, including the cat. "Ready to go see Grammy and Grampa?"

"Grammyeeeeeeeeeeeeeee!" Ellie shrieked into Jolie's ear. She wouldn't be able to hear out of that one for a while.

Jolie's parents were thrilled to keep Ellie on the weekends. They had decorated Jolie's old bedroom in pink ruffles and lace and filled it with toys and books. Since Ellie was their only grandchild, they lavished attention on her. Jolie protested sometimes, but it did very little good. Their response was always, "But we couldn't do it for you, Jolie, and now that we are able, we want to." Unlike many of the mothers of her friends, Jolie's mother had been a stay-at-home mom and her father had worked in a pipe factory all of her life, so his income had been just enough to support them without many of the extras that her friends enjoyed. Having their child raised and major bills paid meant they relished getting to spoil their only grandchild.

Not that Jolie didn't benefit from all the time Ellie spent with her grandparents, not to mention the clothes and other necessities they often provided. Jolie's hourly paycheck couldn't have covered all their needs, let alone their wants. But thanks to her parents, she was able to drive a car with no payments, dress herself and her daughter in nice clothes, and even enjoy a night out once in a while, in spite of rent and daycare. If she was careful, there was sometimes even money left over for herself or the house although her mother also enjoyed buying things for Jolie and her home.

"THERE'S GRAMMY!" As they pulled into her parents' driveway, Jolie could see Mrs. McCray peeking out the front window. It was late for them, but the evening was young for Jolie. This is what the night shift did to people, turn them into night owls. Grammy must have been missing her granddaughter. She was at the car door before Jolie put the car into park.

"How are my girls?" Grammy opened the rear passenger door to reach for Ellie, who laughed in delight and kicked her chubby legs.

"Doing great, Mom," Jolie replied even though she knew no one was listening. Her mother was baby-talking and Ellie was chattering. Jolie joked to her parents that it was sickening, this little love triangle between them and Ellie, but she was thankful. So many children these days didn't get to experience the doting, steady love of grandparents.

Hauling Ellie's bag of toys, clothes, food, and diapers to the house, she knew she had overpacked again. Mrs. McCray would have already stocked up on diapers and food, and it was very likely that new clothes and toys were waiting in Ellie's room.

Her father was inside watching a baseball game. He switched off the television and rose from his recliner, a familiar, exaggerated groan bringing another giggle from Ellie.

"G'ampa!" Ellie almost leapt from Grammy's arms but Grammy held tight until Grampa could take the little girl from her. Mr. McCray was not what one might call tall, but he wasn't short, either. Built stocky, he was still mightily strong in spite of his 65 years, and still a handsome man.

"Hi, Pumpkin." Grampa situated Ellie so that she perched on his strong forearm. Then he leaned over and placed a kiss on Jolie's cheek. "You're all dressed up," he noted. "Hot date?"

Jolie blushed. "Actually, I'm not sure if he is hot, but yes, I do have a date." She dropped Ellie's heavy bag on the couch.

"Not sure? Must be one of them blind dates, then." His eyebrows rose in that familiar disdainful expression of his. Jolie doubted that he would approve even if it was the President of the United States. He would say the President was too old for her.

"G'ampa, I got a new dress," Ellie announced. She placed her chubby little hands on either side of his mouth and turned his face toward hers. "Lissen, G'ampa!"

"I am listening, Pumpkin!" He roared with laughter at the indignant toddler. "That is a beautiful new dress! Did Grammy buy that for you?"

"She's had dinner and a bath," Jolie continued, "but there's applesauce and crackers in her bag if she gets hungry."

"I'm sure we will find something if she gets hungry," Grammy assured her.

It was pointless to argue with her mother about feeding Ellie. She would give Ellie whatever she wanted no matter what Jolie said. But hopefully she knew better than to give her too much sugar before bedtime if she wanted to get any sleep that night.

"Where are you going on this date, Sweetheart? Is he picking you up here?"

Prying disguised as innocent curiosity, Jolie thought. Yep, that's Mom. "No, we are meeting Kaycie and Tim at Kaycie's apartment and then we will go out."

"Dinner and a movie?" she prodded.

"No, Mom, probably to Q's." *Here it comes.*

"Not that honky tonk. Why would you want to go there of all places?"

Jolie rolled her eyes and took a deep breath, but Grampa jumped in before she had to defend herself. "Now, Jeanie," he said to his sweetheart of over 35 years, "they are young and that is their idea of fun. Jolie, you go out and have a good time, and don't worry about Puss 'n' Boots here. We'll take good care of her. We'll see you tomorrow afternoon sometime, okay, Sugar?" He winked.

Grammy pursed her lips. "Just be careful." Jolie nodded and then kissed her daughter before heading out the door.

As Jolie tripped down the porch steps, she could hear her mother's high-pitched protesting and her father's booming laugh. She hoped their light bickering would not have an adverse effect on Ellie, even though she had grown up in the midst of it. Either way, she knew that Ellie would be in good hands. Tonight she would try to forget that she was a struggling single mom and try to have a good time. That is, if she could stop the butterflies that were now dive-bombing inside her stomach.

When she arrived at Kaycie's apartment complex, there was not an empty parking space to be found. She ended up having to park two buildings away. She didn't mind the walk, but she made sure she had her pepper spray in hand before putting out her cigarette and opening the car door. As she popped some breath mints into her mouth, she wondered if everyone was there waiting on her. If he was there waiting on her.

Kaycie opened the door just a few seconds after Jolie tapped on it with shaking fingers.

"Hey, Girlfriend! Come on in! Sorry, but we started without you!" Kaycie giggled, stepping back, beer in hand. "Wanna beer?"

"No, thank you." Kaycie knew Jolie didn't drink. Oh well. It would be nice to know if her date was here yet. She glanced around.

But it was only Tim sitting on the couch watching the same game that Grampa had been watching. The Rangers were on a winning streak. "Hey, Tim, what's up?"

"Not much here. How are you?" Always the gentleman, he rose from the couch to give her a little kiss on the cheek, something Jolie had to get used to. Most men these days just gave a little upwards nod and stayed put.

"I'm good." She fell into the deep fluffy chair opposite the couch where Tim had been sitting. Kaycie's furniture was much nicer than hers, but then she had wealthy parents who had given her a trust fund which paid all her bills and furnished her apartment for her. Even so, Jolie did not envy her because the relationship between Kaycie and her parents was not the best. They seemed more eager to give things than themselves, so Jolie did not let it bother her that Kaycie's place was nicer; at least most of the time she didn't.

"So, Kaycie, have you heard anything about Jay today?"

Kaycie plopped down next to Tim. "No, I haven't. I guess he is still in the hospital. Lucas said he was going to call first thing tomorrow and find out something. I hope the surgery went okay."

"Surely we would have heard something if it hadn't. I guess we won't be getting our regular days off any time soon. Who is working tomorrow night?"

"Looks like me and Lucas are. I don't think anyone will have to give up their days off. There are four of us, so it should be okay. They got somebody from the third shift to work with Lucas tonight so you and I could be off." Kaycie downed the rest of her beer. Wonder how many that makes it, Jolie mused.

"Aren't you going to ask about your date?" Kaycie asked as she got up.

Jolie shrugged but she thought she was going to be sick if the suspense didn't kill her first. Where is he? "I guess he's not here yet?" She attempted to keep her voice from rising an octave.

"Well, duh," Kaycie laughed, crossing in front of her in the direction of the kitchen. "He called and said his babysitter was late, but he should on his way now. Don't you want to know anything about him? You haven't asked me any questions!"

Babysitter? Alarm bells sounded and red flags billowed. She thought she might explode with all the nervous energy. Kaycie never said a word about him having a kid! Or was it two? Or maybe more?

"He has kids?" She stilled her tapping foot. How long had she been doing that?

"I didn't mention that?" Kaycie laughed again from the kitchen. In her small apartment, the kitchen was only a few steps from the living and dining areas. "Well, no?" Jolie drew out the two syllables.

"What's wrong? You have a kid, too, you know. That's why I thought he would be perfect for you."

That doesn't mean I want more, especially someone else's. "How many?" *Jolie was almost afraid to ask.*

"Just one. A little girl. I thought you two might have a lot in common. I think she is about the same age as Ellie, too. How about a Coke?" Kaycie handed her a bottle.

"Thanks." Jolie accepted the soda. Maybe his having a kid Ellie's age was a good thing.

Jolie's butterflies settled a little as the alarm bells stopped clanging. They had left a dull headache. She wondered if she was still up to a night at Q's. It would be loud and smoke-filled, the perfect fuel for a headache. Hopefully this one would go away soon.

Kaycie settled in next to Tim and, as they began to canoodle a bit, Jolie zoned out, trying to collect her thoughts and settle her nerves. She should trust Kaycie. After all, they had been friends through The Divorce, and Kaycie had rescued her from the brink of insanity more than once. Kaycie wouldn't suggest a match-up unless she was fairly certain it was a good one for Jolie. Her mind wandered, recalling the day they had met.

THE ZOO CURATOR in charge of the night shifts stood and extended his hand over his desk. Jolie rose from the chair opposite him and shook his hand. "Thank you for coming in this afternoon, Ms. Sowell. I will be in touch shortly."

"Thank you, Mr. Lopez, for the interview. I really appreciate it. I would really love to work here. If you need any more information, please call me. I look forward to hearing from you." Inside she was screaming, *I NEED THIS JOB! HIRE ME NOW!*

30

Lopez smiled. Wondering what that meant, Jolie scooted out of his office as fast as she could. Why didn't he say something? Like, "We would love to have you as an employee," or "You are hired?" Why didn't he stop her from leaving and hire her on the spot? Dejected, she trudged through the parking lot toward her car, the car that was almost out of gas and she down to her last one hundred dollars. She just could not bring herself to ask her parents again for help. To make matters worse, it was late October and the zoo was about to let all its part-time summer help go and implement the winter schedule, which meant the zoo would close two hours earlier. They just didn't need extra employees. To punctuate her dejection, it began to rain.

A squeal jerked her out of her thoughts. Looking up, she beheld a brunette running toward her with her head down in an effort to dodge raindrops. It was too late to get out of the way.

The impact of their collision sent the young woman sprawling on the concrete and caused Jolie to lose her balance for a moment, but she was able to right herself before she fell.

"Excuse me! Are you okay?" Jolie bent to help her up, but the girl pulled herself away and sputtered in anger. Jolie's face burned with embarrassment.

Scrambling up with very little grace, the brunette glared at Jolie. "Why don't you watch where you're going next time? I tore my stinkin' new pants!"

"What?" Jolie retorted in astonishment, her temper flaring. "I'm not the one flying across the parking lot with my head down, not watching. You ran into me!"

The girl squinted at her. Uh oh. I'm about to get punched in the face by this girl. Jolie flinched.

31

To her surprise, the girl burst into laughter. "You should see your hair!" *She pointed to Jolie's head.*

Taken aback, Jolie stammered, "Wwwwhat?"

"Your hair! It's all frizzy!" The girl laughed even harder.

"Well," Jolie countered in surprise, "your mascara is running down your face!"

"Jerk!" But the girl was still grinning.

"Back at you!" Jolie had to giggle. This girl was crazy!

The girl wiped her hands on her "stinking" pants and extended her right hand toward Jolie. "I'm Kaycie."

Jolie shook her hand. "Jolie." She noticed that Kaycie was wearing a zoo employee shirt and ID tag, and had keys, gloves, and a flashlight hanging from her belt.

"So why don't we get out of this stinkin' rain?" Having regained her balance, Kaycie stepped toward the office building entrance.

Jolie stood her ground. "I was just leaving." Was "stinking" the word of the day?

"Are you new here?"

"No. I mean, I wish I was. I just interviewed for a job." *Was that a wise thing to say? Was this Kaycie someone important? Have I just made a capital blunder by denying that she had been in the wrong?*

"Well, I work here. I was just going to sign my time card that I always forget to do until Lopez calls me. Why don't you wait a minute and we can go have some coffee and I can tell you who else you need to talk to?"

It was still raining. I must look a mess. But she nodded. This girl may have what I need to get hired. "Okay, I'll just wait in my car until you come back out. It's that Taurus over there." *Jolie pointed to her car.*

"Cool. I'll be right back."

As Kaycie disappeared into the building, Jolie tried to keep herself from becoming too hopeful. But why would a complete stranger who blamed her for an accident want to be friendly? Maybe it was because they were about the same age. Maybe Kaycie could see the desperation in Jolie's eyes. Or maybe she was just a nice person. Nah, Jolie thought. No one did something nice without expecting something in return. But for Kaycie, what was it?

Kaycie was interesting, though. In spite of her damp hair, her smeared makeup, and her shapeless zoo uniform, she was attractive with a charming smile that immediately put Jolie at ease. Perhaps this was the beginning of a friendship, something Jolie desperately needed. Being a new mom separated from her husband and without a job was lonely indeed. The last time she could say she had a best friend was in high school, and she missed being able to share secrets with a female her own age. Her mother was a great listener, and her daughter was a captive audience, but she definitely needed someone her own age to confide in.

Suddenly a face appeared in her driver side window, startling her. It was Kaycie, back from signing her time card. Jolie rolled down the window as quickly as she could. "Come on!" Kaycie exclaimed. She turned and zigzagged to her little pickup truck three spaces down, trying to avoid raindrops.

Jolie grabbed her purse and followed, raindrops spattering her face. She hopped into Kaycie's truck as fast as she could, hanging her purse strap on the window frame corner as she tried to slide in. A fierce pain shot through her shoulder as she felt her arm yanked by the strap. "Ow!" She wrenched the strap free and slammed the door.

"Are you all right?" Dark, almost black, dripping ringlets circled Kaycie's damp face. Her porcelain skin glistened with the moisture in the air, setting off dark eyes, eyebrows, and rosy cheeks and lips. She could have passed for Snow White.

Jolie settled in, wincing and rubbing her shoulder. "Yes, I think so. Everything is still attached." She inspected her soaked canvas bag. "This seems to be okay, darn it. I would love for it to come apart so I would have an excuse to get a new one."

Kaycie laughed as she started the truck. "Girl, I have so many purses I could give you ten and not miss them!" She grew serious again. "Are you sure you are okay?"

"I'm positive." Jolie smiled. "I guess I won't sue you. Especially if you give me a purse."

"Doesn't matter, you wouldn't get anything if you did," Kaycie said with a grin. "Let's get some coffee. Then I will take you to my apartment and let you pick out a few bags. If you want to, that is."

Over steaming skinny lattes they became acquainted, learning about each other's families, Jolie describing her broken marriage and little girl, and both commiserating over men. They found that they both loved classic rock music, vintage clothing and decor, and the actor Colin Farrell. They both loved to travel, but Kaycie had been more places with her corporate jet-setting parents. They had grown up as only children and had longed for a sister to play with. Jolie decided she had found the confidante she had been seeking.

At the end of that day, Jolie had acquired two designer purses from Kaycie's closet as well as a job. Instead of telling Jolie who else to talk to, Kaycie had called Mr. Lopez and persuaded him that the night department needed an extra hand.

TIM AND KAYCIE'S giggling and horseplay brought Jolie back to the present. They didn't even notice when she got up and headed to the bathroom. Amazing. She looked the same as she had when she left her home earlier, no hair out of place. Smoothing more lip gloss over the lips she thought were too pale and too thin, she wondered when her date would arrive. Or maybe he had chickened out like she felt like doing.

A few minutes later when she returned to the living room, she found she had no need to wonder. There he stood, the most attractive man she had ever seen, talking with Tim and Kaycie. He stood taller than both of them, his white button-down shirt and dark jeans hugging his muscular body in all the right places. Light brown hair curled slightly over the top of his shirt collar, and as he turned to look at her, the skin around his dark brown eyes crinkled as he smiled. Straight white teeth against tanned skin, a lighter-haired version of Colin Farrell himself. This could be good, she thought as she returned his smile.

Chapter Four

"THERE YOU ARE!" Kaycie cried as she realized that Cade's attention had shifted away from her and Tim. "Jolie, come here and meet Cade Bishop."

"Jolie Sowell." As Jolie stepped forward to shake his outstretched hand in greeting, she was amazed at how normal she sounded. Not shrill or nervous or strained like she felt. His eyes were cool and twinkling in their confidence, his hand strong and warm as he gripped hers. She hoped he couldn't tell how nervous she was. She had not ever really dated and didn't really understand what a blind date was until Kaycie had set this one up.

Ellie had been the product of a tryst with one of the sackers at the grocery store where she worked as a cashier during her freshman year of college. They had married quickly, lasted a rocky year, and then divorced as soon as she found out that his dallyings had not ended with her. She had not dated in high school, too shy and introverted, preferring hiding behind her more outgoing friends and pining for her current crush in her room at night. Sean's attentions at the store had been flattering and surprising, and she fell fast for his charms. Her father had insisted on the marriage; Jolie suspected that there had been a threat involved but neither her father nor her husband would own up to it. So now the real dating process would begin if her nerves could stand it.

"My pleasure, indeed," Cade replied smoothly as Kaycie and Tim sat down together in one overstuffed chair, leaving the sofa for Jolie and Cade. Cade sank into the sofa, leaned back comfortably, and took a sip of the soda Kaycie had offered him. He stretched one arm across the back of the sofa and crossed an ankle over the opposite knee.

Jolie flushed as she perched herself on the edge of the sofa at least a couple of feet from him. Words failed her. She glanced at Kaycie, who smiled encouragingly at her. Why did I ever agree to this? Jolie thought miserably.

"So, Jolie, Kaycie tells me that you work with her at the zoo. That must be an exciting place to work." His eyes, though twinkling, bore steadily into hers. Disarming, perhaps. Charming, not quite. More unsettling than anything. Yet his smile and those crinkles around his eyes charmed the heck out of her.

"Yes, it can be at times," Jolie agreed, again her voice sounding calmer than she felt.

"Especially when a tree falls on your boss!" Kaycie interjected. They all laughed, even though Jolie felt slightly uncomfortable laughing at Jay's misfortune.

"How is Jay doing?" Cade directed his question to Jolie.

"You know him?" Jolie felt herself beginning to relax.

"Only through Kaycie's conversations. I feel like I know him from listening to her talk about work."

"He should be going home from the hospital soon," Kaycie said. "I haven't talked to Lucas today, so Jay may be home already. He will be hobbling around for a while but he should be okay."

"Well, that is good news." Cade turned to Jolie. "I suppose we should get going." He stood and reached for her hand. Jolie glanced quickly at Kaycie, who smiled mischievously. So they all were not going to Q's, obviously. She would get Kaycie later.

Tim, newly absorbed in the Rangers game on Kaycie's 60-inch television screen, lifted his chin in acknowledgement. "Later, bro.' Have a good time, kids."

"More fun than I will have with Tim glued to the game, I hope!" Kaycie got up and walked the couple to the door. "Good to see you, Cade. Take care of my girl here." Handing Jolie the purse she had forgotten, she winked. "I'll call you tomorrow."

She was pleasantly surprised to find that his choice of transportation was a classic 1973 Oldsmobile Cutlass just like the one she had seen in her parents' photo albums.

"I love your car!" She slid easily into the leather bucket seat while Cade shut the door behind her.

"You like this?" He grinned as he eased into the driver's seat. What was that old saying: the way to a man's heart is through his stomach? Appreciating his ride had to be a close second.

"I love it! My dad had one of these back in the day. He said it was the sweetest car he ever had. Where did you find it?" She ran her hand appreciatively across the dash in front of her.

"Your dad had one of these?"

Jolie nodded, smiling and remembering the old photographs of her father standing in front of his car with his arms wrapped around her

38

mother, him sporting long bushy hair, long sideburns, and both of them wearing wide-legged bell bottoms. "He sure did. It was green with a white vinyl top."

"Nice. I've seen pictures of those. I got this one from an estate sale, if you can believe that. I had to do a little bit of restoration but basically she was in pristine condition. The only thing I did was replace the vinyl top and seats with leather and have her repainted. She only had sixty thousand miles on her when I bought her. I'm really proud of her." He started the car, its 350 Rocket engine roaring to life and then settling to a throaty purr.

"You should be. She is a beauty." Jolie breathed deeply, relaxing a little more. How bad could this guy be if he loved a classic car like the one Daddy had? She knew her dad would approve. She couldn't wait to show him. Whoa, better slow down. It's not just about the car.

"I hope you like Italian," Cade said as he maneuvered the car out of the parking lot. "There's this new place I've wanted to try. It's a homestyle Italian place. I heard they have great fettuccini alfredo." He glanced at her hopefully, causing her stomach to do a little somersault. Her eyes lingered on his lips. Then she marveled that she could even think such thoughts after the hurt she had experienced with her ex. She was still human, after all. The long-suppressed needs were beginning to make themselves known as his eyes held hers for a moment.

"Italian sounds perfect."

"Fantastic," he murmured, his eyes moving back to the road. As he gripped the steering wheel she noticed how tanned his arms were under the rolled-up sleeves of his crisp white shirt. Fine dark hair extended down the back of his hands, neatly manicured nails tipped the ends of

strong, thick fingers on large hands. Hands that reminded her of her father. Why do I keep comparing him to my dad?

He handled the car easily in the evening traffic, Jolie noting that he did not become ruffled in the slightest when another car zipped in front of him, cutting him off as he attempted to change lanes. He braked suddenly, avoiding a collision, and then backed off, allowing the car to go on.

"Well, I was going to take that street, but. . ." He grinned at her, setting off another storm of butterflies in her stomach. *"No problem, we can take the next one."* But she noticed as his grip tightened on the steering wheel.

BISTRO ITALIANA TURNED out to be a quaint little two-story house turned restaurant in the historic section of town. Twinkling white lights and the music of a jazz band led them down a cobblestone path to the front porch where they were greeted by a tuxedo-clad host who showed them to a secluded table off the patio. Ceiling fans and portable air conditioning units kept them from noticing the July evening heat. A canopy of sheer white fabric sprinkled with tiny white lights undulated gently overhead as candles flickered from the centers of round tables draped in the same billowy white fabric. The only thing missing was the beach, but to Jolie's delight there was a bubbling fountain with a waterfall not far from their table. *What a perfect setting for a first date.*

The conversation was quiet and relaxed, just like the atmosphere. Cade asked polite questions about her work and her family, even showing interest in Ellie. She learned that he worked at a local bank, but was also self-employed as a handyman. As if that weren't enough, he was also an aspiring writer, not yet published but nevertheless hopeful. He was secretly working on a do-it-yourself home repair book.

"As if there are not enough of those lying around gathering dust," he laughed, poking fun at himself. "And I guess it's not a secret now."

"I'm sure your book will have your unique spin on things," Jolie countered. "There may be lots of books out there, but none by you. And I promise not to tell anyone!" She blushed, hoping she was not being gushy. She hated gushy.

He didn't seem to notice as he flashed his bright smile at her.

The food arrived, and they lost themselves in the taste of authentic home-cooked Italian cuisine. Jolie's butterflies had disappeared— probably the wine—so she dug in with gusto, hoping her table manners were up to par. The smile on Cade's face showed his approval.

He put down his fork and wiped his mouth with his napkin. "How is your dinner?"

"Wonderful! It's so good, I'm afraid I look like a pig gobbling it up!" Oh brother, could she have said anything more lame?

Cade laughed. "There is no way you could look like a pig. Enjoy yourself. I'm enjoying watching you."

As she blushed from head to toe, Cade leaned over the table to wipe a bit of creamy sauce from her lip. His touch gave her a jolt, and then she wondered if he'd noticed. As he leaned back, she thought his thumb had lingered just a little longer than necessary on her lip. Hadn't it?

"Sorry, you had a bit of something. . ." he murmured, turning his attention to his plate. She took a sip of wine and turned her flushed face toward the mist of the fountain, willing it to float over to their table. Where was a breeze when you needed one?

"That's okay. I would hate to carry take-out on my lip." That was *lame, too. Can I not do better than this?*

He chuckled. Either he was being extremely polite or he actually had the same lame sense of humor she had. She could blame her father for that, but when her dad made a joke, everyone loved it. She just seemed to stick her foot in her mouth. Maybe it was because she was female. Or maybe she needed a few years on her.

Suddenly she realized that she had learned very little about Cade, other than what he did for a living. She was dying to know about his little girl, but more importantly, about his ex, about his marriage and divorce, where he came from. She decided to summon what little courage she had left and ask.

"So. . ." she ventured, but he had started to speak as well.

"Go ahead." He motioned with his fork.

"No, that's okay. It wasn't important." She did not want to ask personal questions if he wanted to talk about something else.

"Now that I cannot believe." He laid his fork down and took a sip of wine. "Are you sure?" After she nodded, he went on. "I was just going to ask if you would like dessert or another glass of wine."

Feeling flushed, Jolie was positive she did not need another glass of wine, and she was too full from the meal to even consider dessert, so she refused politely and excused herself to the ladies room, deciding to leave the personal history questions for later. The butterflies returned. While she was at dinner there was no doubt as to what was happening, but now dinner was done, she returned to her earlier state of near panic. No matter how perfect the evening had gone so far, she was afraid of what she might be expected to give in return. After all, that was how Ellie had come about. She emptied her protesting bladder and, after checking herself in the mirror, reapplied lip gloss.

She certainly didn't expect what came next.

"I hope you don't mind if we call it a night," Cade said as they walked to his car. "Maybe Kaycie mentioned to you that I had babysitter trouble tonight. I finally was able to secure one but she just texted me that she needs to get home earlier than she thought." He paused before opening the passenger side door for her. The expression on his face showed genuine regret at having to end the evening so early.

Jolie felt the need to reassure him in spite of the disappointment surprising her. "No, I understand, Cade. Totally. I have a little one, too, remember. Babysitters are difficult to find."

"Unless you have willing grandparents nearby," he said with a wink. "But thank you for understanding. Having kids certainly puts a damper on dating at times. I would prefer to continue our evening with a movie or a walk in the park." He opened the door and she slipped inside. As she waited for him to come around to the driver side, she realized something. In spite of her nervousness and fear of doing or saying the wrong thing, she really did not want the evening to end.

She settled back and then was aware of a pleasant electric charge as his hand rested upon hers. The gear shift in the console made it easy for him to reach her hand as it rested on her purse on the left side of her seat. She was glad she had not moved her purse to her lap as she usually did. His warm hand on hers felt right. Just right.

A short drive later and after some pleasant conversation where Jolie learned some about Cade and his daughter Maddie, they were back at Kaycie's apartment complex. Jolie directed him to where her car was parked. She wondered if he felt the same way she did about the date ending. Would there be any more dates? Will he want to kiss?

She was afraid to turn and look at him, but his fingers gently reached over and turned her chin towards him. Again the electricity, becoming familiar, becoming addicting.

His eyes with their lids half closed smoldered as he leaned close. He is going to kiss me, Jolie realized as alarm bells went off in her head. His lips touched hers for a moment, making them tingle and leaving her longing for more. As he leaned back, she breathed in his scent, willing it sealed into her memory. The feelings he stirred within her scared her.

Embarrassed that he might suspect she wanted more, she scrambled out of the car. She needed to think. Think. Not feel. Her feelings frightened her. But he would not allow her to leave right away. He was there grasping her hands as soon as she stood up outside the car. How did he get here so fast?

"I hope you had an enjoyable evening, Jolie." Her name on his lips was like music. Before she could answer he went on. "I certainly did."

"Yes, I had a great time," Jolie managed to say. Does he want my number? Will he ask me out again?

"Goodnight, then. Have a safe trip home." With that, he turned and walked around his car, opened the door, and got in. Then he backed out of the parking space and drove off, leaving her standing there. Dreamily she turned to unlock her car and realized that she didn't have her keys. And her hands were empty. She didn't have her purse. It was in the car, riding away with Cade.

After her momentary panic, she thought she could call her parents to pick her up, as inconvenient as that would be for them. Nope, her cell phone was in her purse, and her purse. . . The only solution was to go back to Kaycie's apartment to use her phone. She scanned the dimly lit parking lot for Kaycie's car. The compact SUV wasn't in sight. Refusing to panic, Jolie told herself that Kaycie had probably left her car at Tim's. She looked around again, hoping to see a familiar pickup that might be Tim's, but of the several trucks in the parking lot, she couldn't remember what his looked like. Besides, it was dark, and the lights in the parking lot were not very bright.

So it was up the stairs to Kaycie's apartment. After Jolie knocked several times hoping she didn't arouse a grouchy neighbor, finally a tousled Kaycie opened the door a crack.

"Hey," she said, clutching a towel to her chest. She looked confused. Obviously, she did not expect to see Jolie. Then her expression changed to concern. "Is everything okay?"

"Kaycie, I need to use your phone. I left my purse in Cade's car and I need to call my parents."

Kaycie rolled her eyes and opened the door wider for her friend. As Jolie entered the room, Kaycie hurriedly wrapped the towel around her damp body. Jolie had obviously interrupted her bath.

"Is Tim still here?"

"Yup," came the answer to her question as Tim entered the room with a towel around his waist. Jolie's face reddened as Kaycie shut the door and turned to him.

"Hey, honey, could you call Cade real quick? Jolie left her purse in his car." As he turned to get his phone from the bedroom, Kaycie frowned. "What time is it?"

"It's still early, around nine, I think. He had to go relieve the babysitter," Jolie replied.

"Really?" Kaycie frowned. "Did you have a good time? Where did he take you?"

Oh boy, here it comes. Jolie took a deep breath.

"Wait, hold that thought," Kaycie held up her palm as if to stop Jolie's words. "Let me get my pajamas on."

Jolie sank onto a dining room chair as Kaycie disappeared into the bedroom. She wondered if Tim was able to get Cade on the phone and if Cade would be irritated with her. Will he bring the purse over tonight, or will he make me wait? How will I function without my phone, driver's license, and keys? Will this make such a bad impression that he won't want to see me again?

She certainly did not want to call her parents. She didn't want to make them have to get out this late at night. She could just stay at Kaycie's but she had obviously interrupted their private time together and didn't want to ruin the entire night for them. I'm such a dodo sometimes.

She was fidgeting and feeling foolish when Kaycie finally came out of the bedroom in silk pajamas.

"Tim can't get hold of Cade." Kaycie plopped down in the chair next to Jolie. "He left a message. Maybe Cade turned off his phone so it wouldn't wake up Maddie."

"Great." Jolie sighed. "I guess I will have to call Daddy."

"You can stay here."

That was definitely out of the question with Tim spending the night. Jolie didn't consider herself a prude, but she didn't want to be a part of what Tim and Kaycie were doing. "No, I should go on home. May I use your phone?"

"Tim will take you home. Right, honey?"

46

Both girls jumped as someone pounded on the door the apartment.

"I bet that's Cade bringing your purse!" Kaycie literally hopped to the door and flung it open. "Cade! It is you!" She did a double take. He wasn't carrying anything. "You didn't bring Jolie's purse?"

"Purse?" A confused look crossed his face. "Is Jolie here?"

Jolie shoved Kaycie away from the door. The sight of Cade took her breath away.

"Jolie! Thank God! I saw your car still here and I hoped no one had gotten you!" To Jolie's utter surprise, he wrapped her in his arms and buried his face in her hair. Everyone except Cade faded away. Jolie's long dulled senses awakened as his musky male scent filled her nostrils. Something stirred deep within her.

"How stupid and thoughtless," Cade muttered. He pulled himself away, his dark eyes melting hers. Shaken, she was glad his hands were clutching her upper arms. Otherwise her knees may have given way.

"I was halfway home when I realized that I had left you alone in the parking lot without seeing you safely in your car! How thoughtless of me! I drove like a madman getting back here to make sure you were okay. Thank God!" Anguish twisted his handsome face.

"Good grief, Cade! She is fine!" Kaycie scoffed. "Come in and let me close the door before the neighbors call the police or something."

Jolie found her voice as they sank into the couch. Kaycie discreetly left the room and closed her bedroom door to give them privacy.

"There was no need to worry, Cade. I'm a big girl, and I would have been long gone, but, like an idiot, I left my purse in your car, so I couldn't get into mine. I had to ask Kaycie to use her phone because my phone is in my purse, too, and. . ."

Cade's lips on hers stopped her rambling. Not a long kiss but a bit lingering, one she felt down to her toes, and then deep inside. But then he pulled away gently. "If I hadn't driven off like a fool, we would have realized that you didn't have your purse. It's all my fault. I am so sorry. Please forgive me."

Jolie nodded, touched by his concern and chagrin.

"Let's go get your purse, shall we?" He stood and pulled her up.

Cade ushered Jolie down to his car where he retrieved her purse, waited as she dug out her phone and keys, and then helped her into her car. Then he kissed her fingers, closed her door, and watched her drive away. No words were spoken in those few minutes, but Jolie drove home feeling as if she had just experienced the most romantic evening of her entire life.

KAYCIE AND JOLIE arrived at work at the same time the next afternoon. Funny how she hadn't really noticed the heat last night during her date. Tonight the air was so heavy with humidity it was hard to breathe. Jolie wasn't even supposed to be there, this being her usual night off, but Lucas had called at the last minute asking her to trade nights off with him so he could celebrate his suddenly-remembered anniversary with his wife. Jolie and Kaycie enjoyed picking that subject to death for a few hours.

Soon the subject changed. As the girls went through the evening routine of picking up food bowls, checking on baby animals, treating sick animals, and cleaning certain exhibit areas, Jolie described her evening with Cade. Jolie picked Kaycie's brain about Cade's background, but all Kaycie could tell her is that Tim had met him at the bank several months ago after Cade had broken up with his wife. As Cade handled a new bank account for Tim, they had hit it off and become friends.

Kaycie seemed pleased that the date had gone well. "So, did he say anything about going out again?" she asked as they washed the remaining food bowls and set them out to dry.

"No, actually he didn't, but I feel like he will." Jolie actually felt very confident that he would. How could he not, after kissing me like he did?

"So," Kaycie leaned closer to Jolie, who was stacking some dry bowls the day shift keepers had left out, "is he a good kisser?"

Jolie blushed. "I am not going to discuss that!"

Kaycie laughed. "I knew he would be. Those lips are made for kissing. Not that Tim's aren't great, but Cade has the best lips ever!"

"Okay, back off now," Jolie laughed. She turned serious. "Have you heard anything about Jay? When is he supposed to come back to work?"

IN HIS RECLINER at home, Jay wondered the same thing. He was tired of world news, sports programs, and outdoor shows. He was getting used to crutches, but building his strength back up was taking forever. The confinement was making him cranky, his wife receiving the brunt of it. He hated that, but her ability to move around easily and come and go freely irritated him. This time at home could have been a great time to bond with his baby girl, but she was scared of the large cast on his leg and the crutches. The walls were closing in and there was nothing he could do about it.

At least things seemed to be going well at the zoo in his absence. His keepers had been there a while, so he had no doubt that they would continue to do their jobs without needing constant supervision. He hoped they wouldn't forget to check with the curators for extra duties such as caring for new surgeries or babies, but even if they did, the curators would be sure to notify them. He just felt that he was slacking off by not being there. He was not one to take sick days; in fact, he usually received reimbursement every year by cashing in his unused sick days. His family depended on that extra money for home repairs or vacations. There wouldn't be any of that this year.

Four-year-old Laci appeared in front of him. "Daddy, do you need anything? She placed her hands on her little hips and cocked her blonde head.

"Do I need anything?" She always brought a smile to his face, no matter his mood.

"Mommy said," she announced in the most grown-up voice she could muster.

"All I need right now is a big hug from my best girl!" Jay reached for her. She scrambled up into his lap, careful not to bump the cast, wrapped her arms around his neck, kissed him on the mouth with puckered lips, then settling back into his arms. The scent of her freshly shampooed hair reminded him of Molly.

"Am I big, Daddy?" She turned her angelic face up toward him, her blue eyes trusting and innocent. She would believe anything he told her.

"Yes, Sweetheart, you are growing bigger every day. I don't know how much longer I can hold you in my lap!" He kissed the top of her head.

"Aw, Daddy, I'll never be too big for that!" She reached for a book lying on the end table. "Let's read, Daddy!"

Thoughts of work evaporated as they entered the Wonderful World of Disney and the story of "Beauty and the Beast." How could he have even thought he was wasting his time? He was building precious memories with his little girl. As they turned the pages and the aroma of a home-cooked dinner wafted through the house, the thought never entered his mind that something might be going wrong at work.

KAYCIE AND JOLIE and Jolie had split up to get the work done faster. They had worked the night shift for so long that being alone in the dark had become a non-issue. But as Jolie entered the squirrel monkey's holding area to do a headcount, she slipped on something as she reached for the light switch.

Her stomach flip-flopped as the light revealed a gruesome sight. A tiny squirrel monkey lay at her feet in a puddle of blood, its tiny limbs splayed unnaturally, its eyes fixed. What in the world? She swallowed the bile that threatened and grabbed her radio. "Kaycie! Kaycie! Code 3! Squirrel monkey house!"

Chapter Five

JOLIE KNELT TO examine the poor little squirrel monkey, its fur matted with sticky blood. The blood on the floor had not completely dried yet. *How did it get out, and how did it die? There was no evidence of a bite from a larger animal.*

"What is it?" Kaycie skidded to a stop at the door of the squirrel monkey house, her expression one of dread. Code 3 always meant a dead animal. She knelt beside Jolie. "What happened?"

"I just found it like this."

"Did you check the locks? Did someone leave the door open?"

Jolie jumped to her feet. "Not yet. I just came in and found this little guy." She moved to the doors of the holding area, checking to see if they had been left open. Kaycie tried to check for a pulse on the tiny animal, but it was impossible. Its little chest was still anyway. She joined Jolie at the enclosure and began to count the other monkeys after Jolie found that the locks were secure.

The squirrel monkeys bouncing from tree limb to tree limb to cage wires and back made it almost impossible to get an accurate count, but finally Jolie and Kaycie agreed on the number. It was the usual number minus one. But how had the little guy gotten out and away from the others? Jay would certainly want to know. The day supervisor would want to know. The Curator of Mammals would want to know. Most important and scariest for Jolie, Kaycie, and Jay, the General Curator and Director would want to know.

Kaycie and Jolie took photos with Kaycie's cell phone, found two pair of rubber gloves, and then carefully wrapped the dead squirrel monkey in a towel before slipping it into a gallon freezer bag and placing it into the refrigerator in the vet wing. The zoo vet would have to do a necropsy to determine the cause of death for the report that would be done. They had to rule out disease in order to protect the other animals, and to find out if another animal had somehow wandered into the zoo or escaped from another area and killed the monkey.

This was the most difficult part of working at a zoo for Jolie: handling a dead animal and putting it into the fridge. Besides being sad, it just seemed weird to her. Who puts dead animals in refrigerators? Kaycie was always quick to remind her that all beef, chicken, and fish in the freezer at home were dead animals. Still. . .

Cleaning up the blood made her gag a few times before the chore was done. Kaycie tried to lighten the duty by cracking jokes, but Jolie was not in the mood. This wasn't a normal animal death by natural causes. Something weird had happened here tonight, and it gave Jolie the willies.

AS SHE LOGGED into the computer in Jay's office to search for the form she needed to fill out, Jolie breathed a prayer of thanks for Kaycie, who was willing to clean the reptile and aquarium buildings with all the window glass and carpeted floors without her help. Jolie busied herself writing the unpleasant report, wondering what the day supervisor and Jay would do when they found out. She left a note at the bottom of the form, requesting a phone call if they found out what happened before she returned to work.

THE NEXT DAY Molly Latimer helped her husband dress and get to his recliner before fixing breakfast for him and the girls. He had become reacclimated to a daytime schedule since his hospital stay and worried that going back to the night shift when he recovered would be a challenge. It was strange to see the morning sunshine and his wife and girls in their pajamas in the mornings. Sipping his coffee, he watched Molly as she moved around the kitchen getting breakfast together for everyone. The sight of her without makeup, her hair clipped back loosely while tending to his children filled him with pride and admiration. "Good Morning, America" blared the morning news at him, distracting him from hopeful thoughts of private time with his wife later.

In a few minutes, Laci skipped into the den, stopping at his recliner. Jelly and chocolate milk covered her face, but her expression was serious, so Jay stifled the urge to smile. "What is it, Pumpkin?"

"I have some activities planned for you today," she announced. "But first, I have to brush my teeth and make my bed."

"Activities?" This should be interesting.

"It's a surprise," Laci said, lisping a little. Jay's grin widened.

"Laci. . ." warned her mother from the kitchen. Laci skipped off to do her chores before her mother had to tell her again.

"See you in a few." Jay chuckled, taking another sip of his coffee.

"Want a warm-up?" Molly appeared in the arched doorway between dining room and den with the coffee pot.

"That would be great." He grinned as she walked over to him. As she refilled his cup, he said in mock disappointment, "Oh, you meant the coffee. . ."

"You're so bad," she teased, setting the carafe on a magazine next to Jay's chair. She leaned over to give him a light kiss but was swiftly pulled into her husband's lap.

After a lingering kiss Molly righted herself. "You must be feeling better!" An irritated cry echoed from the dining room.

"Uh oh, break over," Jay muttered, giving Molly a little push to help her out of the recliner.

"We'll finish this later," Molly promised, touching his lips with her finger. She grabbed the carafe and swept into the dining room, swaying her hips for Jay's benefit. She flashed him a smile just as she disappeared around the corner to rescue Liza from the confines of her high chair. He smiled. I'm a lucky man.

Laci wasted no time finishing her chores. As soon as her mother declared that her face, teeth, and bed had passed inspection, Laci filled her little red wagon full of games, storybooks, coloring books, dolls, stuffed animals, and a tea set and pulled it into the den in front of Jay's chair.

"Daddy," she whispered again and again until he opened his eyes. The pain medication the doctor had given him made him drowsy. Laci's face loomed close and fuzzy at first and then grew clearer. "Daddy, wake up!" She was frowning and had her arms crossed in front.

"Laci, remember Daddy takes medicine that makes him sleepy." Molly passed by with Liza on her hip. "We need to let him rest so he can get better."

"Okay." Dejected, Laci began to pull the wagon back toward her room.

"Wait, honey, I'm all rested. I think I'm ready for some activities now." Jay winked at Molly as a big smile spread across Laci's face.

Jay spent the rest of the morning dutifully playing Candyland and Chutes and Ladders, coloring three pages of puppies and kittens, reading aloud fairy tales, and sharing "tea" with all manner of dolls and stuffed animals. Finally, just before lunch, Laci decided that they would watch a DVD, so after she picked out the movie and popped it into the player all by herself, she settled into Jay's lap. As the characters carried out their adventures on the screen, Jay and Laci both drifted off to sleep.

Jay awakened to Molly gently shaking his shoulder. It must be lunchtime already, he thought, trying to shift his weight without disturbing Laci. His right leg had gone to sleep. But Molly handed him the phone. He looked at her quizzically while covering the mouthpiece. "Who is it?"

"I don't know. Some place wanting a reference on somebody that used to work for you? I think that's what they said." She lifted Laci easily from his lap and carried her to the kitchen so they could fix their lunches.

"This is Jay Latimer," Jay spoke into the receiver.

"Mitch Walker with Outdoor Safaris," came the voice of the caller. "How are you today?"

"I'm not interested, but thanks for calling," Jay said, preparing to hang up.

"Wait, I'm not a telemarketer!" the voice interjected quickly. "I need to talk with you about a former employee of yours."

"Oh?"

"Yes, his name is Cory Bennett. Do you know him?"

"Yes, I do. He worked for me a few years ago."

"What can you tell me about this young man? Was he a dependable employee? Why did he leave? Would you hire him again?"

Cory Bennett. Jay had been very impressed when he interviewed for the second shift. He had actually pushed Lopez into hiring him when Lopez wavered between Bennett and another applicant. Bennett had been one of the first members of the night shift. Jay and Cory and two other men had established the routines with the day supervisors' input. The four of them had to prove to the curators that the night shift was not only necessary for continuous care and security, but that there were plenty of projects to keep them busy when there were no sick, injured, or newborn animals needing special care.

They had done such a good job at night that zoo administrators added a second night shift, now known as the third shift, and got rid of paid security. Night shift workers now provided zoo security along with their regular duties.

But Cory Bennett had turned out to be much different from the person he had presented himself to be at the beginning. An attractive and fit young man in his mid-twenties, Cory not only was able to take on the physical demands of extreme temperatures and frequent heavy lifting, he worked well with the female keepers and supervisors. He was good at making coworkers feel important and competent and soon became one of the most popular keepers at the zoo, which irritated the other guys who worked on Jay's shift. But Cory ignored their remarks about him being a ladies' man or sycophant. Jay valued him because he was a responsible and energetic team player.

Things changed after a few months. Cory began dating one of the female keepers on the day shift. He seemed to fall head over heels at first, constantly talking about how lucky he was to have met her, how much he liked her, and then how he thought he loved her and wanted to ask her to move in with him. From what he told Jay and the other guys he was staying at her place most nights after work, and then he would hang out at the zoo during the day a few hours before work so that he could spend more time with her.

Although Jay would have liked to advise him about his relationship which seemed to be getting kind of weird, he knew it was none of his business. However, he felt obligated to inform Cory that he shouldn't be hanging around the zoo during his hours off, especially distracting another keeper from her job.

Cory's normally congenial demeanor changed abruptly when Jay confronted him. "Is that an order, sir? Or just a suggestion? Because if it is a suggestion, I am going to say mind your own business."

"You may consider it a directive from your supervisor, Mr. Bennett. And I hope you will follow it before this has to go further, if you get my meaning." Jay had a short fuse when his workers challenging his authority.

They were standing in the lounge getting ready to go to work that evening. The day keepers were clocking out and gathering their things. Jay had not intended for everyone to hear, but Cory's voice rose with emotion as he slammed his locker shut. "You can call me on the radio when you need me," he said loud enough for everyone to hear.

"You know what time we start," Jay replied, refusing to allow him the upper hand. "I'll look for you then."

Cory remained sullen the rest of that night, speaking only when he had to and doing the minimum to fulfill his duties. The other guys were quiet as well, not really knowing what had set him off, but not wanting to escalate the problem. This went on for a few days. Cory apparently had heeded Jay's warning to stay out of the zoo until it was time to work, but he would not make any effort to engage in conversation and did only what he had to do to keep his job.

Then one afternoon Cory bounded into the lounge as if nothing had ever happened, smiling and whistling and greeting everyone he saw. Jay and the other two guys stared at him as he clocked in and put his things in his locker.

"'Sup, Dudes?" Cory practically danced as he popped his locker shut.

At that moment a petite brunette young woman in a zoo uniform sauntered over and put her arms around Cory's waist. Cory's eyes lit up with adoration as he wrapped his arms around her, and then they moved away from everyone for more private conversation. Cory remained in a good mood for a few weeks. His work productivity even returned to its original quality.

"I guess we need to make sure he has a girl at all times," Lucas remarked one night at break after Cory went into the restroom, leaving the rest of them alone in the lounge.

"Yeah, he certainly has been in a better mood lately," Jay agreed. "Is she the same one he was seeing a couple of weeks ago?"

Lucas shrugged. "I don't remember."

The other keeper at the table, Sam, nodded in agreement. "That girl he's seein', ain't she married?" He gathered up his trash.

"Is she?" Startled, Jay glanced over at Lucas, who shrugged again.

"That's what I heard," Sam said.

Jay made a mental note to check into what Sam had said. Although it was really none of his or the zoo's business, it would become their business if things went sour.

Jay did check into it, and it turned out that the young lady, Jessica Webb, was indeed married, her husband employed as a bouncer at a local nightclub. Not good for old Cory should hubby find out. But does Cory know that she is married? Jay decided to mention it, even though he was sure Cory would remind him to mind his own business, and probably not very politely.

It turned out that he didn't have to tell Cory anything except that he was fired. When Jay passed the restrooms near the giraffe exhibit on his evening rounds, he noticed the ladies restsroom light on. Weird. No ladies on this shift. Maybe it was left on accidentally. The instant he opened the door, a woman giggled inside one of the stalls. "Shhh!" came a loud male whisper from the same stall.

You have got to be kidding. Jay entered and stood in front of the occupied stall. "Okay, come on out." This was one of those moments when it was no fun being the boss.

The door finally opened after a few seconds of dead silence. Cory stepped out first, lipstick marks on his face. His palm went up before Jay could say anything. Jessica followed him out, her gaze on the floor, her cheeks red with embarrassment.

Jay's indignance grew. How dare this guy ignore employee rules and do this on company time? How dare he take advantage of his fellow employees? He knew that tonight was a big night for them. Not only did they have their own routine, but they had been asked by three different departments to do additional tasks which took time and attention away from their regular duties. He would see to it that Cory paid for this time

60

he had taken away from the other guys. On second thought, he would see to it that this never happened again because Cory would be gone.

"I'll just walk her to her car and then I'll get back to work," Cory said.

"I don't think so. Jessica, your supervisor will deal with you tomorrow. I'll have Lucas see you to your car."

Jay took his radio from his belt and opened the restroom door. "Wait at that table, please." Without a word and with her head down she exited the restroom and sat at a nearby picnic table. She would be okay there until Lucas arrived. Allowing the restroom door to close, Jay turned to Cory, who wisely had kept his tongue.

"You have involved yourself in fraternizing with other employees on the job, strictly forbidden in the handbook. I think Lopez will agree with me on my decision to terminate your employment," Jay said, his eyes challenging Cory to dare to defend himself.

Cory just stared at him, his eyes narrowing, almost threatening in their intensity. "You won't have to bother consulting Mr. Lopez. I quit."

"Then you will need to report to work tomorrow for a conference with Lopez and me. You can bring your keys and uniform with you. You will have to fill out an exit report."

"You can stuff your exit report. I am out of here. This job is for losers anyway." With that, he stalked out, flinging the door open by punching it with his fist.

Jay followed. Jessica had already gone, apparently unwilling to wait for Lucas. Cory lost no time in grabbing his stuff from his locker and getting to his car before Jay made it to the lounge. Lucas was right behind him.

"Jessica wasn't there when I got there." He followed Jay into his office just off the lounge. "Is everything okay?"

Jay inhaled deeply. "I found Cory with her in the ladies' restroom. He won't be coming back." Jay unloaded his keys, flashlight, and radio onto his desk, settling down to write an incident report. Looking up at Lucas, he said, "I wonder how I am supposed to write that two employees were being romantic in the restroom?" He would now be shorthanded and have to look into hiring someone else. Night keeper applicants were few and far between, too.

"There is something else," Lucas said. "I hate to add to your troubles, but Sam and I saw Cory teasing one of the tamarinds the other night. I keep forgetting to report it."

"Teasing?" Jay frowned. Teasing any animal was not a good thing, but for Lucas to think it serious enough to report? They all were guilty of playing with some of the animals, which could sometimes be called teasing, but usually was considered enrichment and encouraged by zoo officials. Giving bored zoo animals some stimulation and new activity was usually a good thing.

"We saw Cory trap one with a net and spray it with a water hose. We thought it was going to drown, but he finally let it go. I don't think this is the first time he has done something like that, either. Sam has seen him do other things."

Jay's jaw dropped. "How much water?" No one messed with those cute little tamarinds, at least not on his watch.

"One of the fire hoses. Like I said, I thought it was going to drown before he stopped."

"Why didn't you stop him?" Would he need to discipline Lucas for not reporting this?

"We did. We made enough noise to let him know we were coming so he stopped. He doesn't know we saw him. He wrapped the tamarind in a towel and told us that he found him struggling in a water bowl."

Jay called Sam on the radio. In a few minutes he had Lucas and Sam sitting in front of him. Sam confirmed the tamarind story, so Jay prodded him for information about the other things Lucas had mentioned. "Tell me everything you have seen."

"Just stupid stuff like knocking the macaws off their perches and causing some hoof stock to run into fences. Nothing life-threatening." Sam glanced at Lucas. It was clear that he didn't want to be involved.

"Cory is already gone, Sam, but I need any other information you may have," Jay prompted.

"Well, there is that one flamingo." Sam squirmed in his chair.

Jay's eyebrows raised. "Flamingo?" The one everyone thought had gotten caught in some branches during a storm and broken its legs? The poor thing had to be euthanized.

"Yeah, that one that had the broken legs? Cory said that he caught it and picked it up and threw it down because it wouldn't come in during the storm. I don't think he meant to break its legs, though." Sam looked as guilty as if he had committed the deed himself. "I suppose I should have told you."

"Yes, you should have. Anything else?"

Neither Lucas nor Sam had anything else to say, so Jay sent them back to work with a warning that if they failed to report similar incidents in the future it could mean disciplinary action. As Jay expected but hoped wouldn't be the case, Cory never came in for his termination conference. No one ever heard from him again, not even Jessica, who was given a severe warning but allowed to keep her job. Jay never knew if the bouncer husband was ever aware of the affair, but he heard that she divorced not long after that.

"NO." JAY SPOKE into the phone receiver. "I would not hire him again. But that is all I will say about him."

"I understand. Thank you for your time, Mr. Latimer."

As he hung up, Jay felt a twinge of pity for Cory, but it soon faded. If he had been responsible for the flamingo's broken legs, he had no business working at a job involving animals. Besides, that, since when was it okay to get romantic with a coworker right there on company property during work hours?

The phone rang again, breaking into his thoughts. Who is it this time? "I got it," he called in case Molly tried to answer it.

"Hey, Latimer, this is Lopez. How are you doing?"

"Hey, Lopez! I'm getting along all right. I have a doctor's appointment next week and I'm hoping she will release me to get back to work. What's going on?"

"Have any of your guys called you?"

Uh oh, that doesn't sound good. Jay frowned. "No, they haven't."

There was a pause. "Jolie found a dead squirrel monkey last night." Another pause.

"That happens. Was it Gramps?" Jay responded. That squirrel monkey was getting old. Poor Jolie, she really hates when animals die on her watch.

"No, actually it was one of the younger females. And she was killed, maybe strangled. Jolie found her outside the holding area on the floor just inside the door. She was bleeding and looked like her neck had been broken. The vet is coming this afternoon to do the necropsy, so we really aren't sure yet. But it sure looks suspicious."

"So, you think someone actually would kill a tiny squirrel monkey on purpose? How would they have caught it and gotten it out of the area?" Jay froze. Did Lopez think one of his guys did it?

Chapter Six

LOPEZ HESITATED. JAY knew that he would know what Jay's next question was. Lopez was well acquainted with Jay's quick defensiveness when it came to his crew.

"So you think my guys might be responsible?" Jay sat up straighter in his recliner.

"We don't know who is responsible, Jay, but we are not ruling anything out, either. We have launched a full investigation and will be questioning everyone. No one is accusing your crew, so keep your pants on. I will keep you posted as we get more information."

Jay had very little to say. He wished he could be there to make sure that his guys were getting fair treatment. Although he knew that Lopez would do everything he could to make sure they did, Lopez stayed mostly in his office, not out in the zoo where supervisors protected their own crews and were quick to point fingers at the other shifts when there was trouble.

He would just have to relax and hope that Lopez kept things from getting crazy. Jay would call his crew and get their stories and then all he could do was wait for his doctor to give him the go-ahead to return to work. But first things first. Here came Laci with his lunch on a plate. It was lunchtime in the Latimer house.

JOLIE OPENED HER eyes, aware of a small foot pushing up on her jaw. Ellie was a fitful sleeper and had never been one to stay under the covers or in one direction. This morning her reddish blonde hair was splayed across Jolie's leg as she lay on her back with her feet in Jolie's face. Jolie tickled the bottom of Ellie's foot with the ends of her own hair until the child stirred and turned over.

Ellie had adapted to Jolie's schedule of staying up late and sleeping late, which was nice for Jolie but hard on her parents when Ellie stayed there.

Jolie glanced at the clock on the nightstand. Time to get some laundry and housework done before she had to get dressed for work. Then it hit her. A flashback of last night's gruesome discovery. The poor little squirrel monkey probably lying on a metal table now undergoing a necropsy. There would be all kinds of questions. She'd better call her mother and make arrangements to drop Ellie off early. She would need to get to work early and face the barrage of questions from the supervisors, curators, vet, and director. A knot formed in her stomach.

Ellie slept through Jolie's phone call to her mom, her shower, blow-drying and flat-ironing her hair—little good that would do in this summer humidity—and then getting dressed. Jolie was applying the finishing touches to her makeup when she heard a sleepy "G'mornin', Mommy."

"Hey, Sleepyhead!" Jolie turned from the mirror to see Ellie standing in the doorway of the bathroom in her nightgown rubbing her eyes. So adorable.

"Are you hungry, Sweet Pea?" She bent down to give her daughter a kiss on the top of the head.

As Ellie nodded, Jolie set down her mascara wand and took her baby's hand. "Let's go get you some breakfast, okay?"

"Where goin', Mama?" Ellie's voice was husky as she followed her mother's lead. "Date again?"

Jolie looked down at her sharply. Why would she ask that? And then she realized. She did not normally wear makeup. She had just had the extra time this morning and thought a little added confidence wouldn't hurt as she endured the interrogation at work. Funny that Ellie noticed.

"No, Sweetie, no date. I have to go to work early today. And you get to see Grammy and Grampa early today! Isn't that great?" Jolie tried to sound excited instead of nervous like she felt.

"Grammy and Grampa!" Ellie squealed. As they entered the kitchen she climbed easily onto the chair and into her booster seat. "Cheerios!" She slapped the table with both hands. "Cheerios! Cheerios!" she chanted.

"Okay, okay," Jolie laughed. "Cheerios it is!" She poured some of the O-shaped oat cereal into a small plastic bowl decorated with Minnie Mouse, courtesy of Grammy. After adding a few ounces of milk, she set the bowl and a spoon in front of Ellie, who dutifully spooned up every bite while Jolie sipped her coffee and watched her.

About a half hour later, after Ellie was dressed, her bag packed, and the cat fed and watered, Jolie and Ellie headed to her parents' house. Of course, they wanted to know all the details about why Jolie had to go to work early, so she busied Ellie with toys and quietly told them about finding the dead monkey. Now her parents would worry even more about her. They already did not like her working nights. She knew she would be hearing more about this later.

Jolie parked her old Taurus in the only shady spot left in the parking lot. As she climbed out of the car, the midday heat and humidity seemed determined to suffocate her.

She threw her cigarette butt down on the asphalt and squashed it with her foot, only feeling a trace of guilt for littering. There were parking lot attendants for that. She had hoped that a smoke before work would calm her nerves as it usually did, but not today. She would have to smoke several more to quell these butterflies. If it was possible, they were worse today than they were the night she met Cade.

Cade. Think of his beautiful eyes. Maybe that will help. He hadn't called since their date, but it had only been a couple of days. She wouldn't fret about it yet. But she really wanted to hear from him and hoped that he felt the same about her. But right now she had a report to explain. She went straight to Lopez's office and knocked on the door.

IT WAS A rare event when the doorbell rang at the Latimer house. Molly opened the front door to find Toni standing there with a covered dish. Images of their first meeting flooded her memory. "Hey, Toni, come in!"

"I hope this is a good time. I brought Jay's favorite dessert."

"Brownies with vanilla icing? Any time is a good time for those."

Molly took the dish and ushered Toni into the den where Jay napped in his recliner. Laci was stretched out in front of him on the floor quietly coloring a picture with Liza watching and "helping" her. Cartoons played at a low volume on the television. Even with the toys scattered around the den, there was an atmosphere of peace in the home that left Toni in awe. Molly was living Toni's dream and didn't know it.

Despite their quiet exchange, Jay stirred and opened his eyes. Laci immediately noticed.

"Daddy, look what I am making for you!" She held up her coloring creation, a picture of their home and family. Liza babbled in agreement, turning a crayon over and over with her chubby little fingers.

"Yeah, I see." Noticing Molly and Toni entering the room, he pulled himself up and ran a hand through his hair, hoping he didn't look too bad. More important, he hoped he didn't smell bad. How long has it been since I took a shower?

"Don't move." Toni held up her hand. "I just brought you my brownies. I thought at least you could put some meat on your bones while you are recuperating. How are you feeling?"

"Brownies! The ones with vanilla icing?"

"The very ones."

Molly set the plate of brownies on the coffee table and then settled cross-legged on the floor next to the girls.

"So, how are you doing?" Toni repeated.

"I'm doing okay. I'm getting tired of this recliner, though. I wish I could move around more. I need a shave, too. Sorry I'm not more presentable."

"Oh my, don't worry about that!" Toni scoffed. "Is the doctor keeping you from moving around?"

"Yes, apparently there was some internal bruising. I see him in a couple of days. I hope he will let me get back to work."

"There's no need to rush it, is there?" Toni glanced at Molly.

"Daddy, I like it when you stay home," Laci declared. She didn't miss a word.

"I know, Sugar Pie, but I really need to be working. You guys have to eat, you know." He winked.

"We have lots of food already, Daddy. Mommy went to the store last week," Laci informed him, as if that settled it.

"Yeah, Daddy," Molly said, smiling. Jay rolled his eyes.

"So, how is Kent these days? What is he up to? Still driving that truck? I haven't talked to him in ages," Jay said.

"Doing great, just driving that rig all over the place. How about you? Is your staff keeping you up on what is happening at the zoo?"

Jay shifted to try and find a more comfortable position. This recliner was getting old. He longed to just get outside. As soon as he could, he was going for a run. Maybe by Christmas? "I haven't heard much, actually. But I have a good staff. They are taking care of business."

"I bet you want to get back, though, huh?"

"He can't wait," Molly said. At Jay's quizzical look, she laughed. "You know you can't! The zoo is your life!"

Jay smiled and shook his head. "Yes, I love the zoo, but my life is my family. I love spending time with my girls." He leaned toward Molly and she leaned over so he could kiss her on the cheek. "Hey, wanna get me some milk and a brownie?" He put on his best little boy smile.

"I knew that was coming." Molly rose from the floor.

"I want some!" Laci cried. Liza joined in with illegible cries.

"Okay, come with me," Molly lifted Liza to her hip and followed Laci to the kitchen. She turned to Toni before entering the kitchen.

"Would you like some milk? Or I can fix us some coffee."Would coffee be too much trouble?"

"Coming right up."

That left Toni alone with Jay, and neither one was very comfortable with that. Jay really needed to go to the bathroom but he wasn't about to ask Toni to help him do that. When Toni mumbled something, suddenly jumped up, and grabbed the plate of brownies to take to Molly in the kitchen, he breathed a sigh of relief. He leaned back and closed his eyes. Molly would soon be back and she could help him get out of the recliner. It felt good to close his eyes. Why am I so tired? Will I ever be myself again?

WHEN MOLLY RETURNED with a plate of brownies and glass of milk, she found Jay asleep again. She set the plate and glass on the coffee table and gently shook him. "Jay?"

He stirred and squinted. "Mm?" He grunted.

"Here are your brownies and milk."

"Thanks, honey." Was it the pain medication making him so groggy? He was down to only one pill a day but he still seemed to sleep a lot.

Molly helped him straighten up in the chair and then placed the plate and glass within reach. "I'm going to go to the kitchen with Toni and the girls. Will you be okay by yourself out here?" She smoothed his hair back. He would need a haircut soon, and he definitely needed a shave.

"In a minute, can you help me get to the bathroom?" It was almost pitiful the way he looked up at her, and her heart went out to him. It must be awful for him to be so dependent on her. She kissed him on the forehead.

72

"Of course, honey. Just let me know when you are ready." Returning to the kitchen and seeing Toni's expression of concern, she wanted to pour out her heart, to tell Toni about the way she felt seeing her husband so helpless, about having to take care of the girls and him, about having to remain positive when she wanted to cry, and about having no one to talk to about her own needs. But she couldn't. Not with the girls right there with them. Tears threatened when she noticed Toni's concern, but she choked them back and fixed a smile on her face.

"Are they good?" Chocolate brownie pieces and vanilla frosting covered their faces and the countertop. Milk mustaches added to the mess. She should have had a camera ready.

"What a mess!" she laughed.

"It's my fault, isn't it?" Toni grimaced. "Shall I get some wet paper towels?"

"It's okay," Molly assured her. "This is completely normal in our house."

"I'm not as messy as Liza," Laci announced proudly through her milk mustache decorated with chocolate and vanilla bits. "Am I, Mommy?"

Glancing from Laci to Liza and back again, Molly and Toni looked at each other and burst into laughter. The gooey snack had given both children milk mustaches and brown-tipped noses and chins. There might have been less of a mess on the countertop or on their hands, but it was hard to tell. Even the hair around their faces sported bits of chocolate.

"I don't know about that," Molly told Laci. "But it's nothing that some soap and water won't fix."

Toni volunteered to take the girls to the bathroom and clean them up after their snack while Molly went to check on Jay. As Toni and the girls headed toward the bathroom, Molly helped Jay out of the recliner and onto his crutches and followed him as he headed to the master bath.

Jay himself was sporting some bits of chocolate on his own chin, which was badly in need of a shave.

"Look at you," she said as she brushed the chocolate off his face. He braced himself against the bathroom sink counter, leaned the crutches against the wall, and pulled her close.

"I miss you," he murmured as he began to kiss her neck.

"But I've been right here," she teased, wrapping her arms around him. Then as his hand in the small of her back pressed her closer, she realized that she had been missing him, too. His mouth moved to hers and lingered there, making her forget that Toni and the girls were in the bathroom down the hall. Either Jay remembered they had company, or he realized his physical limitations. He pulled back, tenderly pushing a tendril of Molly's blonde hair behind her ear.

"You better check on Toni. The girls may have her wrapped up in duct tape and toilet paper by now."

Molly giggled and kissed him on the nose. "Just call if you need anything."

"I'll be fine. I think I will take a bath and shave this woolly face."

"Take it easy and don't get too tired." Molly bent to get him a towel from the bottom of the cabinet.

When Jay patted her upturned bottom, she jumped, feigning indignance, and then punched the towel into his chest. "Behave yourself, Latimer. Plenty of time for that later."

"Hopefully sooner than later," he growled, winking at her as she shut the door behind her.

JOLIE LAUGHED IN nervous relief as she left Lopez's office. It hadn't been an interrogation after all. He and the other curators believed everything she told them and didn't question her story. They did not seem to believe that she or Kaycie had anything to do with the squirrel monkey's death. Lopez thanked her for the way she handled the situation and for writing the full sequence of events and a detailed description of what she had found. After asking the others if they had any questions, which they did not, he thanked her for coming in early and encouraged her to take a long break before reporting to work.

Jolie decided to return to her parents' house and visit for a while before work. She still had a couple of hours, and maybe her mother had something to eat. She was suddenly famished and couldn't face another frozen entrée.

As she drove the five miles from the zoo to her mother's, her cell phone rang from the depths of her purse. Cade. She answered and started searching for a place to pull over. There was no hands-free system in her old car.

"Jolie?" A masculine voice greeted her. "It's Cade." She whipped her car into a convenience store parking lot.

"Cade," was all she could manage. She had begun to wonder if she was going to hear from him at all.

"Cade Bishop."

"Yes! How are you?" Jolie found her manners. She fought the urge to start chattering. Stay calm, she instructed herself.

"I would really like to see you."

Her stomach somersaulted and stood for cheers. Her old car began to whine as it sat with the air conditioner running, so she turned it off. It would get unbearably hot inside the car soon, but she didn't want to roll the window down since it had a manual crank. "I would like to see you, too," she admitted, fighting a wave of nausea. Nerves.

"Do you have plans for lunch?"

As if I could eat anything now. "I'm on my way to my parents' house," she blurted, hoping they wouldn't mind if she brought a guest. They would probably be overjoyed that she was bringing a man with her. "Would you like to meet me there?"

She gave him directions to the McCray residence and was amazed when they arrived simultaneously. As she predicted, her parents were gracious and happy to meet Cade, who seemed to impress them. Ellie was shy and stuck close to her mother.

Mrs. McCray rose to the occasion by bringing out leftover roast beef, which she sliced for thick sandwiches and served with fresh vegetables from their garden. For dessert she served a pecan pie that she had fixed for Jolie's father the day before. She always seemed prepared for company.

Jolie's parents learned all they could about Cade without being nosy or offending Jolie. Ellie warmed up to Cade and kept them all entertained until too soon it was time for Jolie to go to work. Cade got up to leave as well, thanking her folks for the excellent meal and then promising Ellie to get her and his daughter together to play. Ellie clapped her hands in glee and then gave Jolie a goodbye kiss before Cade and Jolie went out the front door.

Jolie embraced her parents and whispered to them how much she appreciated their hospitality. They just smiled. "Have a good night at work, honey. We'll see you later." Her mother beamed with optimism.

Cade then walked Jolie to her car. "Thank you for inviting me here." He faced her, holding both of her hands. "It was wonderful meeting your folks and your daughter."

Jolie suddenly realized what introducing her parents to him must have implied. They had only been on one date, and already he was meeting her folks. What a great way to scare him off, because of course it made her look desperate. What had she been thinking? She had to fix this right away.

"I hope you don't take it the wrong way," she ventured. "I was headed over here when you called, and Mom always has plenty of food, and they love company. . ."

Cade put a finger to her lips. "Say no more. It was lovely."

Her heart jumped in her throat as he leaned in to lightly brush her lips with his. The heady scent of his cologne awakened her nostrils as he moved back. "I'll call you," he promised as he opened her door for her.

She nodded and scooted into the hot car, and then watched him as he shut the door and turned to get into his own car. She didn't even notice that she had not turned on the air until she was halfway to work. She was too intent on watching the classic Olds behind her until it turned down another street. As she lost sight of his car, she realized that she was baking and switched on the air. How will I be able to concentrate on work after this? Her lips still tingled from his touch.

Chapter Seven

JOLIE PRACTICALLY FLOATED from her car to the lounge where she put her purse and lunch in her locker, clocked in, and grabbed her radio. She was still early, so there was no one in the lounge yet, no one from the first shift clocking out, and no one from her shift clocking in.

She hooked her radio, keys, gloves, hose nozzle, flashlight, and multi-tool on her belt and headed into the restroom where she twisted her unruly frizzed locks into a bun and secured it with an Allen wrench from her key carabiner. So plain my name should be Jane, she thought as her reflection in the mirror stared back at her. What could a man like Cade see in her? At least she had put on makeup today for the questioning session with the curators, but the drab brown color of her zoo uniform did absolutely nothing for her complexion. Her mascara was already smearing from the heat, probably caused by the tiny droplets of sweat under her eyes. A few minutes in the outdoors putting up the animals for the night and she would be soaked from head to toe, her shirt, Bermuda shorts, and socks wringing wet. No fainting Southern belle, her body had adapted well to the heat and she produced the perspiration to prove it.

When night fell and the atmosphere cooled a bit, her damp clothing was a blessing, cooling her off until she sometimes got chills even on a hot summer night. If she hadn't been driving that old jalopy of hers, she might be a little concerned about soiling the interior with sweat and grime on her way home.

As her critical eye pointed out every perceived flaw, she completely missed the attractiveness of her petite and shapely frame, her bright green eyes, and heart-shaped full lips. Even her hair in its frizziest state created a red halo that set off her green eyes perfectly. It was this picture that Cade took with him back to work.

AS A BANKER and self-employed handyman, he had little time to spend with his daughter Maddie, much less time to date. But Maddie attended a wonderful daycare run by a grandmotherly woman who cared for Maddie and only three more children in her home. Mrs. Johnson did not mind when Cade was late picking her up or when he needed her on the occasional weekend while he worked on building his home repair business.

He hoped someday to have enough steady business to quit his job at the bank. To some it appeared to be a great job, indoors in the air conditioning, clean and respectable with great hours. It was stifling to Cade, who enjoyed being outdoors and working with his hands. Moving back to Timber City and anxious for a job so he could take full custody of Maddie, the bank position offered him the stability and respectability that the court was looking for. When the employment agency told him about the job as bank loan officer, he jumped at it. After a year he would be able to take advantage of benefits such as insurance and paid vacation time, which would give him even more opportunity to fulfill his dream of owning his own business.

His work buddy, the loan officer in the next cubicle, checked his watch and arched his eyebrow when Cade walked in. "One hour, ten minutes?"

"So now you're the lunch hour police?" Cade seated himself at his desk. Good. The loan packet for his newest client was now on his desk waiting for signatures.

"Sorry, man, I'm just tired of always being under the microscope myself," Mark said. "Sarah called me in the other day for being five minutes late from lunch."

Yeah, well, you are always late from lunch, and late getting to work as well, Cade thought. Getting to feel the softness of Jolie's lips was totally worth a call into his supervisor's office. So was the opportunity to meet her family. But he would have to be careful. Sarah would certainly notice.

Time to get back to work. As he flipped through a client packet to find their phone number, his mind wandered back to the woman who was beginning to become an obsession. Her eyes, her mouth, her hair, her figure, her scent—he couldn't get her out of his mind. Picking up the phone, he dialed Jolie's number instead of his client's.

He let it ring until her voicemail picked up, but suddenly Sarah strode out of her office and headed toward him. "It's Cade. Call me back when you can." He hung up the phone just as Sarah stopped in front of his desk.

Sarah Dearborn had earned her position as bank vice president by adopting a no-nonsense, nonsmiling, suit-and-pumps-wearing, hair-pulled-back-so-tight-she-would-never-need-a-facelift persona. She alone possessed the bank's power to hire and fire, which meant an admonition from her struck fear into her employees. Apparently Cade's ten-minutes-over lunch hour had ruffled her feathers. He decided to feign innocence.

"Hey, Sarah," he said, moving papers from one stack to another in an attempt to appear busy.

"Hello, Cade." She tapped the knuckles on her left hand with a pencil in her right as she stared at him for a few seconds. Well, out with it, Cade thought. Enough suspense. To be honest, if he had to describe her appearance, she was a fairly attractive lady.

"Did you find the Smithfield packet I left on your desk?"

"Yes, I was just about to call Mr. Smithfield and set up an appointment to sign the papers." Surely there had to be more. Was she going to ignore his ten-minute tardiness from lunch? Wasn't there going to be a detention assigned? He almost smiled at the thought.

"You probably haven't had a chance to look through it, but I believe a page was left out. Would you please double check and let me know if I need to look at it again before you call him? Thanks." She wheeled around and headed back to her office as Cade nodded in agreement.

When her door shut behind her, Mark spoke up. "What was that? You got off scot-free, you lucky dog!" Cade chuckled and began leafing through the loan packet. "You owe me, Bishop!"

"Not a chance," Cade replied. "Watch and learn, Lasater. Don't you have work to do?"

"More than you can imagine," Mark retorted.

Cade shrugged. The Smithfield loan. Much as he hated to admit it, Sarah had a sharp eye. He had indeed overlooked a page of the packet. Turning to his computer, he dashed off an email to her explaining which page it was and that he could easily add it without her needing to look at it. Then he pulled up the file, printed the page, removed the staple from the packet, and inserted it where it needed to be. When he picked up the phone though, he dialed Jolie's number again instead of Smithfield. He needed to hear her voice.

JOLIE COULDN'T WAIT to fill Kaycie in on the details of her impromptu lunch date with Cade, so when Kaycie got to the lounge a few minutes late, Jolie could hardly contain herself. "Where have you been? I've been waiting for you!"

"What are you talking about? I'm always ten minutes late. What's up?"

"You'll never guess who I had lunch with today." She wiggled from side to side in anticipation.

Kaycie slipped her time card through the clock and into the slot below Jolie's. She then tossed her lunch tote into the refrigerator and headed across the lounge to her locker. "Hm, your parents?" She was stalling and Jolie knew it.

"Cade!" Jolie exclaimed in exasperation. "He called to ask what I was doing for lunch and when I told him I was going to my parents' house, he agreed to meet me there!"

"Fantastic! See, I knew you guys would hit it off." Kaycie slammed her locker shut after getting her gear together.

"I guess you were right. I think my folks really liked him, and he was very good with them and Ellie. You don't think he will read too much into it, do you? I mean, me inviting him to meet my parents and all?"

"What is this, the 1950's? I think he is smart enough to realize that it was just a coincidence since he asked you where you were going.

Besides that, what if he does read something into it? Aren't you looking for the same thing he is looking for?"

She had a point. Her jeans pocket vibrated. Someone was calling her. Her heartbeat quickened. No one ever called her. She hoped nothing was wrong with Ellie or her parents. She pulled the phone out of her pocket. The number wasn't familiar at all.

"I'm going to talk to Lopez to see if there is any news on Jay. Meet me on the terrace," Kaycie said as she headed out the door.

Jolie nodded as she answered the phone. "Hello?"

"Jolie?"

Cade.

"Hi." She tried to hide the excitement she felt.

"I hope you won't get into trouble because I called you at work. I just wanted to hear your voice again. I really enjoyed lunch with you and your folks." He paused. She could hear his breath and it made her heart beat a little faster. "I can't stop thinking about you."

Was she dreaming? Could this handsome, available man really be saying this to her? Please don't let me screw this up, she prayed, closing her eyes. Dare she say it? "I feel the same way."

"When can I see you again?" Then his tone changed. "Yes, sir, I can certainly schedule this for tomorrow afternoon. How about 2:30? Great! I will see you then." Jolie realized that he was pretending to talk to a customer. She took the lead, surprising herself.

"Call me when you get off work." Then she hung up to keep him from getting into trouble. His attention had given her new confidence to be coy and hopefully mysterious. It was time for her to get to work as well, or else she would be hearing it from Kaycie. And Lucas might tell Jay on her.

Kaycie was just leaving Lopez's office when Jolie got to the terrace overlooking the giraffe, elephant, and African lion exhibits. Deep moats separated the three areas, but from a distance it appeared that the three species lived as they do in the wild, with plenty of trees and an expansive grassy area to wander. Tall bamboo plants with taller pine trees and mighty oak trees behind them surrounded the acreage while hanging baskets full of trailing flowers were scattered around the terrace. It was a beautiful area of the zoo, which was probably the reason Lopez and the other curators had their offices there just off the terrace.

"Did you find out anything?" Jolie asked. "Is Jay coming back any time soon?"

"Lopez said he talked to Jay this morning and he has a doctor's appointment next week. He hopes the doctor will release him to come back to work then." Kaycie looked around. "Have you seen Lucas yet?"

"No, I haven't."

"Speak of the devil." Kaycie laughed. They turned to see Lucas lumbering up to the terrace, adjusting his tool belt. He grinned and waved. "Wonder what makes him so late today?"

LUCAS HAD AWAKENED late that morning to the sound of the vacuum cleaner running in the other room. The bedroom door was shut but he could still hear the high-pitched whirr. He had asked Deana so many times he had lost count not to vacuum while he was trying to sleep. Glancing at the clock, he realized that he had slept an hour longer than he intended to. Maybe this was Deana's way of sounding the alarm for him. He would let it go this time. He should be up anyway.

The shower felt especially good this morning. He hoped Deana still had some coffee in the pot waiting for him. Stepping out of the shower, he wrapped a towel around his waist and ventured into the den, not noticing that his hair was still dripping. Deana was wrapping the vacuum cleaner cord around the hooks on the back of the vacuum, unaware that he had come out of the bedroom and bath.

"Hey, beautiful," he said as he goosed her.

She emitted the cry he had hoped for. As she whirled around, he caught her against him and held her captive as she squirmed, pretending to want to escape. "Lucas! How am I supposed to get my work done?"

"This is your work," he growled, nuzzling her neck. Her pregnancy had done nothing to squelch his desire for his wife. If anything, it had made her more attractive to him. But he released her after only a few moments, leaving her face and neck damp from his wet hair. "I need to call Jay and see if I am still on to start my vacation tomorrow."

"Vacation? You're going to be on vacation? Did you tell me that?"

Lucas could tell the wheels in her head were spinning. "Don't panic, honey. I really didn't plan on us going anywhere. I thought it would be a great time to finish the baby's room and do some repairs on the house before the baby comes." He smiled. "And spend some time with my honey before the baby comes and she forgets I exist."

"That will never happen," she pouted, plopping down on the couch. "You are going to be chief diaper changer." She smiled up at him.

Lucas grimaced and plopped down beside her, wet towel and all. "We will see about that. Besides, I don't know if Jay will be able to come back so I can take off a week."

"Well, you go ahead and call him and I'll get you some coffee." With a slight push from behind, Deana rose from the sofa awkwardly and headed toward the tiny kitchen.

That's my girl, Lucas thought, getting up and heading back to the bedroom to get his cell phone. Although not working and living with a zookeeper husband meant there was not a lot of income, she had made the conscious choice to quit her job as a schoolteacher as soon as she had discovered she was pregnant. Lucas worried about making ends meet but he appreciated her decision to become a full-time wife and mother. There were certainly times when he wished there was more money coming in, but he loved her being home when he woke up and when he got home. He loved the house being clean and orderly, and he loved the little things she did like bringing his coffee to him, setting his clothes out for him, and even staying up late to greet him when he got home from work.

No doubt the baby would change things. It would demand all her attention for a long while, and her body would go through lots of changes, physically and emotionally, but he was ready. He couldn't wait to meet his son or daughter.

After finding his cell phone in the last night's work pants, he sat down on the bed and dialed Jay's number. "Hey, man!" he heard as Jay answered the phone. Jay sounded cheerful.

"Hey, Boss. How are you doing?"

"Better every day. Is everything going okay?"

"Going great, but we miss our boss."

"I miss you guys, too. I'm hoping the doc will release me after I see her in a few days."

"In a few days? I guess I won't be able to take my week off, then, huh?"

Jay sighed and Lucas heard it. Maybe he shouldn't have called. The last thing Jay needed to be doing was worrying about giving him some time off. "I forgot all about that, Lucas. When was your vacation supposed to start?"

"Actually tomorrow. But it can wait. I didn't really have any plans other than doing some stuff around the house."

"Let me think about it. Maybe I can figure out something."

"Nah, just forget about it," Lucas replied. "It's no big deal. It can wait until you are back at work and feeling like yourself again."

"Nope, by that time Deana might have delivered and you won't be able to get anything done. I will call Lopez and get back to you."

"Are you sure?" Lucas really hated to put Jay out. Deana came into the bedroom and set a steaming mug of coffee on the nightstand. She ruffled his hair and drifted out.

"Yeah, I'll call you in a bit."

KAYCIE AND JOLIE stared at Lucas until he reached the terrace. "What?"

"Don't say anything to us about being late," Kaycie baited him.

"I'm late one day and you are late four out of five days a week and you tell me not to say anything? Ha!" Lucas wiped the sweat from his brow with a bandana he pulled from his pocket. "Wonder when this heat will break? It's getting old."

"I know, right?" Kaycie shook her head. "I think I've lost ten pounds with all this sweating!"

Jolie rolled her eyes. "As if you had ten pounds to lose in the first place."

"Women and their weight," Lucas muttered, rolling his eyes as well.

"Hey, I talked to Lopez just now and he said the doctor might release Jay to come back next week," Kaycie informed him.

"I just talked to him this morning. He sounded good," Lucas replied.

Several parents walked by, some pushing strollers of red-faced toddlers, trailed by red-faced preschoolers clutching dripping snow-cones that had stained their chins and shirts. The preschoolers were entranced by the sight of three bona fide zookeepers standing right there in front of them. One of them stopped to stare, and he kept staring for several seconds.

"What's up, little guy?" Kaycie knelt to face him.

"Are you a real zookeeper?" His mother hadn't noticed yet that he wasn't following her.

"Sure am. We all are. This is Lucas and this is Jolie. I'm Kaycie. What's your name?"

"Are you gonna feed the lions?" The little boy ignored her question.

"Yes, we will later on," Jolie told him.

"You're not afraid?"

"No, because they are behind bars in their holding areas." What a cute kid. Lucas wondered if this is what he had to look forward to. He couldn't wait.

"What's a holding area?" the little boy persisted, full of questions.

"It's a safe place where the animals stay at night after they eat their dinner," Lucas explained. What will my little one look like? Will it be a boy? Will he have curly brown hair like mine or fine blonde hair like Deana's? He stared at the little boy's face, marveling at its innocence

and beauty. Suddenly he wanted the baby to come now, yesterday. He wanted to meet the product of his union with the love of his life. The little boy had no clue what thoughts were running through Lucas's mind, while Jolie's and Kaycie's mouths dropped open in astonishment at this new facet of Lucas's personality.

"Will you show me?"

"Jonathan!" It was the panicked cry of a mother who has lost her child in a crowd. "Jonathan!" Almost hysterical.

Jolie and Kaycie saw her immediately, running here and there, frantically searching for her baby, her eyes wide with fear.

"We have him!" Kaycie shouted, raising her arm to get the lady's attention. "He's over here!"

The mother was there in the blink of an eye, grabbing the boy in a frightened hug so tight he cried out. "Mommy, you're hurting me!"

She released him immediately. "Sorry, baby, but I thought you were lost! You scared me!" She stood, facing the keepers and extending one hand while the other gripped her child's shoulder.

"Thank you so much. I just knew someone had grabbed him."

"Mommy, they feed the lions! I get to see!"

At the sharp look from the mother, Lucas shook his head. "Sorry, little dude, we can't let you see us feed the lions. But you know what? If you will come back at around 2:00 one afternoon, you can see the otters get fed." He patted Jonathan's head.

"But I want to see the lions eat an antelope!" The kid's face twisted into a scowl as he let out a howl. Jolie and Kaycie glanced at each other. "Mommy! Make him let me see the lions eat!" he wailed.

Mom shook her head, grabbed the child's hand and began to pull him away. At his protests and stalling, she promised him a trip to the gift shop if he cooperated. He immediately straightened up and complied.

JOLIE AND KAYCIE exchanged amused looks and headed for the west side where they would start gathering food bowls from the Texas area. It was Jolie's favorite area because she loved the river otters, bobcats, and alligators more than any other animals in the zoo.

She loved seeing the river otters scurrying over the rocks and leaping into the water where visitors could see their underwater antics through the thick plexiglass wall. The otters sometimes even seemed to enjoy the attention, but most of the time they were so nonchalant they preferred to sleep even when crowds of people had come to the zoo just to see them swimming.

The bobcats intrigued Jolie because they seemed like housecats until they reached through the piano wire and grabbed a visitor's hat, sunglasses, or camera with lightning speed. There was no way to retrieve such an item for visitors who ignored the signs posted. Occasionally a visitor would protest, whining that their camera or sunglasses were very expensive, but all Jolie and Kaycie could do was shrug and point to the signs: "Caution: animals are wild. Please stay behind the barriers. Not responsible for lost items."

Either the visitor would threaten to report them to the zoo administrators, or they would grin sheepishly and go on. Threats were unfounded, but Jolie just figured it made the embarrassment a little less difficult to endure. Keepers would retrieve the items at feeding time when the cats were in their holding areas to eat and sleep, but most of the time the items were not in good shape. Occasionally Jolie brought stuffed animal toys home to Ellie that had not been destroyed by the bobcats. After a cycle or two in the washer and dryer they turned out almost as good as new.

Kaycie and Jolie split up to retrieve food bowls and spray down areas. Just as one went toward the otter exhibit and the other headed to the bobcats, an earsplitting scream sent their hearts into their throats.

Chapter Eight

KAYCIE AND JOLIE jumped back so fast they almost collided. Looking both ways, they tried to figure out which direction the scream came from, and then they heard it again. It was around the corner of the boardwalk near the bobcat exhibit. Curious visitors began moving in that direction as Kaycie and Jolie bolted toward that area. They had to weave in and out of people and then push their way through to the front of the exhibit where a woman was crying and pointing. Kaycie reached the woman first. Jolie was right behind her.

"What is it?" Kaycie demanded. It had better be good to cause this much of a stir. All the woman could do was point. Jolie and Kaycie saw it at the same time. Two of their bobcats were standing over another one lying on the ground. For a second it appeared that the one on the ground was asleep or sick and the others were guarding it. But as Jolie stared, she realized that a good deal of blood covered the one on the ground. There was also blood on the mouths and noses of the other two standing over it.

Jolie glanced at Kaycie, who had come to the same conclusion. Time to get the public away from the exhibit.

"Okay, people, let's move on," Kaycie shouted. No one was listening. She shouted again, louder this time. "Come on, people, we need you to move away from this exhibit, please." Some glanced around to see if anyone else was going to move. Jolie sprang into action and grabbed her radio.

"Code 4, bobcat exhibit. Code 4, bobcat exhibit." She repeated it once more, and soon keepers and armed security guards surrounded the throng of people, directing them away from the exhibit toward the concessions and aquarium building.

Kaycie took off around the exhibit to the door leading into the holding area to try and get the cats to come in, though she knew it was hopeless. They would never leave their fresh dinner for thawed-out generic prey meat. She had never in her wildest imagination thought that bobcats would become cannibalistic, though. She supposed it was because they had never had the opportunity. But how did they get the opportunity? Last night all three bobcats seemed as healthy as could be.

This was just too weird. And, of course, a crowd of people had seen it. Not good, because the news channels were sure to get word and soon be there to find out all they could.

Jolie joined Kaycie in the building. "They're not going to come in."

"I know but I thought it was worth a try anyway."

Jolie wondered if they should return outside to make sure that someone was questioning the woman who screamed, but it probably didn't matter, because the woman would already be gone, hustled on with everyone else.

Jolie flopped down onto a stool by the supervisor's desk. "What is happening around here? This is the second animal we have lost in two weeks."

"It's probably just a coincidence. Sometimes animals attack their own when they detect weakness. It's their way of keeping the gene pool strong." Kaycie locked the door that led directly into the cage area and turned to face Jolie.

"You're right. But they all looked so healthy and playful yesterday." She got up to go back outside, Kaycie following her. They both knew the curators would be looking for them. Exhaustion threatened to overtake Jolie as she trudged through the door from the cat house.

Security guards were busy roping off the area when the ladies emerged. The curators had not arrived yet. A glance at the cats revealed a grisly scene they would not soon forget. Nature was not kind at times, and it was a hard lesson to learn. The security guards refrained from speaking, probably out of respect for the sensitivity of keepers about their charges. They just nodded in greeting and went on about their task.

The women trudged up the hill toward the otter exhibit without really knowing what to do next. Should they wait for the curators or go on about their work? Jolie worried about the small children who may have witnessed the grisly scene. She shuddered to think of Ellie seeing something like that. Maybe they wouldn't understand what had happened. Suddenly Jolie heard her name. "Jolie! Wait!" Lucas sprinted towards them. "Kaycie! Hold up!"

They remained silent as he caught up with him, huffing and puffing from the heat and the weight of the tools he carried around his waist. "Come on." He grabbed their hands and pulled them to the otter house fence, then fumbled with his keys before finding the one that unlocked the gate, and then another which unlocked the door to the otter house. Shoving them past himself, he quickly closed the gate, locked it, and then closed the door and bolted it from the inside.

"Hey!" Kaycie protested. "What are you doing?"

"I'm keeping you out of trouble. Lopez has put out a call for the lady who started the screaming and got the crowd around the exhibit. He also wants to know who the first keepers on the scene were and who called Code 4. He is already threatening to fire Martinez."

Diego Martinez was the supervisor of cats, and it was his crew's responsibility to pick up on any abnormal animal behavior before it turned into a crisis. Obviously, no one had reported any strange behavior from the bobcats and now the public had witnessed a horrific cannibalism in animals who were usually as peaceful as housecats. It spelled bad publicity for the zoo.

"Fire Martinez? He wasn't even there!" Kaycie stood with her hands on her hips, as if ready to fight someone. "Who put the burr under Lopez's saddle?"

"Lopez has to report to the director. He's worried about his job. Oates hates bad publicity," Lucas said.

General curator and director and also one-time owner Bradford W. Oates had sold the zoo to the city years ago to avoid willing it to his delinquent son. One condition of the sale had been that he remained zoo director until he was no longer able or no longer interested.

"I get it." Jolie rubbed her arm where Lucas had grabbed her.

Lucas noticed. "I'm sorry if I was too rough with you girls. I didn't mean to be. I just didn't want you to be in the line of fire. Lopez needs to calm down before he gets to see you."

"Because he is wanting to fire someone and he thinks we could have prevented the whole thing?" Kaycie's mouth drew up as it did when she was angry. Jolie sighed.

"Thank you, Lucas. Thanks for having our backs." Jolie threw her arms around him, catching him off guard and causing him to blush. Lucas's shirt was pretty wet but the odor was more pleasant than unpleasant, Jolie noticed. Weird that I should notice that.

"Yeah, thanks, buddy. We owe you one," Kaycie agreed.

"Y'all should stay here--at least until the zoo closes. You can close the gates and clean this area while you wait," Lucas suggested.

"Gee thanks," Kaycie smirked.

"Better than being bored or worried." Lucas shrugged his wide shoulders.

"She's kidding, Lucas. We were going to clean this area anyway. That is why we were so close to the action. Right, Kaycie?"

"Yeah, that's right. Actually, I was headed right here. We can keep ourselves busy. I've been meaning to scrub that mold off the ceiling anyway."

Satisfied, Lucas turned toward the door to leave. "It's only 45 minutes until closing time. I'm going to try and get hold of Jay before anybody else does." He unbolted the door and exited the building.

Jolie and Kaycie got to work spraying the otter area down with water and a little bleach and when they were satisfied that it was clean enough, they pulled bandanas out of their pockets and tied them over their hair. After finding brushes and a bucket, they donned gloves and face masks before filling the bucket with water and bleach. Then they began scrubbing the walls and ceiling.

Just as Jolie believed her arm was going to fall off from the overhead scrubbing, her cell phone vibrated in her jeans pocket. She stopped, removed her glove, and pulled her phone out, something she would never do in front of Jay or Lucas or anybody else in the zoo but Kaycie. Kaycie stopped scrubbing as well, interested to see who was calling.

As always when she received a phone call at work, Jolie's stomach lurched, thinking it was bad news about Ellie or her parents. But this time the screen read "Cade." She was glad she had thought to save his number the last time he had called.

Cade, she mouthed. Kaycie nodded and winked and returned to scrubbing as Jolie turned away.

"Hello?"

"Hey, darlin,' can you talk or should I let you go?" His voice seemed lower and huskier than usual, causing her heart to flutter.

"Hi, Cade! No, I can talk." Jolie glanced over at Kaycie, who made swishing sounds with the scrub brush as she worked.

Cade regaled her with the tale of his late return from lunch and his coworker hoping he would get into trouble with his supervisor, which didn't happen. "When are your days off?" he asked.

"Unfortunately not until Wednesday and Thursday."

"Actually, that is excellent. It will give me time to plan your surprise."

"My surprise?" Jolie's curiosity piqued.

"Yes, ma'am, and don't ask me what it is because it is a surprise," Cade teased. "Is 10:00 a.m. too early?"

"No, it isn't, but don't you have to work?"

"I have vacation days coming. Not to worry, my dear. I will pick you up at 10:00. You can dress very casually. Ellie can come, too."

That had been her next question. She liked to spend her days off with Ellie since she felt she didn't give her daughter enough of her time. "Will Maddie be coming as well?"

"Yes, so I will see you Wednesday morning." And without waiting for her to say goodbye, he hung up.

Jolie promptly informed Kaycie of her special surprise being planned by Cade. Kaycie shared her excitement with a high five.

JAY HOPED THAT Dr. Packer would allow him to return to work after this visit. He hadn't even entertained the thought that he wouldn't. But Dr. Packer asked him a few questions which helped him see for himself that he wasn't ready for a work release. Yes, he was still on pain medication. Yes, he was still heavily dependent on the crutches. Yes, he slept much of the day. Yes, he still needed assistance moving around the house and taking care of personal needs. Yes, putting weight on his leg was excruciating, even with pain meds. It appeared that he would not be able to return to work for a while. Dr. Packer was sympathetic but unwavering. "If you want complete use and mobility of your leg, you must give it time to heal properly." Jay nodded in unhappy acknowledgement.

MOLLY WAS AT a loss. She realized that Jay was getting bored and restless, but he was having mood swings as well. He had become increasingly irritable, and when he saw that his supervisor from the zoo had left a message on their answering machine, Jay got so tense and grumpy that he practically barked at her and Laci. Startled by the sudden outburst, Laci burst into tears, making the tension even worse. Without a word Molly helped him into his recliner and then turned to take care of Laci. Of course, hearing Laci's tears, Liza began wailing from the playard where Molly had placed her while getting Jay out of the car and into the house. Molly understood Jay's frustration and helplessness, but there was no excuse for upsetting the children.

"You could at least try to be nicer to your daughters," Molly whispered before turning to Laci. "Come on, honey, I'm sure Daddy didn't mean to hurt your feelings. It's just that his leg still hurts." She guided Laci toward the playard, picked up Liza, and led them into the kitchen. Maybe some lunch would make them all feel better.

FEELING LIKE A louse for making his girls cry, Jay rubbed his eyes. I'm going to grow roots in this stupid recliner, he thought. He picked up the phone and dialed Lopez's number.

"Lopez," came the gruff answer.

"Yeah, it's Jay Latimer. You left a message?"

Lopez cleared his throat. "We've lost another animal, Jay. A bobcat. A visitor spotted the other two bobcats feeding on one. Jolie and Kaycie were the ones who called for help."

Jay took advantage of the pause as anger welled up inside him. What was it, Slam Jay Latimer Day? "You don't have to say it, Lopez. You think my girls are responsible, don't you?"

Silence.

"Or Lucas Slade?" Unbelievable. He couldn't seriously think. . .

"I have to pin this on somebody, Jay. Oates has gotten wind of it and he wants answers. Once this hits the news we may all lose our jobs."

"Well, you better pin it on somebody else. Has anyone thought that it could be someone on the third shift or one of the day keepers? How many employees have been hired and quit in the last few months? It could be anyone!" Jay's voice rose with emotion.

"I just called to let you know that we are investigating every possible lead. Your loyalty to your crew is admirable, Jay, but you may have to face the fact that you may have an animal killer on your watch."

"You want to know what I think?" Without waiting for him to reply, he continued: "I think you should--"

"Jay!" Molly shouted from the kitchen doorway. He stopped short, glancing over to see Molly's widened eyes and shaking head, with Laci clinging to her blouse and Liza on her hip. He had been about to say something ugly without thinking of the little ears that would hear it. He took a deep breath.

"Do what you have to do, Lopez. I would bet my life on my crew—in fact, my crew saved my life just a few weeks ago--but go ahead and interrogate me and them. By the time you figure out that it isn't us, another animal will have died. Maybe more." With that, Jay hung up. He looked over at his family. Molly frowned at him as she patted the back of Laci's head, who had buried her face in her mother's blouse. Only Liza acted as if nothing was amiss.

He would have run to Molly and folded her into his arms if he could have gotten up by himself. He wanted to lift Laci up and twirl her around and around and make her giggle until she hiccupped. Instead all he could do was run his hand over his face and wish he could take back the words that had made Laci cry. Just as he was going to call them over to his chair, Molly turned and disappeared into the kitchen with the girls. Silence loomed heavy in the kitchen where noisy chatter usually reigned. Jay lay his head back against the headrest and closed his eyes. Hot tears stung the back of his lids as he fought to hold them back.

Then he felt a light touch on his arm. Opening his eyes he beheld the beautiful face of his older daughter shyly gazing at him as she held a plate out to him. As her bottom lip trembled he realized that she was afraid of him. Her mother must have instructed her to bring him the plate.

He took the plate from her and set it on the table on the other side of the chair. With the other hand, he cupped her small head and leaned over to plant a kiss on her forehead. "Laci, Daddy is so sorry."

She nodded, a big tear slipping down her cheek. "'S okay, Daddy." Her little voice wavered, breaking his heart.

"Come here, Sweetheart," he said, his voice unnaturally husky. As Laci clambered into his lap, he snuggled her close to his heart, lay his head on top of hers, and allowed the tears to flow.

Molly watched from the kitchen, tears escaping her eyes. She hugged Liza close and then turned to put her in the high chair, but thought again. She went into the den and knelt down beside Jay's chair with Liza. Jay lifted his head from Laci's and gazed into Molly's hurt, moist eyes.

"I'm sorry, baby," he whispered to her before her lips met his for a quick and salty kiss.

"Hungwy!" Liza cried, ending the quiet moment. Laci's giggles soon made lunchtime at the Latimer house somewhat normal again.

WEDNESDAY MORNING, CADE and Maddie arrived at Jolie's little house promptly at ten. When they climbed up the wooden porch steps and knocked on the door, they heard a shriek and some scrambling around on the hardwood floors. A few seconds later, Jolie opened the door a crack. He was holding his little girl, and she was adorable.

"Good morning!" Jolie smiled as she peered around the edge of the door. "Hang on, okay?" The door shut on his confused face before he could reply. At least there was a screen door to soften the blow.

"Is he early?" Jolie asked no one in particular as she ran back into her bedroom to pull on denim Bermuda shorts and a fitted tee. Ellie had climbed down from her booster seat and was about to "help" the cat eat its breakfast. "Ellie! Come here, Sweetie! Let's get you dressed!"

Jolie popped into the bathroom to check her face and hair before opening the front door. She would brush her teeth and do her makeup and hair in a second after letting Cade in and getting Ellie dressed.

She was all apologies when she finally opened the door. "I am so sorry I kept you waiting. I guess I didn't realize how late it was getting. Come on in and make yourselves comfortable. I still need to get Ellie dressed and finish up myself." She hoped Cade didn't mind seeing her without makeup. It was pretty early in the relationship to shock him like this, but the fact that she was even thinking in terms of relationships was even scarier.

"Take your time." Cade sank into a well-worn chair in the tiny living room. "We'll just wait right here, huh, Maddie? Look, there is a baby doll right over there."

As Maddie scrambled down from his lap to investigate, Cade stood up again and extended his arm toward Jolie. But my teeth aren't brushed, she protested silently as she moved closer and took his hand. He brushed her closed lips with his own, intoxicating her with the scent of his cologne. She could have melted into his arms and stayed there all day in total contentment.

Cade moved back after a moment, though he still held her hand as he rested his forehead against hers.

The tender greeting didn't last long. A piercing screech filled the air as Ellie pattered into the room towards Maddie. "Mine! Mine!" She snatched the baby doll away, which knocked Maddie off balance, sending her down hard on the floor. At least her diapered bottom cushioned the impact, but she wailed as if she were mortally wounded. "Mine! My doll!" Ellie continued to scream.

As Cade rushed to Maddie's aid, Jolie grabbed Ellie and her baby doll and whisked her back to the bedroom to dress her and try to make her understand that what she had just done was wrong. Cade checked Maddie for injuries and then settled on the couch to console the little girl. Hopefully the day will go better than this, Jolie thought as she explained to Ellie the importance of sharing.

It couldn't have gone better. The two toddlers became fast friends once Jolie convinced them that there were enough baby dolls to go around. She allowed Ellie to have the newest doll her Grammy had given her and gave Maddie another less-favored but just as nice one from Ellie's collection. Cade still would not reveal what his surprise was, so Jolie resigned herself to the fact that she would find out soon enough and settled back into the seat to wait while the girls chattered in their car seats in the backseat.

To the girls' delight and Jolie's surprise, Cade had also brought along his English bulldog Jack, who rode in the back seat between the girls' car seats. Content to sit and endure the toddler girls' pulling on his ears and patting his back a little too hard, he just sat there, panting and dripping saliva onto the towel-covered leather seat.

Cade drove them out of town into the country and finally through the gates of a state park. He paid the day fee, and as they rode deeper into the pine forest, Jolie found herself relaxing. Soon a large lake came into view. Cade pulled into a well-shaded spot overlooking the lake. There was even a children's play area just a few feet away so they could relax and still keep an eye on the girls.

Jolie exited the car after waiting for Cade to open the door, expecting a hot blast of summer air, but surprisingly there was a pleasant breeze coming off the lake. The children's area was even shaded.

"This is wonderful!" she said before turning to fold the seats forward and unbuckle the girls. Jack jumped out of the car and ran around in circles, enjoying his new-found freedom.

"I hoped you would like it here," Cade said as he opened the trunk.

Soon the girls were playing on swings, a short slide, stacked tires, and other items which Cade and Jolie inspected carefully before letting them go. He spread a large quilt on a cushion of soft pine needles and motioned for Jolie to sit down. He then plopped down beside her, close enough so that she could feel the hair on his arms and tanned shorts-clad legs. It tickled and left her skin tingling. When he kicked off his flip flops she followed suit.

She stretched out her own long legs and noticed they were not tanned like his. At least she had shaved them yesterday so that hadn't been an issue that morning during her rush. Jack trotted between her and Cade and then over to the girls as if checking on everyone.

"How did you know about this place?" Jolie had heard of a state park nearby but had never visited. Her parents had never been into the whole picnicking, camping, swimming thing. If she went swimming, it was always at the city pool, which lately had not been well-kept. The only pool Ellie knew was the plastic kind from the dollar store.

"I used to come here as a teenager. My friends and I would hang out at the swimming area watching the girls." Cade turned to her and laughed. "You know how teenage boys are."

She smiled, trying to imagine him as a teenager.

"But even then I noticed how nice it would be to bring a family here someday. This is the first time I have brought Maddie here. I scoped it out a few days ago and found this spot. I'm glad you like it."

The girls were having a big time out in the play area. Cade covered Jolie's hand resting on the quilt next to his with his own hand and squeezed it. Jolie's gaze shifted from the girls to him, his dark eyes mesmerizing. "Thank you for coming with me and Maddie today."

With that, he leaned over to kiss her. Instinctively, her lips parted, allowing him deeper access into her mouth and into her heart. To her, this was the point of no return, and she did not hesitate. A flood of emotion and heat filled her mind and body as she allowed herself to feel again.

If it hadn't been for Ellie and the all-powerful motherly protective instinct, emotion would have totally taken over any rational thought. But Jolie pulled herself out of the emotional tsunami she was experiencing just before she lost herself. "Wait." A quick glance to the girls revealed that they were playing as if nothing had happened. As if the world had not stopped spinning with that one kiss. As if her heart had not burst out of its hardened shell, the one created by the man who had put her through The Divorce. As if her heart was not betraying her by making her break her own promise to herself to never be that vulnerable again. As if the future had not just taken on new promise.

Cade leaned back, his own breath ragged and quick. "I'm sorry. I thought--. Please forgive me."

"There's nothing to forgive." She hesitated. "You are wonderful. This is wonderful. I just--." She stopped.

"You don't have to explain. I understand."

And she really thought he did, as Ellie and Maddie came running back to them as fast as their toddler legs could carry them. "Thirsthy, thirsthy," Ellie cried, throwing herself against Jolie.

"Thirsthy, too, Daddy." Maddie fell onto her daddy's lap.

Cade fell backwards laughing as Maddie repeated herself. Ellie continued to repeat herself as well. Jack jumped around as best he could with his stocky body and licked the girls' faces.

"I hope you came prepared!" Jolie shouted over the din.

Cade scrambled up, set Maddie next to Jolie and Ellie, and retrieved an ice chest from the trunk of his car. Setting it down next to the quilt, he opened it to reveal bottles of water, sippy cups, juice boxes, chips, cookies, fruit, and a zippered plastic bag full of sandwiches.

"I have to say I'm impressed." Jolie watched as Cade poured water into two sippy cups and handed one to each child. The chatter ceased as the girls satisfied their thirst. Jolie took a bottle offered by Cade. He even poured some water in a plastic bowl for the dog. If she weren't careful, Cade would shatter everything she had decided about men after Sean. She settled back and let Cade serve her and Ellie and Maddie a delicious lunch that he had prepared just for them. She could certainly get used to this.

Chapter Nine

DEANA SHOOK HER husband. He had slept way too long and would be late to work. Lucas grunted and turned away from her. Okay, that's it. She grabbed the covers and yanked them off, feeling the muscles pull in her stretched-out abdomen. Her stretchmarks had their own stretchmarks.

"All right, slacker! Time to get up!" She clutched her belly with one hand and tossed a pillow at his head with the other. Then she eased herself down on the bed beside him.

Grinning, he tossed the pillow back at her, then gently pulled her against him. Her belly was getting so big she couldn't wiggle out of his grasp even if she tried.

"Aren't you going to get up today?" She faced him with her head on his pillow. "You're going to be late, you know. Don't you care if Junior has a roof over his head and food in his mouth?"

Lucas groaned and pulled the covers over his head.

"Come on, baby, you need to get your shower. It's getting late." Deana attempted to sit up.

"My vacation starts today," Lucas informed her. "I guess I forgot to tell you. I've got plenty of time. Just relax." He eased her into his arms. Once his lips claimed hers, it would be awhile before either one of them were up.

MOLLY STOOD IN the checkout line at the grocery store trying to pay for her purchases when the machine wouldn't accept her debit card. "Denied." She frowned and inserted it into the chip reader again.

Laci was picking up every item strategically placed at child's eye level while Liza drooled animal crackers.

"Wait, I didn't scan those animal crackers," the cashier said, tapping her foot.

"I brought those from home," Molly said. Then she handed her card to the cashier and asked as nice as she could. "Could you try running this? The card reader isn't working."

The cashier scanned Molly's card on her machine. "It was denied, ma'am." The cashier handed the card back and just stood there, staring at Molly and waiting for her to do something about it.

"Can you please try it again?" Molly's face burned with embarrassment. There were several people in line behind them, and although no one had said anything, she could see the impatience in their faces.

"Can I buy this, Mommy?" Laci held up a ring pop.

"No!" Molly waited for the cashier to run the card again. Laci pouted.

The cashier, no older than twenty in Molly's estimation, mechanically rescanned the card. Then she turned back to Molly, handing her the card. "Still denied."

"That's impossible!" Molly dug in her wallet and pulled out their only credit card, the one they used only for emergencies. "Here, use this one." She tried handing it to the girl.

"Just swipe or insert it, please."

Molly rolled her eyes as she swiped the card through the machine on the counter. Accepted. Finally. But Jay wouldn't be happy when he saw the credit card bill. She would have to call the bank when she got home.

"Mommy, can I buy this?" Laci tugged on Molly's shirt while holding up a container of kid's lip gloss. Thank goodness Liza was still happily chewing the animal crackers.

"I said no," Molly repeated in a lowered voice. Laci folded her arms and pouted as hard as she could.

Molly scribbled her signature on the screen and took the receipt from the cashier. Enduring the stares from the people waiting behind her, she wheeled her shopping cart out of the lane and toward the exit. Laci followed at a distance but stepped it up when Molly turned around. "Come on, Laci. Let's go."

She had planned to treat the girls to McDonald's but if her debit card was not working she couldn't do that. She didn't have enough cash to cover it. Glad that she hadn't told them about the treat, she headed straight home to put the groceries away and call the bank. Maybe Jay would know something.

JAY WAS FINALLY going back to work. After he practically begged the doctor, she finally relented on the condition that he stay off his feet or leg as much as possible. "Unless you want to limp and have an uneven gait the rest of your life," she warned.

"I hear you, I hear you, and I will stay off of it, I promise. I just need to be there and not stuck at home in my recliner getting fat and watching TV 24/7." He practically floated out of the exam room, as well as he could on crutches.

Molly balked at having to cut the left leg off all his work pants to accommodate his cast. "We'll have to buy all new work pants when you get the cast off."

He pulled her close and kissed her on the forehead. "I suppose I could just wear my boxers. At least it would be cooler."

"Very funny," she snorted as she tossed the cut pants at him. "The zoo would probably make a lot more money from people coming to see your white leg hobbling around!"

"All right, that's it." Jay pulled her down on the bed where he sat and tickled her until she gasped for mercy.

IT TOOK HIM a while to get out of his truck. Thank goodness it was his left leg that had been broken and not his right. At least he could still drive, although it was quite a trick to get his left leg under the steering wheel and dash. He was also able to lean on his crutches to bring his right leg out. He was exhausted by the time he made it to his office. At least he was early enough to get inside his office before the day keepers came in the lounge to clock out. He needed time to catch his breath and cool off a bit before greeting anyone.

Jay had called Lopez to let him know that he would be coming in to work, so Lopez agreed to meet with him at 5:00 that evening, which left time for Jay to sort through all the mail that had been dumped onto his desk. He also had 154 messages in his email inbox. That by itself could take all night.

It was good to sit in his chair again. His office was nothing fancy, really just a closet off the keepers' lounge, but it felt like home. His large office chair was worn but comfortable and it fit him perfectly. Framed photos of Molly and the girls surrounded him—several on his desk, some on the window sill, and some on the shelf next to the desk.

As he sorted through his mail, he heard keepers coming in to clock out and grab their things. It was quitting time. Lopez would be here any second. He almost opened the door to greet the keepers, but after second thought he remained in his chair. It would be an effort to get up and open the door, and he just didn't feel like having all the attention he would attract by being back at work. He decided to just sit and wait for Lopez and allow himself to enjoy being back at his desk for a little while.

As soon as he got still, the hurtful words he had hurled at his wife when she confessed to him about having to use the credit card for groceries resounded in his head. When she told him that her bank card had been declined, he panicked, realizing that his last paycheck had run out and nothing was coming in to replace it. He would get workman's comp for the injury, but the money wouldn't appear in the bank for weeks. He had forgotten to explain to Molly about their need to stop spending until the account was back up.

"Credit card! And how do you expect us to keep making that payment! Obviously if we don't have the money in our bank account we can't afford to make a credit card payment!" Jay roared when she told him she had used the Mastercard to pay for the groceries when the debit card wouldn't work.

Hurt and shock showed in her face but she was quick to defend herself. Her spunkiness was one of the things that had first attracted him to her. But all it did at that moment was fuel his anger.

"I had no idea we didn't have enough money in the bank to cover the groceries! I just thought there was a mistake! I had no other way to pay!" she cried, tears welling in her eyes. She had quickly wiped them away. Thank goodness she hadn't brought this up until the groceries were put away and the girls were down for their naps. She hoped they wouldn't wake up hearing their parents arguing.

"Why didn't you just leave them there?" Jay continued. "It doesn't take a rocket scientist to realize that if the card is declined there isn't any money to back it up!" He hated himself for what he was doing to her, but it was almost like he couldn't help himself. She had to know the pain and worry he was going through trying to heal while continuing to support his family without being able to work.

"You're right. I am not a rocket scientist and I suppose I should have realized. But the girls were hungry and I just wanted to get out of there and get them home. The people in the line behind me were getting more impatient every second. It never occurred to me that I could leave the groceries there. I have never been in that situation before, Jay Latimer. Maybe you should have given me a clue that I shouldn't buy groceries for our family until you said it was okay. Maybe you should just do all the shopping from now on since I am too stupid to do it!" With that, Molly retreated to their bedroom where she slammed the door shut and allowed the angry tears to fall.

All Jay could do was sit in his recliner with his own demeaning words replaying over and over in his mind while the image of Molly's tortured face haunted him. He was finally able to bring himself to use his phone to transfer funds from savings to checking so he could pay the grocery bill which had been charged to the Mastercard. Fortunately when the zoo went to automatic check deposit a few years ago, he had also set up a savings account to set aside a small amount from each paycheck. He had gotten out of his usual daily habit of checking his accounts, so when the checking account got low and Molly went to buy groceries there wasn't enough and the card was declined. It was his mistake and an easy fix, but instead of admitting it and fixing it, he had erupted at Molly.

He should have made the effort to get out of the recliner and go to the bedroom to try to make amends, but he closed his eyes, overcome with fatigue. She had been embarrassed and humiliated, and it was his fault.

JAY WAS PONDERING how to smooth things over after another night spent in his recliner when Lopez knocked on the office door and opened it before Jay could respond. He had Bradford Oates with him. This can't be good, Jay thought as he grabbed his crutches.

"Please," Oates said in his booming voice while extending his hand to shake Jay's. "Don't get up." He sat down in the further of the two chairs across from Jay's desk. Lopez closed the door behind them and sat down in the closer chair.

"Thank you, Sir," Jay replied. "How have you been, Mr. Oates?" It has been a while."

"Yes, it has, yes, it has. I've been well. I understand you were recently injured in a storm here at the zoo, and I want to express my sympathies for the pain and inconvenience you have undergone."

"Thank you. I have received excellent treatment and am very happy to be back at work." He glanced at Lopez, knowing that Oates normally would not be here in person to wish him a quick recovery. Lopez seemed a bit nervous.

"Mr. Oates and I wanted to visit with you about the recent animal deaths here at the zoo." Lopez raised a palm quickly as Jay opened his mouth to reply. "Let's hear what Mr. Oates has to say first, shall we?"

Oates reached for a handkerchief from his suit pocket and wiped his brow. Apparently the walk from the parking lot to Lopez's office to Jay's office had been an effort in the late August heat. "Latimer, I have always held the highest esteem for you and your crew. However, the events of late have had me up at night wondering which animal will be the next victim of this twisted scheme. Necropsy results have shown that none of our animals died of natural causes, and we cannot escape the fact that these dead animals have been found by your workers."

Jay's brow furrowed. "Sir. . ."

"You know your crew better than anyone, Latimer, so I am going to trust your judgment on this, and trust if you hear anything you will let us know." He smiled, his already double chin doubling.

Jay exhaled, relaxing a bit. This was better than he expected, certainly better than he usually got from Lopez and the other curators.

"I still want you and your crew to undergo a lie detector screening, though," Oates continued, "just to be sure."

No doubt Lopez's idea. Jay stared at his immediate supervisor.

Lopez shifted in his seat and stared at the hem of the pant leg on his knee.

"Of course." Jay continued to stare at Lopez, whose eyes remained locked on his pants hem. "When would you like for this to happen?"

"Lopez will set it up and let you know. Is there anything else, Lopez? I'm a busy man."

Lopez shook his head and rose without a word, Oates following. Oates extended his hand again to Jay and thanked him for his time. Lopez left without a word, which didn't surprise Jay at all.

Chapter Ten

THAT WAS A short vacation, Lucas mused as he drove to work. As short as it was, he had enjoyed the time spent with Deana fixing up the nursery and doing small repair projects he had been putting off. He had helped Deana do a thorough house cleaning as well, since her large belly and swollen legs and ankles made it uncomfortable to bend and stand for very long.

He hated leaving Deana home alone so close to delivery but she had instructions to call him as soon as she started feeling contractions or if her water broke. He was only a few minutes away and could get home fast, so at least that was some consolation. Jay was a good boss, too, and he had already told Lucas and the others that he considered family his first priority, so whatever they needed to do they should do it and he would worry about the workplace. Jay would understand if Lucas had to suddenly leave work to be with Deana when it was time.

At least the summer heat was beginning to abate. Lately the evenings had been cooler with just a hint of the coming fall. Lucas loved fall, when the nighttime lows would fall into the 40's and 50's with daytime highs in the 70's or 80's. It was so much easier to work in those temperatures, and everyone seemed to get along better when heat was not an issue. A bad thing about fall was that leaves would fall into the moats and ponds, stop up the pumps and drains, and leave a messy residue. He welcomed that if it meant cooler temperatures and fewer visitors.

He entered the keepers' lounge and spotted Jay in his office just off to the right. His mood brightened. When had Jay come back?

"Hey, Boss!" He knocked on the door jamb before he entered. "How long have you been back?"

JAY LOOKED UP from the latest memo from Lopez informing him that his crew would undergo lie detector screening beginning the next morning at 9:00. They would love having to get up early for that. But seeing Lucas brought a grin to his face.

"Hey, Lucas! Back from vacation today? Did you have a good one?"

"It was great. We took one of them 'staycations' and did a lot of work on the house. Deana's getting ready to pop so we had to get everything ready."

"Already? Seems like you just found out she's expecting!" Jay motioned for Lucas to sit down. "Is she feeling okay?" His mind wandered back to when Molly found out she was pregnant with Laci. What a wonderful day that had been, the beginning of parenthood. They had never looked back.

"She's feeling huge," Lucas laughed. "And having false contractions, backaches, and swelling. The doctor said all that is normal, though."

"If she's like Molly, she thinks the baby won't come soon enough."

"She says every day that maybe today will be the day," Lucas agreed before changing the subject. "How long have you been back and how are you feeling?"

"I've been back a couple of days. I'm feeling okay except for having to hobble around on crutches. It's getting old, but my arms are getting a good workout." Jay flexed his right arm. "I guess you guys will have to continue doing the physical work for me."

"Not a problem, Boss. I'm just glad you are back."

Jay knew he meant it. He picked up the memo. "You guys are going to have to come in early tomorrow for lie detector tests. They don't really believe our shift is responsible for the animals dying, but they want to test everybody to be sure."

Lucas nodded. He expected as much.

"When you see Jolie and Kaycie today, could you please ask them to come and see me as well?"

"No need. We're right here," Kaycie announced as she and Jolie filled his doorway. Kaycie let out a little screech and threw her arms around Jay's neck, almost knocking him back in his rolling office chair. Jolie immediately grabbed her shoulders to pull her off.

"Kaycie, careful! He's hurt!"

Kaycie backed away, growing red with embarrassment.

"I'm so sorry! Are you okay? I'm just so glad you are back!"

"I'm just fine," Jay laughed.

Jolie leaned over and placed a gentle kiss on his cheek. "It's really good to see you. You'll just have to excuse Kaycie."

"She's never been one to hold back, has she?"

"Is there something you need to tell us? We heard you asking Lucas to tell us to come by." Kaycie had recovered her composure.

"Yes, I need all of you to come in early tomorrow morning for lie detector tests. Can you be here at 9:00?"

"Why so early?" Jolie wondered aloud.

"I guess they want to have plenty of time to question all of us," Jay replied. "Maybe I can get Lopez to at least feed us lunch."

The three coworkers promised to be there and exited the office, Jolie and Kaycie asking Lucas about his vacation. Jay leaned back in his chair, enjoying the feeling of being back in charge of his own domain. He just wished it was as easy at home as it was at work.

LUCAS BROKE OFF from the girls and headed to the commissary to pick up diets for the cats as the girls headed toward the hoof stock barn. He gathered the bags of meat as well as a bucket of bones. The cats loved their weekly bone night because they got to chew on real prey animal bones which still had some meat on them, something they didn't get to do while captive because their diets were purchased and provided for them instead of hunted and killed in the wild.

As he entered the cat house, through first one locked heavy metal gridded door and then another, he noticed that their favorite cougar, Zoe, would not get up from the corner of her holding area. Usually she was one of the first to greet him, especially on bone night, but he had noticed before his vacation that she had been acting listless and sluggish. Lots of the animals had been acting that way, though, listless and eating less because of the heat.

However, Zoe's head rested on the cold concrete floor as she lay on her side. She didn't respond to the noise he made coming in, and then she didn't respond to his call.

"Zoe, Zoe," he crooned. "It's bone night!" The other cats bellowed in eager anticipation of their food and treat. Zoe did not move. Stepping closer to the heavy gridded wall, he studied her for a moment before realizing that she wasn't breathing, or at least her side was not moving in and out. Her tongue also lay limply and unnaturally out of the side of her mouth. Was she dead?

He dropped the meat packages and bucket of bones, grabbing his radio from his belt. "Code 2, code 2! Cat house!"

He couldn't decide if he should venture into her area or not. His training had taught him never to approach a sick or injured zoo animal alone, as they were even more unpredictable and could lash out in fear, causing severe injury or death to the keeper. But she was so still.

He opened the gates leading from her area to the opposite side and placed the diets in that area, hoping the cats in Zoe's area would transfer to the other area so he could isolate her. It worked. As soon as the other two cougars were in the other areas, he released the gate that separated them and isolated Zoe. Against his better judgment, he inserted a key into the access gate and unlocked it. Rules or not, he had to know whether or not she was still alive.

"Lucas!" he heard before he opened the gate. "Wait!" Kaycie had entered the cat house with Jolie close behind.

He paused as they approached. "What are you doing?" Kaycie demanded.

"It's Zoe. I don't think she is breathing."

"You aren't going in there without backup," Kaycie informed him. Jolie had already disappeared and reappeared with a tranquilizer gun.

"I've got it." Jolie prepared to shoot a tranquilizing dart at the cat if it should become aggressive toward Lucas while he was in the area with her.

The access gate opened with a creak as Lucas entered the area. Slowly, so as not to startle the possibly sleeping mountain lion, he approached her, speaking her name over and over in a low voice. As he stopped next to her, he knelt and put his hand lightly on her side to see if she was breathing. She lay completely still, with no evidence of breath or heartbeat. Lucas picked up one of her paws to check for resistance but it fell limply and heavily on the floor next to her. She did not stir. He then moved her head but still there was no response.

GLANCING BACK AT the girls who stood waiting with bated breath, he stood up and shook his head. Kaycie stepped through the access gate as if to confirm what Lucas was telling them. Zoe was one of her favorites.

Jolie hung back, afraid to hear what she knew was the truth. Zoe was one of her favorites, too. This big cat was the animal she always described to people who wanted to know what her job was like. For a wild animal, she was the sweetest, most gentle creature. Jay constantly reminded them that she was not a domestic cat and she could turn on them without warning. Still, Jolie and Kaycie could not resist petting her through the bars. They loved feeling her soft fur and hearing her low, throaty purr. It was hard to believe that she could be anything but her gentle self. Yet there she was, lying motionless on the cold dirty concrete, concrete which had not yet been rinsed of the urine and feces from the day.

The cat house should reek with the odor of the unwashed floors, but the noses of Jolie and the other keepers had long ago been rendered insensitive to zoo odors. It never failed to surprise her when a visitor complained about the odd smells of a certain area when Jolie noticed nothing at all.

"Ah, Zoe, you can't leave us," Kaycie wailed as she fell to her knees and bent over the mountain lion.

Jolie choked up and knelt beside Kaycie and Zoe.

"I guess we'll have to call Jay," Lucas mumbled.

At that moment the door to the cat house burst open and Jay hobbled in on his crutches.

"What is it?" he thundered.

Jolie hopped up as Lucas turned around to face Jay. "It's Zoe," Jolie sniffed, wiping her eyes with the back of her arm. She still had her rubber cleaning gloves on. A curly lock of hair fell across her forehead, straying from its ponytail.

Kaycie continued to sob as Jay made his way over to them and through the access gate.

"You found her like this?"

"I brought the food and bones and she didn't respond, so I moved the others and came in to check on her," Lucas said.

"But not without us here," Jolie interjected, knowing Jay's penchant for adhering to safety rules.

"Is she breathing?" Jay already knew the answer because of Kaycie's reaction. He wanted to get down on the floor but his leg wouldn't let him.

"I'm afraid not," Lucas replied. "She's gone."

Jay sighed. "Any sign of injury?"

"Not that we could tell," Lucas said, "but we haven't turned her over to look at her other side."

"Let's do that, guys. Come on, Kaycie, we need your help. We can all cry later." His words sounded harsh to Jolie, but they were just what Kaycie needed to pull herself together. She stood up, wiped her tears, and nodded.

The three keepers grabbed Zoe's legs, pulled her away from the wall, and then carefully rolled her to her other side. There was no evidence of injury on that side, either. They all looked at Jay.

"Let's get her to the vet wing. I will meet you there in a few minutes." With that, he and his crutches made it awkwardly out of the area through the access door. They soon heard the sound of the zoo truck starting up.

Lucas broke the silence. "I think there is a tarp in the supply room over there."

Kaycie and Jolie jumped into action, bolting for the supply room where Jolie spotted a rolled-up tarp in the corner. Kaycie helped pull the heavy tarp out of the small room that also doubled as the cat keepers' office. With Lucas's help they rolled Zoe's body into the tarp and then all three of them pulled her out of the house—rather roughly, Jolie thought—and heaved her into the back of the utility truck that they had driven down when they heard Lucas's call for help. Kaycie and Jolie rode silently in the back of the truck with Zoe as Lucas drove to the vet wing.

Jolie's heart went out to Kaycie, whose tear-streaked face was stricken with grief. If she could have she would have wrapped her arms around her friend, but the ride was too bumpy and curvy. Jolie hung on with both hands as the truck wove through the zoo on narrow trails and sidewalks not much wider. Lucas seemed to be driving a little fast, but adrenaline was probably to blame. Getting Zoe's lifeless body to the vet wing a few minutes later would not have changed anything.

When the truck screeched to a stop, Lucas slammed it into park and jumped out to help the girls down and gently carry Zoe into the vet wing's refrigerated closet, designed especially for situations like this.

Jay was waiting inside. He had unlocked the closet and held the door open while leaning on his crutches as the three keepers dragged the big cat inside. Kaycie wept as they exited the small cold room and watched Jay shut the door and lock it. He met Lucas's eyes and nodded toward the keepers' lounge.

"Come on, K," Lucas grabbed Kaycie's shoulders and gently moved her toward the truck. It was a short drive back to the lounge, where Jay and Lucas disappeared into Jay's office to make the report and call the zoo veterinarian who would need to perform a necropsy as soon as possible to determine the cause of death.

Unconcerned about returning to work, Jolie and Kaycie sank into the dilapidated lounge couch. Jolie put her arms around Kaycie, not really knowing what to say. They had lost a good friend; in fact, they had lost one of their reasons to show up at work every day.

AFTER CALLING LOPEZ and explaining what had happened, Jay sent them all home with a reminder to return at 9:00 in the morning for lie detector testing. Lopez was not happy when Jay awakened him in the middle of the night to tell him about another animal death. Fortunately he was too groggy to give Jay the full inquisition, but he wanted to see him at 8:00 in the morning.

An hour and a shower later, Molly stirred as Jay slipped under the sheets. Feeling some grief himself over the loss of Zoe and needing comfort, he reached for her. She was so soft and warm. But she pushed him away and turned over with a mumbled protest. She must have had a long day herself, he thought, leaving her alone. Lately it seemed that all her days were too long and too crowded for him. He was beginning to miss the closeness they had once shared. Was it him? Was it the lack of money? I'll figure it out later, he thought as he drifted off to sleep.

ACROSS TOWN, JOLIE climbed into bed after smoking two cigarettes, one on the way home and one on her front porch. She had hoped the two smokes and a hot shower would help her relax after the trauma of losing a favorite zoo animal. It was too late to pick Ellie up from her parents' so she would be able to sleep without being awakened through the night by chubby wayward arms and legs. However, she lay sleepless for what seemed a long while mulling over the night's events and the fact that she hadn't heard from Cade in several days.

WHEN LUCAS DROVE into his driveway, he was surprised to see the bedroom lamps on through the windows. Deana was usually in deep slumber when he got home, although lately she slept fitfully, unable to find a comfortable position now that the baby was so big. Even though he was a few hours early tonight, she still should have been in bed by now. She had been tired lately with the baby and its drain on her tiny body. It occurred to him that something might be wrong. He pulled into his usual space under the flimsy tin carport he had fashioned for his old

1981 someday-to-be-restored pickup, shoved it into park, and sprinted to the back door.

"Deana?" he called as he entered the kitchen. At least she had remembered to lock the back door. She probably could not hear him over the noise of the window air conditioning unit in the bedroom window. He hurried through the kitchen and living room, finding the bedroom door closed, which was a bit unusual. Maybe she was having hot flashes again.

When he burst through the bedroom door, what he found sent him back outside to vomit off the back porch for a few seconds before he headed to his truck to grab the sawed-off 410 shotgun he kept behind the seat.

Chapter Eleven

AS LUCAS RETURNED to the back door he could hear Deana wailing from inside the house. In a rage he almost tore the storm door off its hinges as he re-entered the kitchen. A disheveled young man darted like a rabbit through the living room and out the front door holding his shoes and shirt with one hand, and his jeans up with the other. Lucas pointed the shotgun at him.

"No, man, don't shoot--it's all good!" the young man shouted as he struggled with the front door.

Without a word from Lucas, the barrel of the sawed-off shotgun followed the boy out of the house and down the front steps. He was lucky he hadn't been shot. But even in his rage, Lucas knew that he didn't want the police showing up. He needed to handle this on his own. He stomped into the bedroom.

Deana's eyes widened in horror as she saw the shotgun in Lucas's hands. "Lucas, no! I didn't mean it! He means nothing to me. I love you!"

Baby or not, Lucas wanted her to fear him. All those times when she said she couldn't be with him because of the discomfort. All lies. She had a boy on the side. Was the baby she carried even his? Bile rose again in his throat but he choked it down. Show no weakness. He moved toward her.

"Baby, no." Deana scrambled back toward the headboard of the bed she was sitting on. Their bed. Their soiled, dirty, filthy bed.

"It's nothing! Really!" How dare she call him "baby" right now?

"Who is he?" Lucas thundered, unable to contain himself any longer. "How long has this been going on?"

She could not take her eyes off the gun. "Put the gun down, baby, so I can explain," Deana said, still moving back. Against the headboard now and unable to move any further, she grasped the comforter to her breast as she cowered.

Lucas could see that he would get nowhere with her until he lost the gun, so he set it on the floor and moved closer to the bed, towering over her. Tears coursed down her cheeks, smearing the makeup she must have applied especially for her boyfriend.

"Who is he?" Lucas spat. He wanted to shake her until she told him everything, but then he wasn't sure he wanted to know everything. Was their entire life together a lie? He had given her everything within his power to give—the house, the privilege of staying home, occasional shopping money. . .had it not been enough? He practically doted on her. Was his love not enough?

"Some guy I met," she choked.

"Some guy you met. And how many guys have you met? How many have you had here? How long has this been going on?"

Deana broke down into sobs, clutching her belly. "I'm not supposed to get upset," she managed to say between sobs.

"Oh, really? Is that so? Maybe you should have thought of that. Should I even care since I am not even sure who the baby's father is now?"

"Lucas, I never loved anybody but you! It just gets so boring here alone." She couldn't look at him.

"So he's not the first then," Lucas muttered, feeling pain as if a knife were twisting in his chest. Numb, impervious to his sobbing wreck of an unfaithful wife, he turned away from the bed and went to the closet where he rummaged around until he found an old duffel bag. He grabbed a couple pairs of jeans and two work shirts, stuffed them in, and then retrieved a few pair of underwear and socks from the dresser, which he also stuffed inside the bag.

Deana watched him as he went into the bathroom for his razor and toothbrush. "Where are you going?" she croaked as he zipped up the bag.

"Have a good life, Deana."

"Wait!" Deana scrambled off the bed as he picked up the shotgun and headed toward the back door. "You can't leave me now, like this! I'm about to have this baby! Your baby!"

He turned toward her, the shotgun pointed toward her again. She shrank back, unsure of what he would do. "Since we don't know whose baby it is, Deana, you are on your own. I do not have it in me to stay here with you. When the baby comes you can have a DNA test done and if it is mine I will fight for custody." He turned away, and then turned back to add, "You don't deserve my child."

He crossed the living room, yanked open the front door, and then slammed it behind him, rattling the windows of the old house. His young pregnant wife remained on the bed, her face streaked with tears and smeared makeup. He didn't care.

Lucas drove his old truck back to the zoo parking lot and stayed inside it the rest of that sleepless night. He would get the rest of his things some other time, some other day. Right now he didn't care if he ever got the rest of his things out of that house. For a brief second he considered using the shotgun on himself but he refused to give Deana that much power over him. The rage which had consumed him the moment he discovered his wife in bed with that kid—he looked no older than 18—had evaporated. Only numbness remained. He felt disconnected from everything, including himself. He was afraid to feel anything, afraid of what he might do if he did.

NINE A.M. CAME early for Jolie. She hadn't seen her little girl since yesterday morning and she missed the morning chatter. She threw on the first jeans and top she found, grabbed a mug of coffee and her purse, and headed out of the house to start her car. She would call Ellie on the way to work.

But there was a red Cutlass in the driveway blocking her Taurus when she exited the house. Cade. What was he doing here? She glanced at the cell phone in her hand to see if she had missed his call or had a text message waiting. Nothing. Her heart hammered with anticipation as he got out of the car. Could he have grown more handsome since she had seen him last? She bounced down the porch steps toward him. He met her halfway and folded her into his arms, planting a lingering kiss on her upturned mouth.

"Surprised to see me?" he asked after a delicious minute. He smelled so good. He felt so good. His arms around her felt so. . .right. It had been so long since she had felt this way. It scared her a little.

"Yes!" she managed after catching her breath.

"Where are you going so early, Sweetheart?" He kept her body close while brushing a wayward tendril of hair away from her mouth.

"I have to be at work early today. We are taking lie detector tests this morning." Oops. *Maybe she had said too much.*

"Because of the dead bobcat?"

"You know about that?" How would he know about that?

"I saw it on the news last night," he continued as if reading her thoughts. "Awful. Do they think a zoo employee might be to blame?"

Jolie's elation plummeted. So it was on the news. Work would be impossible now. Jay would be under so much pressure. Dread overcame her. She wanted to drag Cade with her back inside the house and hide from the world.

He noticed the change. "What's wrong?" He tilted her chin up with his index finger, sending tremors through her body. His touch was as exciting as his kisses.

"It's just that the zoo administrators hate bad publicity about the zoo. They want to keep a happy family-friendly public image, you know. I suppose it was bound to happen since a zoo visitor discovered the dead bobcat."

"I'm sure it will blow over soon. Would you like for me to drive you to work?"

Jolie frowned. "Don't you have to go to work?"

"I just stopped by because I wanted to see you before work. It's been several days and I've missed you." His gaze held hers. "I do have to be at work, but I could drive you to yours first."

Jolie placed a palm on the side of his face, enjoying the feel of his rough facial stubble. His sun-lightened hair fell over his forehead as he gazed down at her.

"I don't want you to be late," she said. "Besides, I will probably go to my parents' after I am done so I can be with Ellie before it is time for my shift."

"Are you sure? I really don't mind."

Jolie nodded.

"You're a good mother. I'll call you," he promised as he bent to kiss her goodbye. It was another lingering kiss that caused her heart to beat wildly and her knees to turn to jelly. When he finally released her, she wondered if she could make it to her car by herself. Taking her hand, he walked her to her car and opened the door for her. Once she was safely inside, he bent to give her a quick kiss.

"Have a good day at work," he said. "I'm sure everything will be fine."

She watched him as he returned to his own car, completely forgetting about phoning Ellie until she pulled into the zoo parking lot. Right, good mother, she berated herself. She would definitely go to her mother's afterwards and spend the day with her baby.

Jolie was the first to arrive at Jay's office. No one was in the keepers' lounge, so she placed her purse in her locker and sat on the couch to wait for someone else to arrive. She didn't remember Jay saying to meet anywhere else. His office door was closed but she could hear muffled voices behind it. She wondered if it was Lopez in there talking with Jay about the news story.

As she checked her social media on her phone, Lucas came dragging through the door to the lounge. She almost gasped at his appearance. She had never seen him look so bad. His hair was a mess, his face was unshaven, and his clothes looked and smelled like he had worn them yesterday and slept in them. He averted his eyes, avoiding looking at her and greeting her.

"Hi, Lucas," she ventured. "Is everything okay?"

He glared at her before disappearing into the men's room without a word. Weird. Was he the one responsible for the animals? Had he confessed?

Jay's office door opened and Jay stuck his head out, looking around the lounge before settling his gaze upon Jolie. "Are you the only one who showed up?" She could see another man in his office with a machine, apparently the lie detector. Lopez was not there. She breathed a little easier before answering Jay's question.

She didn't have to because Lucas exited the men's room just then. She noted Jay's quick recovery after his shock at seeing Lucas so disheveled. So Lucas hadn't confessed. She sighed in relief.

"Anybody seen Kaycie?" Jay asked, not addressing Lucas's appearance. It didn't matter anyway. It wouldn't affect the lie detector test.

Both shook their heads, neither having heard from Kaycie since she left early yesterday. "Want me to call her?" Jolie offered.

"Would you please? We'll start with Lucas." Jay motioned for the big man to come on into his office, shutting the door behind him as Jolie dialed Kaycie's number.

There was no answer so Jolie sent her a quick text message. Didn't Kaycie realize that if she didn't show up it made her look guilty? But Kaycie was so upset over Zoe, she probably wasn't even thinking about that. She might have even completely forgotten about the test. Jolie hit redial.

This time a groggy-sounding Kaycie answered the phone. "Hello?"

"Hey, it's Jolie. Did you forget we are taking lie detector tests today?"

There was a low groan and a hesitation. "Can I please talk to Jay?"

"He's in his office with Lucas and the testing guy right now, but I can ask him to call you when they come out. Are you okay, girlfriend?"

"Just wonderful. Please tell Jay I won't be in today. He can call me if he wants." She hung up before Jolie could say anything else.

Lucas came out of Jay's office. It was her turn. Her hands began to shake.

JOLIE ARRIVED AT her parents' house just in time for lunch. The lie detector test questions had been easy until he began to question her on her relationships with the other employees, even her supervisor. Her hands began to sweat on those questions, but she told the truth, hoping not to offend Jay with her honesty. At least the test had come back negative. She couldn't be accused of having anything to do with the animal deaths, or murders, as the official had called them. The word gave her the creeps. Obviously none of the recent deaths were considered accidental or natural, but they hadn't heard anything from Zoe's necropsy yet.

She snuffed out her second cigarette in the car's ash tray, gathered her purse and keys, and headed up to her parents' porch. The sound of Ellie's chatter put a smile on her face. She relaxed a little.

"Mommeeeee!" Ellie yelled as Jolie let herself in the side door off the kitchen. She was sitting at the table in her booster seat with a peanut butter and jelly sandwich in one hand. Her face and other hand were smeared with jelly. She beamed at Jolie, peanut butter, jelly, and bread stuck between her teeth.

"Hey, Pumpkin!" When Jolie reached her, she gingerly kissed her on her sticky cheek while trying to avoid the sticky hands that reached for her.

"How did it go, Jolie?" Her mother moved Ellie's sippy cup away from the edge of the table.

"It was fine. I got all worked up for nothing."

Jolie told her mother about the testing as best she could as Ellie chattered about feeding the ducks in the pond with Grampa.

"Come on, Silly Bear," Jolie told Ellie when she finished her sandwich and the few Fritos that were on her plate. "Did you finish your milk?"

"Yes, ma'am," Ellie replied politely. Jolie grinned and glanced at her mother. They had been working on manners. "Can I have a cookie?"

"It's 'may I'," Mrs. McCray responded. "Say: 'May I have a cookie?'"

"May I have a cookie?" Ellie repeated obediently.

Mrs. McCray started to reply before stopping herself and deferring to Jolie. "How many cookies have you had today?" Jolie asked her daughter.

Ellie cocked her head as if trying to remember. "I gave her one cookie at about 10:00 this morning," Mrs. McCray admitted. "But she had a good breakfast. . .bacon and eggs and a biscuit with butter and jelly."

"Okay, Pumpkin, you may have one cookie. But let's get you cleaned up a little first."

"Yay!" Ellie clapped her sticky hands as Mrs. McCray went to get a dampened paper towel. After Jolie wiped Ellie's face and hands, she lifted her from the booster seat and handed her the peanut butter cookie her mother had gotten from the cookie jar. As Ellie toddled off to watch "Sesame Street," which was already on in the den, Jolie proceeded to wipe off the table and booster seat.

As Mrs. McCray began putting the fixings for grown-up sandwiches on the table Jolie told her mother about Jay returning to work and about Zoe's death. Her mother was an attentive listener, especially when from the kitchen table she could see Ellie contentedly watching TV as she munched on her cookie in the den. At the moment Ellie was singing and dancing with Elmo.

"You haven't said much about your gentleman friend," Mrs. McCray coaxed. "Are you still seeing him? Ellie hasn't said anything since your picnic."

"She talked about that?" Jolie said in amazement.

"Of course! She told me about her new friend Maddie--Cade's daughter, right? She wants to go on another picnic soon. Cade seems to be a very nice man, by the way."

"He is," Jolie agreed, her stomach fluttering a bit at the mention of his name.

"And a good father," her mother continued.

Jolie looked at her and shook her head. "Okay, Mom, I get the hint."

"Hint about what?" Jolie's father came through the kitchen door and tossed his keys on the countertop.

"Where's my best girl?" he boomed after giving Jolie a kiss on the top of the head.

"Grampa!" Ellie came running in from the den. She leapt into his arms and began chattering. Without waiting for a reply from Jolie or her mother, he carried his granddaughter into the den, responding to her chatter with appropriate "uh-huh's" and "you don't say's" in all the right places. He was an expert in Ellie-speak.

"I'm taking this really slow." Jolie said to her mom. "I don't want Ellie to get hurt if it doesn't work out between Cade and me."

"We don't want you to get hurt again," Mrs. McCray replied as she began to assemble turkey sandwiches for the three of them. "Honey, would you get more chips out of the pantry and get us all some iced tea?"

Jolie obeyed. "I really like Cade, but I am kind of afraid of getting too involved, you know?"

"Of course you are, honey. After what you went through with Sean, it's no wonder." She set the plates of sandwiches around the table as Jolie brought three glasses of iced tea to the table.

After the three of them were seated and Mrs. McCray had asked the Lord's blessing on the meal, Jolie relaxed. It was good to be home with her parents. Their unconditional love and support made it so much easier to be a single parent.

"We saw on the news the other night where there have been some unexplained animal killings at the zoo," Mr. McCray said. "What do you think is going on with that?"

Jolie glanced at her mother, who looked down at her plate. What were they up to? "I don't know, but everybody on my shift took a lie detector test this morning."

"Somebody on your shift is killing animals?" He frowned.

"No, of course not, Daddy. But the powers that be want to put the blame on somebody, and it is easy for them to blame us since we are the ones who find the dead animals."

"Mama and I have been talking. . ."

Jolie glanced at her mother who wouldn't look directly at her. Traitor. Jolie shook her head, waiting for the axe to fall.

"We want you to move in with us and look for another job," her father continued. "Mama has cleaned out the guest room." Her mother used the guest room for occasional projects such as sewing and crafts.

"But I don't want to move in here," Jolie balked. "I love my house, and I love my job."

"Your workplace isn't safe," Mr. McCray insisted. "You'll be safer here while you look for a job. I have already talked to Gus at the feed store. He needs help at the counter and he would start you out making almost what you are making at the zoo."

"And the hours would be so much better for you and Ellie," her mother added.

Jolie's temper flared but she held it in check. She didn't need to argue with her father, especially not where Ellie could hear. This is exactly why she had moved out in the first place. Would they ever treat her like a grown-up? "Daddy," she began.

"I'll look after Little Bit while Mama helps you get your things from your house," he continued. "You can put in your two weeks' notice tonight. I want you to meet Gus in the morning." As if that settled it.

"Daddy, I can't leave the zoo now. I am up for a promotion soon. Are you sure you want me and Ellie here all the time? She will wear you guys out even more than she does already."

"You just let us worry about that. We just want our girls safe. Money isn't everything."

Jolie pushed back her chair and stood up. "I'll think about it." *Maybe that will satisfy them for now. "Thanks for lunch."*

"Where are you going?" her mother asked.

"To watch "Sesame Street" with my daughter." She retreated to the den where Ellie was dancing and clapping her hands while singing to the music on the television.

"Mommy, dance!"

"Maybe later, Sweetie." Jolie sank into the sofa as Ellie clapped her hands and shook her bottom. Jolie felt suddenly weary, needing someone to talk to. She considered calling Cade but was unsure if she should be sharing family issues so early in their relationship. As she weighed the pros and cons, she felt her phone vibrate in her jeans pocket. It was Cade.

"Hello?" She kept her voice low so her parents wouldn't hear.

"Hi, Sweetheart," came his sexy drawl through the phone. "I was just thinking about you and wondering how your lie detector test went."

"You're sweet to check on me. And I'm not guilty," she responded. "Hang on a second." She got up from the couch and went outside to the front porch without Ellie noticing. Of course her parents noticed, but they were courteous enough not to react.

"Is your day going well?" she asked once outside. A breeze fluttered her hair. There was even a hint of fall in the air with the latest cool front that had come through. A few crisp leaves fluttered to the ground as if eager for the change of seasons. Even the leaves seemed tired of the relentless Texas heat.

"The usual. You sound a bit down. Are you okay?" Wow. He could *tell by her voice? She would have had to hit Sean over the head with a two by four to get him to notice anything.*

"My parents want me to move in with them and find another job," Jolie blurted. So much for her misgivings about telling him. "They're worried about me staying at the zoo with all the weird stuff that has been going on."

"Really? In that case, I have a proposition for you. I've been thinking about asking you anyway, but now seems like the perfect time."

The word 'proposition' sent Jolie's imagination into overtime. What on earth did he mean by that? She waited for him to continue.

"Why don't you and Ellie come and stay with me and Maddie?"

Her heart slammed into her shoes. She lost the ability to speak.

"Jolie? You there?"

She nodded, and then whispered, "Yes."

"We have plenty of room. You and Ellie could even have your own bedroom and bathroom."

"Gee, I don't know, Cade. I'm not sure if you and I are ready. . ." Jolie stammered, unsure how to put it. She wasn't ready for a full-time relationship. As strong as the physical attraction she felt for him was, she did not think she was ready to sleep with him yet. And she refused to sleep with anyone outside marriage. She had learned her lesson after Sean. God had given that command for a reason. The guilt and complications were not worth it.

"No strings attached, Jolie." He seemed to read her thoughts. "No obligations. I promise."

Could this guy be for real? Could he actually want her to come and live with him without sleeping with him? She would have to consider this carefully. It wasn't just herself she had to think about. What kind of effect would this have on Ellie?

"I appreciate the offer, Cade, I really do, but I am going to have to think about it for a while."

"Of course! I promise I will not pressure you. I won't say another word about it. You can let me know when you are ready, okay?"

"I have to get off the phone." She needed a cigarette in the worst way.

"I'll call you later." She walked back into the den in a daze. Ellie was still bouncing to "Sesame Street" and her parents were still at the kitchen table. Her world had just turned upside down and no one had noticed.

Chapter Twelve

AS JAY HOBBLED into the lounge, what he beheld made him pause. All his workers were present and on time, even Kaycie, but they were all seated apart from each other and completely silent, which was not normal, especially for the girls. Jolie and Kaycie were constantly chattering when they were together. Lucas, who was usually the first to greet him, barely even looked up. He looked like he had slept in his clothes and he badly needed a shave. Jay had never had to do it before, but he would have to talk to Lucas about his appearance.

"What is going on here?" he wondered aloud. "Is something wrong?"

All three of them looked up from their cell phones and shook their heads, but no one spoke.

"Well, all right, whatever it is, we have to get to work. But first, you should know that the lie detection tests came back negative, so whoever is responsible for the animal killings is not one of us, thank goodness. I knew it, but now at least the curators believe me."

There was no response. Not what he expected. Kaycie had taken the test just before work. She should have jumped up and screamed and hugged Jolie. Lucas should have broken into a grin and shook Jay's hand. Weird.

"Lucas, you and I will tackle the elephant moat tonight. Girls, you'll do the otter pond. Let's hit it."

JOLIE AND KAYCIE headed toward the otter exhibit, where they checked to make sure the otters were inside before pulling the drain on the tank. While it was draining they gathered cleaning supplies and then separated to pick up food bowls in adjacent exhibits. Neither had spoken except for polite greetings. Each was too immersed in her own thoughts to worry about the other much, or even notice that the other was preoccupied.

Jolie had major decisions to make: whether to move in with her parents, move in with Cade, or just stay put. Should she keep her job or find something else? Was the zoo too dangerous? Her thoughts kept wandering to Cade and staying there. What would it be like to live in the same house with him, to be there when he woke and when he went to bed, for him to be there when she woke and when she went to bed? Could she stand the proximity without giving in to the lusts of her flesh? Could she continue to be a good example for her daughter? What about his daughter? What would his babysitter think? What would her parents think? Her stomach twisted. What would her parents think?

Jolie picked up the last food bowl from the coati mundis. As she turned to exit the area, a flash of light caught her eye. In the twilight, a light was moving through the outer edge of the hoof stock yard. It looked like a flashlight but no one was supposed to be over there. The hoof stock was in the barn for the night. There was no reason for anyone to be there. She took her radio from her belt and pressed the side button to call. "Location, Jay? Location, Lucas? Location, Kaycie?"

In perfect sequence, the answers came back.

"Giraffe moat," Jay said.

"Giraffe poop," Lucas cracked. Was he coming out of his doldrums?

"Just getting back to the otter pond," came Kaycie's response.

Then who the heck was that out in the hoof stock yard? She hurried back to the otter house to tell Kaycie.

Jay called her back on the radio. "Everything okay, Jolie?"

"I just saw something weird in the hoof stock yard." Jolie's hand on the radio shook. Kaycie's eyes widened.

"I'll be right there."

There was nothing to see when Jay and Lucas got there a couple of minutes later. They even went out to where Jolie saw the light and looked around. When they returned to tell her they hadn't found anything, she felt foolish. Had she imagined it?

"You did the right thing calling me, especially in light of what's been happening around here," Jay assured her. Then he told Lucas to stay with her and asked Kaycie to come with him.

Relieved, Jolie tried to make small talk with Lucas as they began to scrub the floor of the otter pond. "How are things, Lucas? I've noticed you haven't been yourself the last couple of days."

Lucas stopped what he was doing, placed his hands one on top of the other on the end of his mop, and stared at her. He said nothing for a moment, and then to her astonishment, tears began to run down his cheeks—not sweat, but tears.

"Lucas! What is it?" She dropped her mop and rushed over to him. He flung his arms around her, letting loose his pent-up anger and hurt in racking sobs. She couldn't support his bulk so they sank to the concrete, him clinging to her like a child to its mother.

What in the world? Then it struck her. Deana. His wife. Wasn't she expecting a baby? Something must have happened. But there was no way he could talk right now so she just sat there with him, patting him awkwardly as he sobbed. She didn't know what else to do.

After a few minutes, the sobs subsided. Her shirt and jeans were soaked with either his sweat, tears, or drainage from his nose, she couldn't tell. What surprised her is that it didn't bother her.

He finally lifted his head from her breast and sat up straight. "I'm sorry, Jolie. I don't know what came over me." He stared at the concrete floor and wiped his face with a rag he pulled from his pocket.

"Don't be silly. We're friends, aren't we?" She kept staring at him until he met her gaze. "Now tell me what has you so upset. Is it Deana?"

His head jerked up. "She's been cheatin' on me, Jolie. She cheated on me." He repeated the words as if he couldn't believe them himself.

Jolie was speechless. He had a perfect marriage, to hear him tell it. He adored his wife and she adored him. They had always seemed like the perfect couple.

"I'm so sorry," she managed to say.

"I found them together," Lucas continued. "Then I got my gun."

Jolie's eyes widened. She tried to remember if she had heard anything about a shooting on the radio or TV, but she didn't pay much attention to the news. She had enough to worry about without adding the rest of the world to her troubles. She waited for more.

"I didn't shoot him. I just made him think I was going to, and then I left. He was just a kid."

Jolie nodded, at a loss for words.

"I don't even know whose baby it is any more," Lucas continued, more tears welling up. He fought them, wiping his eyes. "I can't go back there."

He could get a DNA test later, but she wouldn't mention that now. "Of course you can't," Jolie agreed. "Where have you been staying?"

"My truck. That's why I look so bad."

"Not anymore," Jolie replied. She would talk to Jay and see if Lucas could stay with him for a while. She would have invited him to her place, but it wouldn't work with Cade being in the picture. Plus her parents would hit the ceiling. Then she realized that he had nowhere to go tonight. She would have to talk to Jay right away.

Not wanting to leave by herself, or to leave Lucas alone, she decided to get him to help her find Jay. He didn't have to know why. But first they needed to finish cleaning the otter pond and start refilling it.

She scrambled to her feet and brought Lucas to his. "Come on, we have to finish this up, and then I want to find Jay. I need to talk to him." Lucas didn't ask why.

"Why don't you go on? I'll finish up here," Lucas suggested as he resumed his scrubbing. Recognizing the look of fear on her face, he thought again. "Or maybe not. Let's finish up and I will go with you."

As she retrieved her mop from the floor, she felt Lucas's hand on her arm.

"Hey, what happened here stays between us, right?"

"Of course," Jolie said. She smiled and patted his hand on her arm, then turned to begin mopping. She heard his sigh of relief.

They worked fast without talking, scrubbing the cement bottom and sides until they gleamed. Jolie returned the mops to the storage closet while Lucas sprayed everything down and then turned on the spigot to refill the pond. Even with the water full on, the pond wouldn't be full until well after the day keepers arrived to turn it off. They checked on the otters one last time before leaving the area to find Jay and Kaycie.

All four of the otters looked up with sleepy eyes as Jolie shone her flashlight over them. Assured that all was well, she followed Lucas out of the area as she called Kaycie on the radio.

"Yo," Kaycie responded. At least she was talking now. She even sounded like herself.

"Location?"

"Lounge. It's break time."

"We'll be right there," Jolie replied, trudging up the hill toward the keepers' lounge.

Once inside the lounge, Lucas headed straight for the vending machines. He hadn't felt like eating for the past two days, and he was suddenly ravenous. Kaycie munched on popcorn while engrossed in a novel, so Jolie went into Jay's office, hoping he was there. He was.

"Hey, Jolie. You okay? You got a little spooked earlier."

"I'm fine. My imagination must be working overtime. Could I talk to you for a minute?"

Jay gazed at her as she closed the door. How did she say this without betraying Lucas's confidence in her? "If I tell you a little bit about a situation, can you help without knowing all the details?"

His brow furrowed. What in the world was she talking about? "Depends on what you are about to tell me."

"You can't ask me any questions. You can only say yes, you will help or no, you won't. Okay?"

He nodded, waiting for her to continue.

147

"Lucas needs a place to stay. It may be just for one night, or it may be for a while. Do you think maybe he could stay with you?" She saw the questions in his eyes. "I can't tell you any more than that."

"I'm sure it will be fine if he stays with me but I need to talk with Molly. How soon?"

"Tonight."

Jay hated to call and wake her up, but Molly would be even more angry if she woke up in the morning to a houseguest. He picked up the phone.

"I'll wait outside," Jolie said as she slipped out.

Lucas sat at the table, his face in his hands, candy wrappers and empty chip packages lying all over the table, along with two empty soda cans. Jolie's heart ached for him. What a horrible turn life could take, and without warning. One minute everything was fine and the next everything was in shambles.

Kaycie still read from one of the many romance novels she had downloaded to her phone. At the moment she was oblivious to everything except what was happening on the page.

Jolie remained standing outside Jay's door, hoping Molly would agree to having Lucas as a houseguest. Otherwise she would have to invite him to stay at her place tonight and try to explain to everyone afterwards.

Jay's door opened, his face drained of color.

Alarmed, Jolie grabbed his arm without thinking. "Jay, what's wrong?"

He hopped to the nearest chair, leaning against the back of it. He had forgotten his crutches. "Lucas, would you please come and stay at my house? Molly has taken the girls and gone back to her parents, and I will need help."

Jolie hated to pry, but she couldn't deal with two grief-stricken men at once. "For a visit, right? Maybe she forgot to mention that she was leaving?"

He looked at her, but his eyes were uncomprehending. "She said she needs to figure out if we should stay together. She said that this has been a long time coming. She said she would let me see the girls in a few weeks. . ." He crumpled into the chair he was leaning upon.

As if coming back to life, Lucas rose, walked into Jay's office, emerged with the crutches, and helped Jay onto them. "Come on," he said, his voice hoarse. "I'll drive you home."

Jay looked at him as if he didn't recognize him, but he pulled his keys off his belt loop, handed them to Lucas, and allowed him and Jolie to help him outside to his truck. Kaycie joined them, her eyes wide with disbelief.

LUCAS TOOK CHARGE and told the girls to get into their vehicles and go on home while he was there to watch them leave. Obediently they darted back into the lounge for their things and then to their cars, which they started up and drove out of the parking lot under his watchful eye. Perhaps having to take care of Jay would help him take care of himself at the same time.

As he drove Jay to his house, Lucas remembered something he had forgotten to tell him. It would just have to wait. Jay was in no condition to talk, much less talk about hiring somebody else for the night shift. Lucas had taken a call earlier from a former zoo employee who specifically wanted to apply for a night shift position. He could not remember the guy's name. He had worked at the Denver Zoo, he had said. Telling Jay about him would just have to wait. There were other things on Jay's mind at the moment.

Chapter Thirteen

JAY OPENED HIS eyes, expecting the smell of coffee and the sound of girly chatter to assault his senses. But there was only silence. Eerie silence. And then it hit him. His family was gone. Two hundred miles away, not coming back without some miracle happening, and his life seemed desperately void of miracles lately.

He wanted to pull the covers over his head and stay there forever, but his bladder would not let him. He hobbled to the bathroom where a glance in the mirror made him realize that he was still in his zoo uniform. Then he remembered Jolie's request that Jay allow Lucas to stay with him, and that Lucas had driven him home in his own truck after the devastating news of Molly's departure. Lucas must be in the house somewhere. Jay supposed he should check on him and see about getting him something to eat.

He splashed his face with cold water. The mirror offered him a disturbing image: a graying, weather-beaten, middle-aged man in need of a shave and shower. Somehow with Molly and the girls around he didn't notice that he was getting older. Was that it? Was Molly watching him age and thinking that she wanted someone younger? She certainly didn't look as old as he did; at 38, she could pass for much younger.

It was easy to blame their problems on his looks but he knew it went deeper than that. It certainly didn't help that he had erupted in anger over her charging groceries on the credit card. She had never liked him working at the zoo and now that he had gotten injured, maybe she had decided that she'd had all she could take. Perhaps in a day or two she would want to talk about it. How could he fix things if he didn't know what was wrong? She would call soon. The girls would miss him, and she would have to call, if for no other reason than to let them talk to him. Then maybe he could convince her to meet him and they could have a long talk together. He had to believe that she wanted to make it work. He had to.

Grabbing his crutches, Jay made his way down the hall into the den where Lucas was sprawled in the recliner with several beer cans littering the floor and side table. He had obviously helped himself to the fridge. Jay tapped Lucas's knee with the end of a crutch. Lucas stirred and squinted one eye open.

"Bad night?"

Lucas grunted and brought the recliner to its upright position.

"Hey, Boss." He followed Jay's eyes around the chair and saw the cans he had dropped.

"Man, I'm sorry. I'll clean all this up, and I'll get you some more beer."

"No, you won't. It's all good. I'm going to fix some coffee. Want some?" Jay headed toward the kitchen where his wife and girls usually were this time of day. It was too quiet.

"That would be great." Lucas eased himself out of the chair with a groan and began picking up the empty cans. After setting them all on the coffee table, he headed down the hall to the girls' bathroom.

Jay got the coffee started and opened the fridge to see what might be in there for breakfast. Molly usually kept it well-stocked when she didn't have to use the credit card. Why does my mind keep bringing that up?

There were about a half-dozen eggs in the carton, a can of biscuits, and half a gallon of milk. Enough for a king's breakfast. He set the eggs, biscuits, and milk on the counter and began digging for the skillet and a pan to put the biscuits in. Now, if he could only remember how to scramble eggs. If only Molly could see this.

JOLIE WOKE UP to her baby girl stroking her face with her chubby fingers and singing "Hush, Little Baby, Don't Say a Word." She giggled as Jolie opened her eyes. Late morning sunshine flooded the bedroom. Jolie caught Ellie in a great big hug.

"How's my sunshine girl?"

Usually Ellie struggled to get away but this time she settled in. Jolie inhaled the delicate smell of her little girl hair, wanting to lock in the memory of that smell forever.

"Fine." Ellie studied her chubby hands.

"Did you get a good night's sleep?"

"Yesth."

"I heard you singing a lullaby song. Did you learn that from Grammy?"

"Yesth, she sings it to me when I take a nap. Mommy, can we get up?" She scrambled out of Jolie's arms and sat up. "It'sth a busthzy day ahead."

"It's a busy day ahead, huh?" Jolie smiled. "Have you checked your calendar?"

Ellie nodded her head, her reddish-blonde curls bouncing. "Come on, Mommy. Let'sth get dressthed!"

KAYCIE AWOKE AS her phone beeped with a new text message. It was a message from Tim. Had it only been a few days since they had talked? It seemed like a lifetime. "Miss u may I come over"

Hurriedly she typed back: "Yes miss u 2"

She crawled out of bed and headed to the shower. Tim was taking off work to come and see her? Maybe an extended lunch hour? Whatever. She didn't care. She couldn't wait to see him.

TONI GLANCED OUT her kitchen window toward the Latimer house. Molly's car was still gone, but Jay's truck was in the driveway. It was weird that Molly hadn't called or answered her phone. She had never left overnight without calling. Maybe her car was in the shop, but that still didn't explain why she wouldn't answer her phone. Toni decided to find out what was going on, nosy neighbor or not. She grabbed her house key and headed across the street to Jay and Molly's house. Kent wasn't home to tell her not to meddle.

HE SETTLED INTO his own private nest, a secret area he had created for himself in the zoo warehouse which was home to all the unwanted furniture, fencing, planters, feeders, carts, and other odds and ends zoo personnel didn't use but might need in the future. He had gathered together some old bean bags from the education department, a table from somebody's office that needed the leg screws tightened, an old coffee maker from the lounge that needed a replacement carafe, and an old microwave oven from concession that had a dial instead of a digital timer. He had chosen a space with an electrical outlet, so power was no problem. He brought in water to make coffee, and snacks and leftovers to heat in the microwave. He kept some books on animal anatomy there, a bag of work gloves, and a couple of knives. It was his version of a man cave, only on zoo property.

After pulling a spiral notebook out of a hole in the seam, he settled into a bean bag and opened the journal. Inside he had placed printed phone photos of Jolie, Kaycie, Lucas, and Jay, along with photos of the animals he had recently killed. He caressed the photos of Jolie and Kaycie.

Kaycie would be first. He wanted to save Jolie for last; she deserved a lot more attention. Lucas and Jay would go together. Jay was too arrogant, and Lucas wanted to be just like him. If he could just get on again at the zoo, it would be so much easier. He had been such a skinny young redneck when he worked there before. Now that he was older and more mature, had gained weight and dyed his hair, maybe Jay wouldn't recognize him.

He turned to the animal photos where he had noted the date for each animal he had killed: squirrel monkey, bobcat, mountain lion, and a young coyote they hadn't found yet. It was so easy; he just put some kind of sedative he had bought online in their food, and then it was easy to slash their throats. Of course, Zoe, the first one, he slowly poisoned until she finally died. There were still some to go before he started with that brunette keeper. As soon as he knew for sure that no one else was around, he would head to the macaws. That one bird had squawked in his ear one too many times.

MOLLY ROLLED INTO her parents' driveway after five long hours of driving. The girls had finally fallen asleep after fussing and whining for half the trip. Tired of holding back the tears, she had spent the last hour crying as they slept, so her face was a swollen, tear-streaked mess, which would probably alarm her mother. She had no time to try and fix it because the porch lights had already flicked on. As she put the SUV in park and removed the keys from the ignition, the interior lights came on, waking up the girls.

"Are we there, Mommy?" Laci's voice was hoarse from sleep. Liza whimpered.

"We're there!" Molly tried to put some enthusiasm into her voice. She was weary, not only from the drive but from the emotional turmoil of the last few weeks. She got out of the car and went around to the back door to get the girls out of their car seats. When Laci's was unbuckled she slid out and took off running toward the porch where Molly's mother was coming out the front door.

"Mimi!" she cried as her grandmother swept her off her feet. Molly's father was right behind her.

Not quite understanding what was going on, but hearing Laci's excitement, Liza kicked her legs impatiently as Molly unbuckled her and lifted her out of the car. Both girls were hungry and tired. Molly hoped her mother was prepared to feed them.

Phil and Mamie Martin embraced their granddaughters and their daughter, saying nothing about her tear-stained face. Molly knew they had noticed, though. Nothing got by them. They must have been bursting with questions but they acted like nothing was amiss.

Once the greetings were done, Molly sank into the sofa in the living room while her parents tended to the girls. Mrs. Martin asked them all if they were hungry and then carried Liza into the kitchen while holding Laci's hand. Mr. Martin remained in the den with his daughter, sitting on the sofa beside her.

"Want to tell me what's going on?" He took her hand in his large, rough but familiar hand.

"Nothing, Daddy." Molly recognized the weariness in her own voice.

"Wrong answer, Molly. You've been crying. What's this all about?"

She couldn't fool him. She might as well come clean, but she said as little as possible, just enough to pacify him for the time being. Of course, anything she said would immediately be shared with her mother unless she put her foot down and insisted her dad keep it a secret. Then she couldn't be sure. She supposed when a person had been married as long as they had been, it was difficult to know when one stopped and the other one began. With that thought, the tears began to threaten again. She took a deep breath. Her father waited patiently, his gaze not wavering from her face.

"I just had to get out of the house. I think Jay and I need some space."

"He's not hurting you or the girls, is he?"

"What? No!" Molly looked at him in disbelief that he would even ask such a thing. "Jay has never hurt me. How could you think such a thing?"

Her father shrugged. "Just eliminating the obvious. So why do you need space?"

Molly went on to explain how Jay had broken his leg at work and been confined at home for weeks, how animals were being killed at the zoo, and then how their bank account had been drained. Hearing that information, her dad jumped in with his usual answer for every problem.

"You need money?"

Molly shook her head, exasperated. "No, Daddy. We'll manage. I just think the stress has gotten to him, you know? He has gotten moody and distant, and he is snapping at me and the girls. I just can't stay in that environment, especially if it hurts the girls, you know? Maybe my leaving for a while will help him get himself together, I don't know. It's okay if we stay here, right?" The tears trickled down her cheeks again.

Phil Martin put his arm around his daughter and pulled her close. "Of course it's okay. You can stay as long as you need."

"I love him, Daddy." She sniffed and wiped her face with the back of her hand. It felt so good to lean on her father once again. She missed being his little girl. She wanted her girls to have the same relationship with their daddy.

"I know you do, Sweetheart." Her father patted her shoulder. "There will be times like these in your marriage. You just have to decide whether it is worth saving. I think you know it is, and I think Jay will realize that, too. He probably already has if he knows you have left. A man's house can get awfully quiet when the wife and kids are gone." He recalled a similar scenario years ago when Molly was a little girl. It hadn't taken him long to mend his ways and beg his wife and daughter to return home.

158

Molly looked up at him. He always knew exactly what to say to make her feel better. "I suppose we will spend the night and go back tomorrow," she said, giving him a kiss on the cheek.

"Not so fast. Give him a chance to miss you, and give us a chance to spend some time with our girls," he laughed, squeezing her shoulders.

Mrs. Martin walked into the den, Laci and Liza in tow. "The girls said that you had not eaten anything, so I fixed some sandwiches. They've already eaten theirs." She set a plate on the coffee table in front of Molly.

"Thanks, Mom." Molly straightened in her seat and picked up the sandwich. Laci, wanting to feel more grown up and take care of her mother, set a glass of water on the table, filled only halfway so she wouldn't spill it. "Thanks, honey," Molly told her. Laci smiled in smug satisfaction.

Molly's parents listened to the girls chatter on about their trip and other things while Molly ate. The girls started yawning so the ladies took them into Molly's old bedroom to put them to bed while Mr. Martin took the dishes into the kitchen. Mrs. Martin bustled about, turning down the bed for Molly and Laci, setting up the portable crib for Liza, getting extra towels, and asking them if they needed anything else before she left the room. In a matter of minutes, Molly and her girls were under the covers and fast asleep.

DEANA HAD DONE nothing for three days. She was miserably pregnant, with the baby due any day now. The doctor had said that her cervix was already dilating and to stay close to home so that she could get to the hospital quickly. She couldn't sleep, and she didn't know if it was because of Lucas leaving her or because of the baby. Exhausted, she sat and lay around the house watching TV and trying to stay cool. The loneliness and impending birth were almost too much to bear.

Why had she been so stupid? That boy she had met at the grocery store had hit on her almost a year ago and after brushing him off for weeks, in a weak and lonely moment she succumbed to his charms. It wasn't the first time she had allowed herself to stray. There had been others. Why couldn't she be the kind of wife she wanted to be? Why was she so weak?

She had never wanted to hurt Lucas. He was the best thing that had ever happened to her, yet for some reason she couldn't seem to control herself when the opportunity to stray presented itself. So now she had lost him. He was right: she didn't even know if he was the father of this baby.

As if the baby heard her thoughts, she suddenly experienced the worst cramping she had ever felt in her life. Grabbing her swollen belly, she felt something give way. A sticky liquid soaked her underwear. Was it her water breaking? As she moved to get her phone, the cramping intensified, and she was horrified to see that it was blood staining her clothes instead of amniotic fluid. She managed to find a friend's number on her phone, but before she could call, she lost consciousness.

JAY SAID GOODNIGHT to his crew. He had decided to stay a little later to finish up some paperwork and check on a flamingo baby that was struggling to survive in the vet wing. He needed to give it one last feeding before the third shift keepers arrived.

The little guy, a fluffy gray ball of down with long legs, in no way resembled an adult flamingo. Jay had to hand it to him; he was a fighter. Jay patiently held the syringe full of blended flamingo diet while the bird lapped it up. He had to be careful that it didn't choke as it gulped the food down, and the fishy liquid ran all over the downy feathers and Jay's hand and arm. It was a nasty, smelly job but not only was the animal's life at stake, these birds were worth thousands of dollars. As Jay finished feeding the bird, he put down the syringe, but as he turned to grab his crutches, his arm bumped the heat lamp that aimed its warmth into the cage for the bird. The lamp crashed to the floor, shattering its ceramic base and bulb.

Jay muttered a curse word and then a quick prayer for forgiveness, realizing that he would have to go to the warehouse to try and find another lamp if he couldn't find another one in the infirmary. After a few minutes of searching, he resigned himself to hobbling out to the mule truck to drive the few hundred yards over to the warehouse where he was sure there must be more. He could have left a note for the third shift, but they would not appreciate it very much. He swept up the mess before heading over to the warehouse.

A few minutes later, Jay unlocked the door of the massive barn-like building and shone his flashlight on the wall, searching for the light switch. Flooding the open gym-like space with light, he began to poke around in search of a good heat lamp. He had almost given up his search when he stumbled upon an area which looked like someone might have taken up residence. How in the world would a homeless person get inside here?

There was a bean bag chair, a table, an old floor mat, a microwave oven, and a coffee maker. Magazines littered the cement floor along with food wrappers, soda bottles and cans. It was amazing that there were no visible droppings. He picked up a piece of paper on which names of animals with their schedules and diets had been scribbled. There was also a raggedy throw on the beanbag. Somebody had been spending quite a bit of time here, and it had to be somebody with a key to the warehouse. A cold tingle raced up and down Jay's spine. Is this where the animal deaths were being planned?

He shivered and hurried out of the warehouse without a heat lamp. After securely locking the warehouse door, he hurried back to the infirmary as fast as he could to make sure the air conditioning was off and to leave a note for the third shift to fix up another heat lamp for the baby flamingo. He then climbed into his truck and phoned Lopez. Voicemail picked up.

"Lopez, this is Latimer. I found something very interesting in the warehouse. It looks like someone has been spending a lot of time there. It may be a long shot, but I wonder if it might be related to the animal killings." He hoped Lopez would check his messages.

As he wheeled toward the exit gate, his headlights revealed a large, brightly colored object in the drive. He slammed his truck into park and got out as fast as his leg and crutches would allow. As he came around his truck to find out what it was, his heart stopped.

It was one of the zoo's prized trained blue and gold macaws, splayed onto the pavement, heaving its last breaths, its fresh blood staining the asphalt. From the amount of blood Jay knew there was no way to save it, but he took off his shirt, wrapped it around the poor bird, and with much difficulty climbed back into his truck. The hair on the back of his neck stood up. He had the distinct feeling that he was being watched.

Chapter Fourteen

AFTER DEPOSITING THE dead bird in the vet wing freezer, Jay left the zoo as fast as he could. He couldn't shake the feeling that someone was watching him, but he was not the superstitious type so he refused to give in to fear. Whoever was trying to intimidate the zookeepers into quaking, fearful shadows of themselves would not have their way with him or his crew. He wished he could confront the person, whoever it was. He would confront him, sooner or later.

How do they get inside the zoo, and how are they able to get close enough to the animals to hurt them? It has to be someone who has keys: a keeper, a former employee, a contract worker from the cleaning service.

Lucas was still up watching some hunting show on TV when Jay came in, which startled him even though Lucas's truck was parked in the driveway. He wasn't used to someone being up when he got home. It hit him again how much he missed his girls. If he didn't have to make all those calls to the vet and Lopez, he would pick up the phone and call them just to hear their voices, even if it did mean waking up everyone in his in-laws' house.

"Hey, Boss," Lucas said as Jay and his crutches passed through the den on his way to the bedroom.

"I found another dead animal tonight."

Lucas groaned and turned off the television to give Jay his full attention.

"Blue and gold macaw." Jay took a deep breath. "Marky."

Lucas shook his head. "You gotta be kidding me. Does Tanya know?" Tanya was the bird curator who practically hand-raised the bird and taught it to talk and do tricks. She would be devastated.

"I haven't called anyone yet. He was just lying there in the drive as I started to leave. I can't believe you guys didn't see him there."

"In the drive?"

"Yeah, right there in the middle of the pavement. I would have had to swerve to miss him. I stopped and gathered him up with my shirt but he was dead by the time I got to the vet wing. I need to call Doc and Lopez."

"So Marky was still alive when you found him?"

"Yeah, it appeared that he had been stabbed. There was blood everywhere." Jay started off toward the bedroom again.

"Then it must have just happened."

Jay paused. "You're right. Otherwise you guys would have seen it. Whoever did it was probably watching me when I found him." That's why he'd had that weird feeling. He shivered.

"Remind me to show you something when we get to work tomorrow," Jay told him as he hopped down the hall with his crutches, leaving Lucas alone to watch television. He wanted to see Lucas's reaction when he showed him the nest he had found. Lucas couldn't possibly be guilty.

Could he? He shut his bedroom door and locked it from the inside. Was he nuts? He unlocked it quickly. Things were beginning to get to him.

Dr. Grantham finally answered the phone after Jay tried three times. Voicemail kept picking up. "Grantham," he grumbled. "This better be good."

Jay identified himself and explained what he had found and then done with the bird carcass. He listened patiently while Dr. Grantham demanded to know why this news could not have waited until morning. Jay resisted the urge to defend himself by citing zoo policy and protocol, but he just apologized and hung up. Grantham would apologize later.

Lopez answered after only two tries, and he sounded alert. He listened carefully to Jay's story and then asked him if he could possibly be at work at 8:00 in the morning. Jay agreed, knowing he would be drilled by his superiors without having had a good night's sleep. But no wasn't an option. He set his phone alarm for 7:00, stripped down to his underwear, and fell into bed, hoping to get a little bit of sleep.

HE REMOVED THE pitchfork from the breast of that awful bird that everyone loved but which had done nothing but squawk in his ear the whole time he was trying to catch it. He had finally impaled it with a pitchfork he'd found nearby in the bird house. Stupid thing took forever to die, but thank goodness it was finally quiet. He had intended to poison it with the rest of the strychnine he had used on Zoe, but it just wouldn't be still and stop that horrible screeching and flapping around. He had no choice but to use the pitchfork.

He was going to leave it dead in the bottom of its holding area, but he suddenly had an idea. He would take it up to the parking lot by the back gate and lounge so the night keepers would find it when they left. He'd had barely enough time to drop it in the parking lot before Lucas, Jolie, and Kaycie came out of the lounge, sending him scurrying behind some bushes. They headed away from the bird, though. Their vehicles were around the corner. Where was Jay? His truck was right there where he would have to see it when he left.

After waiting for what seemed hours crouching in the bushes bordering the dimly lit parking lot, he almost gave up when Jay hopped out of the lounge on crutches. It's about time. He watched as Jay started up his truck and began to drive out of the parking lot. Just as expected, Jay hit his brakes and managed to get out of the truck to investigate the bleeding animal he had almost rolled over.

It was entertaining to see Jay remove his shirt, wrap it around the bird, and get into the truck with it. He watched the truck back up and drive toward the vet wing. He smiled. Another one to mark off his list.

JOLIE CALLED CADE as soon as she got home, hoping he wouldn't mind if she woke him up. She needed to hear his voice. Although she was still trying to figure out how to answer his request for her to move in, she was also feeling especially jumpy and vulnerable, wondering which animal she might find murdered next. There was no way she could sleep. Mustering courage, she hit Cade's number.

"Hello?" His voice with its sleepy raspiness quickened her heartbeat.

"Hey, Cade?" she spoke in a low voice. "Can you talk?"

His voice became more alert. "Of course, baby! What's wrong?"

"I just wanted to hear your voice. I miss you and there is a lot of weird stuff going on at work." She must sound like a scared little girl.

"Want me to come over?"

Is that what I want? She hesitated, knowing what might happen if he were to come over at this time of night. Am I ready for this? "Could you?" she asked before she thought about it too much.

"I'll be right there." Then the phone clicked.

She panicked, unsure about the decision she had just made. She jumped into the shower for a couple of minutes--careful not to get her hair wet--emerged from the bathroom wrapped in a towel, and started running around the house picking things up from the floors and counter tops and stuffing them under the sofa and into cabinets.

She had no time to dress before the doorbell rang. After a quick glance in the mirror, she made sure her towel was secure and then tiptoed to the front door and peered through the peephole. The sight of his disheveled blonde hair, his wrinkled tee shirt thrown over jeans, and his tan feet in flip flops as he stared at the porch floor waiting for her to answer the door made her heart skip a beat. She hesitated, then cracked the door open.

At the sight of her in a bath towel, he took in his breath sharply and smiled. "Hey."

She opened the door wider as he opened the screen door and entered the dimly lit living room. In one smooth movement he had shut the door and wrapped her in his arms, his mouth devouring hers.

His strong male scent coupled with the faint whiff of his cologne sent her senses into overload. She felt herself being lifted in his arms and carried through the house to her bedroom while his tongue caressed hers, then stopping the kissing only to find her bedroom without walking them into a wall. In the bedroom, lit only by the light shining down the hall from the living room and the moonlight filtering through the blinds, he lowered her onto her quilted bed and leaned over her, gazing straight into her eyes.

"Are you sure?" he whispered.

No! her conscience screamed. No! No! No!

But her body had other ideas. His eyes dark and liquid, held hers captive, his body warm and hard. Her fingers traced the muscles of the flexed arms that held him over her, and then they moved lower to find the skin under his tee shirt. His breath caught. Lowering his face to hers, he gently tugged on her lip with his teeth before coming up again and raising his eyebrows. She had not answered him.

"Yes," she finally whispered, surprising herself by placing her hands on the sides of his neck and bringing his face back to hers. This time it was she who explored his mouth as he groaned, his full body length against hers. God, forgive me, she pleaded silently. It had been so long since she had felt this primal need for a man. Unable and unwilling to stop herself, she gave in. She would think about the repercussions tomorrow.

TONIE AND KENT sat at the kitchen table eating breakfast, Toni describing what she had found out about the Latimers.

"Toni, come on, you mean you actually went down and knocked on the door?"

"I certainly did, Kent! It has been days since I saw Molly or the children. They are usually playing out in the yard, or walking out to get the mail, or at least getting the car out to go to the store," Toni insisted.

"So did Molly answer the door?"

"No! Some guy did. I don't know him, but he said he works at the zoo with Jay. He said Molly and the girls weren't there."

"I guess you asked him what he was doing there, and where they were. Was Jay there?"

"The guy said he was busy, so I just thanked him and left. But I asked him to ask Jay to call me and he said he would."

Kent waited but she didn't offer any more information. "Well?"

She frowned. "What?"

"Did he call?"

"Not yet." As Kent donned his "I told you so" expression, she added, "But I know he will."

"Whatever the deal is, it's their business." Kent got up for a second cup of coffee.

"We are supposedly their best friends, though, Kent. Don't you think we should know if something is going on? I mean, shouldn't they have at least called if Molly and the girls were leaving town? Or if they split up and Jay got a new roommate?"

"As usual you are letting your imagination run wild, Toni." Her meddling in other people's business exasperated him. It was strange, though. He had to admit that it wasn't like Jay and Molly to leave town without telling them. He hoped his wife wasn't right about them splitting up. Their marriage seemed to be as solid as anyone's he knew. He had been looking forward to the backyard barbecue that Jay had promised. Of course, no one knew what really happened behind closed doors in another person's marriage.

LUCAS WAS STILL having trouble sleeping. Things had not been settled between him and Deana, and all of his things were still at the house. And why should he be out of that house, when it was she who had betrayed him? His job paid for everything they had. She should be the one to leave if anybody did. But how could he kick a woman who was about to give birth out of the house? Where would she go? There was no family to speak of, at least no one that he would trust to take care of her and the baby. As much as he hated to admit it, he needed to check on her and at least retrieve some of his clothes and things. He dreaded the confrontation, but he decided to go over there before he went to work.

JAY WAS AT work by 8:00 a.m. waiting outside the curator's office when Lopez arrived at work. Jay's eyes had bags under them and he was dragging from lack of sleep, so he gulped coffee from his stainless-steel travel mug. Though it was bitter—yet another reason to miss his wife—she made the best coffee—he guzzled it anyway.

"Come on in." Lopez looked a little rough himself. This succession of dead animals was taking its toll on everyone. "Have you seen Oates or Tanya? They are supposed to be here."

"No, I haven't," Jay replied, dread kicking up a notch.

"They will be here. Why don't you tell me exactly what happened?" Lopez sat down at his desk as Jay sat in one of his nice leather chairs and propped his crutches against the front of the desk. Lopez tapped a pencil on the desk as he waited for Jay to reply.

"I would rather tell the story just once," Jay offered, hoping Lopez would wait.

"I don't blame you," Lopez agreed. He continued to tap the pencil. Finally he stopped, seeming to realize what he was doing. Jay stared at him. "Somebody is killing animals around here and costing us thousands of dollars while putting our jobs in jeopardy. I have to find out who is doing this." His eyes narrowed and sweat popped out on his brow as he gazed at Jay.

"I hear you. I'd like to know that myself." Lopez is going to be fired if he doesn't find out who is doing the killing and stop it, Jay thought. We may all be fired. "I did find something interesting."

Lopez sat up, giving Jay his full attention. "Go on."

"I found a hiding place in the warehouse where someone has been hanging out eating and drinking coffee and looking at books on animals. Very strange, almost like someone has been living there."

"I want to see that right away." Lopez pushed his chair back. "Why didn't you tell me?"

"I am telling you. This is the first time I have seen you." He took his crutches and prepared to get up.

"Not now," Lopez said. "We have to wait—"

"Wait for what?" Oates opened the door, his large presence filling the doorway and hiding the petite bird curator coming in behind him. Lopez jumped to his feet. "For you, sir!" He extended his hand to shake Oates's.

As Jay moved to get up, Oates boomed, "No, no, rest yourself, Latimer." The big man shook Lopez's and Jay's hands and then plopped into the remaining chair, breathing hard. Jay moved to rise for the third time, but Tanya shook her head. "I'll stand," she said in deference to the man with the broken leg.

Oates demanded that Jay explain exactly what happened with the macaw. The death of the macaw would be a hard one to keep secret since Marky was the official mascot for the zoo and frequently featured in newspapers, TV, and billboards. The public would soon start noticing his absence and asking about him. It was easy to find another blue and gold macaw but not one that was trained to do and say the things that Marky did. In time one could be trained but how would they explain his disappearance from the public eye? This time Oates was feeling not only the monetary pressure of losing an animal, but the pressure to please the public. And Oates did not like to be put on the spot.

Tanya asked all kinds of questions about where the bird had been during feeding and cleaning times, how it was found, and many more that Jay could not answer. He almost wished he had not been the one to find the bird, but he was glad the girls hadn't found it. When her tone began to turn accusatory, he snapped.

"All I know is that we cleaned his area and fed him just like we do every night. When I got ready to leave, there he was, bleeding on the parking lot. I wrapped him up in my shirt and put him in the vet wing fridge." His voice had grown louder as he spoke.

Tanya sighed and glanced at Lopez who attempted to defuse the tension.

"No one is blaming you. We're just trying to figure out what happened."

Tanya's frustration showed itself in her bright eyes full of unshed tears.

Oates struggled to get out of the armchair. Once he was standing he announced in no uncertain terms: "Somebody better figure out what is going on or somebody is going to be without a job." As he turned to open the door, he added, "I want to hear something in 48 hours or you are going to be looking for employment elsewhere, Lopez."

He left them sitting and staring at each other. Tanya dabbed at her eyes as she went out the door.

Lopez stared at Jay, his jaw flexing with stress. "Show me that hiding place," he ordered.

JOLIE WOKE TO streams of sunlight bathing her face. She stretched, feeling happy for no apparent reason. Images of last night flooded her memory and she flushed, but as she opened her eyes she realized that the man who had loved her with so much tenderness and passion the night before was no longer lying next to her. She sat up and listened, hoping to hear him in the bathroom or kitchen, but the house was quiet. He had gone.

She lay back, wondering when she would see him again, amazed at how thoroughly loved and cherished she had felt last night. Despite the niggling guilt that threatened to ruin her glow, she refused to feel shame in what they had shared. Maybe it was time to say yes to his invitation to move in with him, no matter what her parents thought. But what does God want? Will He punish me for last night? She pushed the troubling thoughts from her mind and got out of bed. Time to check on Ellie and her parents.

HE WATCHED LOPEZ and Latimer leave the warehouse. What were they doing in there? When they were far enough away, he unlocked the door and hurried to his hiding place in the back. A few things were out of place but his journal was safe inside the bean bag where he kept it. They had discovered his secret place. He would have to relocate. A noise alerted him to the fact that someone was coming in. Had they come back? His heart raced with anticipation as he grabbed a long thick screwdriver and waited.

CUSTODIAN RICK SUTTER unlocked the zoo warehouse in search of another heat lamp for the zoo nursery. New babies seemed to be arriving daily, and each one needed a heat lamp. The nursery had run out. He thought he had seen some lamps piled up in a corner of the warehouse last time he had been inside.

Rick switched on the great overhead lights and began heading toward the far corner of the warehouse where he had last seen the lamps. As he picked his way through the clutter, he wondered if the fire marshal had done an inspection lately. There were paths but they were much narrower than before. He began to hum as he grabbed an empty box and an extension cord. There might be other things in here he needed as well.

Suddenly he felt as if he had been punched hard in the back. He intended to turn around to see who the culprit was, but instead his knees buckled. It astonished him to notice blood dripping out of his mouth onto the floor. As he lay on his side, he lost consciousness, but not before he saw the face of his attacker, strangely familiar somehow. Too bad he would never be able to tell anyone else. The last thing he knew he was being dragged across the floor, over the threshold, and into the blinding sunlight, but then the light dimmed and went out.

LUCAS BANGED ON the door of his little house for what seemed like ten minutes or so, but no one answered. Deana's beat-up old car was in the driveway so she had to be home. Maybe she was sleeping too soundly to hear his knocking. He went around to try the back door and found it unlocked. He had lost count of how many times he had told her to lock the doors. She was either too trusting or extremely forgetful.

The TV was blaring an afternoon talk show. He didn't think she liked the particular program, but who knew? She wasn't in the kitchen, living room, bathroom, or baby's room. Maybe she was in the bedroom.

As he entered that room, the stench of death assaulted his nostrils the same moment he saw her lifeless body lying in a huge pool of dried blood.

"Oh, no! No, no, no, no, no, no, no!" he cried as he ran to her, realizing from her color and her cold skin that there was nothing he could do to save her or the baby. He clapped a hand over his mouth and ran into the bathroom to throw up. What had he done?

JOLIE WHEELED INTO the zoo parking lot but was immediately stopped by a police officer. What in the world was going on? Several police cars with lights flashing dotted the parking lot along with a fire engine and ambulance parked further up the hill on the other side of the lounge and offices near the warehouse.

She rolled down her window. "What's wrong?" she asked the officer.

"ID badge, please."

She fished her badge from the console and presented it for his view. Satisfied, he waved her on. The drive to the hill was barricaded. She parked her car in her usual space near the lounge and looked around for

Kaycie's car. Was she involved in whatever was going on? Her stomach lurched as she thought that something might have happened to Jay or Lucas or Kaycie. She refused to dwell on it. Maybe a visitor had collapsed from the heat or something.

She grabbed her purse and lunch bag and exited her car. Jay was coming out of his office when she entered the lounge. The expression on his face alarmed her.

"Jay! What's going on?" she demanded as he almost walked past her.

He stared at her without saying anything, his eyes flashing with anger.

"Jay?" Her heartbeat quickened in dread. What now?

"Rick's been killed."

Relief that it wasn't Kaycie or Lucas mixed with sadness for Jay. Rick had worked at the zoo for years and was one of Jay's closest zoo buddies. "I'm so sorry, Jay." She touched his arm.

He nodded and moved past her the best he could on his crutches.

The police officer who had stopped her in the parking lot earlier opened the door for Jay, then poked his head inside. "Are you Jolie Sowell?"

"Yes." Hadn't she just shown him her ID badge? He should know her name.

"Do you know a Cade Bishop?"

"Oh, God!" she cried, her hand clutching her throat as her heart plummeted to her stomach.

"He's fine, ma'am. He asked to come into the parking lot to pick you up early. I just wanted to make sure you know him and it is okay with you."

"Yes, I know him." As her panic abated, she watched the police officer wave to the familiar classic car which drove up and parked next to her car. As she trotted down the sidewalk toward him, Cade rolled down the passenger side window.

"Will you come with me, Jolie?" His tone was serious. She couldn't see his eyes behind the dark sunglasses he was wearing. Jolie's brow furrowed, wondering what was going on, but she obediently opened the passenger side door and got in. With all the upheaval no one would even realize she was gone. He quickly backed up his car and drove toward the exit gate.

"I'm taking you home, Sweetheart. I will tell you when we get there."

She wanted to demand that he explain right now, but the look on his face kept her quiet. She would have to show him that she trusted him. It made it easier when he reached over and enclosed her small hand in his. He must have seen her hands shaking. She needed a cigarette badly, but she dared not smoke in Cade's car. She would just have to wait until she got home and hope he didn't mind.

Chapter Fifteen

LUCAS DIALED 911 as soon as he was able to compose himself and stop being sick. He then left a message on Jay's office voicemail telling him that he would not be in. He couldn't bring himself to explain why, and he didn't care if it meant being terminated. He had just found his wife dead, her body decaying with a dead baby inside of her that quite possibly could have been his. How could he have left her at such a critical time? What kind of person left a woman alone who was about to give birth, no matter what she might have done to hurt him? Thoughts of the pain she must have suffered as something went wrong, the fear she experienced as she saw the blood flowing out of her, the thoughts she must have had as she realized her life was bleeding away and she would never be a mother to her baby pounded Lucas's mind and heart like a sledge hammer.

After hours of questioning and investigation by the police, the coroner was finally allowed to take Deana's body out of the house. Lucas sobbed as he watched the body bag zipped, rolled out on a gurney, and shoved into the back of a siren-less ambulance. No emergency sirens or lights were necessary. It was too late for that. The helpless police chief patted him on the back and shook his head.

"I WANT YOU to consider quitting the zoo," Cade said as he took her house key and unlocked the front door for her.

Not believing her ears, she followed him inside. Leaving her standing in the living room as he walked down the hallway, checked the bedrooms and bathrooms and then the kitchen and laundry room, she wondered if she had heard him correctly. She fumbled through her purse, producing a cigarette and lighter.

When he returned to the living room, she sat down next to him after he seated himself on the couch, seeming to ignore the fact that she was smoking.

"What did you say?" She snuffed out the cigarette in an ashtray after two long drags. "And what was all that about?"

He put his arm around her and kissed her on the forehead, almost making her forget the question she had asked him. His scent intoxicated her. As his lips moved to kiss her lightly on the tip of the nose, then her mouth, and then her neck, she summoned willpower and pushed him away.

"Cade, what did you say?" she repeated breathlessly. He smiled and fingered the tiny gold studs in her ears. She pushed his hands away. She wanted an answer.

"I said that I want you to think about quitting your job at the zoo."

Her eyes widened. She remained silent for a few seconds as she stared at him. She wished she hadn't put her cigarette out.

"Quit the zoo?" He can't be serious. "Why would I do that?"

"I could get you on at the bank. You could work days instead of nights. It would be safer, not to mention cleaner and air-conditioned."

"But I am a zookeeper. I would die of boredom in a bank."

Cade chuckled. "So, my job is boring, huh?"

She reddened. "Not for you, I'm sure. But I have to be outdoors. I can't even imagine working inside a building all day shuffling paper or money or whatever and having to dress up every day. Besides, my best friends are at the zoo!"

Cade frowned. "I thought that I was your best friend."

"I thought we were more than friends. I don't kiss my friends like this." She pulled him to her and planted a kiss on his lips.

Cade wrapped his arms around her and slipped his tongue inside her mouth. She pushed him away.

"Cade, I love the zoo. It's my life."

"What about your hours? What are you going to do when Ellie starts school?"

"My parents have agreed to get Ellie to and from school."

"What if they get sick or unable to do that?"

What is up with him? Jolie's good mood darkened. His concern had turned into prying into what was none of his business. Would he be this controlling if she moved in with him?

"I don't want to talk about this anymore." Jolie rose from the couch. "I need you to take me back to work."

Cade grabbed her arm. "Jolie, people are dying. I'm concerned for your safety."

"People are dying? Who besides Rick? And how did you know about him?" Jolie pulled her arm out of his grasp.

"The police officer said that a worker had been killed when I drove up to the gate," Cade said. "I didn't know who, but I panicked when I thought it might be you."

It occurred to Jolie that he must have been planning all along to ask her to quit her job, which was why he showed up unannounced to pick her up. "You came to the zoo to ask me to quit?" *He couldn't have known about Rick being killed before that, and she hadn't mentioned the animals dying. Is he ashamed of dating a zookeeper—a girl who shovels poop for a living?* She stepped back and grabbed her purse. "I think you are embarrassed that I am a zookeeper," *she decided out loud.*

Cade jumped to his feet. "Jolie, I would never be embarrassed of you, no matter what you did! I just thought that you might want a more—" He stopped himself.

"A more respectable job?" *She finished for him.* "It's obvious that you don't know me at all. I'd like for you to leave. I'll call Kaycie to come get me." *Her throat constricted. Have I made a mistake with this man, too?*

"Jolie, I'm sorry. I didn't mean to imply that your job is not respectable. I—"

"Just go." *She turned away, fighting the tears that threatened. She would not cry in front of him. She went to the kitchen, leaving him alone in the living room. Please go, she thought as she grabbed a paper towel to wipe the tears that had fallen. As she picked up her phone she heard the door open and shut, and then his car started.*

"Kaycie?" Jolie asked as someone picked up her call. "I'm at home. Can you come pick me up and take me to work?"

"I'm there," her best friend answered without asking why. *Now that was a best friend.* Jolie wiped the tears that had escaped down her cheeks and poured herself a glass of iced tea. Mindless poop-shoveling was exactly the kind of thing she needed to do right now. She had a lot of thinking to do, and performing her duties as a "fecal transfer technician" as Kaycie called it would offer the perfect opportunity. She lit another cigarette. She really must stop this habit of hers.

MOLLY SAT ON the front porch of her parents' home watching the girls play on the lawn. Liza giggled from her playpen and clapped as Laci danced and jumped like a cheerleader. Molly smiled, wishing she had brought her cell phone with her outdoors so she could snap some pictures.

Mrs. Martin came outside with a tray holding a pitcher of lemonade, two glasses, and two sippy cups. It was pretty warm outside, but there was a breeze and the porch ceiling fans to stir the air even more, so Molly was comfortable. The girls were oblivious to the outside temperatures but at least they played in the shade of the giant oak.

"How about some homemade lemonade?" Molly's mother set the tray on the wicker table next to Molly's rocking chair.

"Mmm, sounds wonderful," Molly replied. "Laci, want some lemonade?"

"Yes, Mommy!" Laci cried, dropping her pom-poms and skipping toward the porch. Liza began to wail, either afraid of being left out or left alone, or both. Molly rose to go and get the baby, but her mother stopped her.

"I'll get her," she volunteered, already halfway down the steps. Molly smiled as she poured Laci a glass of lemonade. She handed the cup to her daughter and settled back into the rocker before pouring herself a glass.

Laci took such a long, gulping drink that Molly worried she would choke. When she finally had her fill, she said "Ahhh" loudly, and wiped her mouth with the back of her hand.

"Is it good?" Molly laughed.

"Good," Laci agreed. Her grandmother came back onto the porch with Liza on her hip. "It's good, Mimi!"

Liza began kicking her feet, expressing her desire for what Laci had. "Want some lemonade, Sweetie?" Mrs. Martin sat in the rocking chair opposite Molly. Liza drank with gusto out of the sippy cup Molly handed her.

"Mmmmmm. . ." Liza hummed as she drank. Laci, Molly, and Mrs. Martin laughed. Molly realized it was the first time she had laughed in days, maybe even weeks.

Molly allowed the girls to play a while longer after she carefully washed the sticky lemonade off their faces and hands. They all had a lunch of grilled cheese sandwiches and fruit inside before Molly put the girls down for their afternoon naps. She could have used a nap herself, having felt tired lately, but she decided to call her best friend instead. Toni was probably beside herself wondering what had happened.

"Where have you been?" Toni demanded. "Why haven't you answered my texts and calls? I've been worried sick about you!"

"I'm so sorry, Toni. I am at my parents' house in Oklahoma," Molly confessed.

"Well you could have told me you were going. Since when do you just run off without telling me?"

"Since I left Jay."

"Are you kidding me?" Toni asked after a shocked pause.

"No, I am not kidding. I just couldn't stand what we were becoming."

"I'm so sorry, honey. I had no idea. I should have been there for you."

"No, no, how could you have possibly known? We looked like the perfect couple. I thought we were."

"He didn't cheat on you, did he?" Molly could hear the indignation in Toni's voice.

"No! Nothing like that. It's just that with his injury and problems at work we started to drift apart. He was getting mean to me and girls. . ."

"He didn't hit you!"

"No! Toni, for Pete's sake! He just started snapping at us and stuff. The girls and I were always upset. I just had to get out for a while. I hope it is temporary, but he doesn't know that."

"Have you talked to him since you left? How long has it been?"

"It's only been a few days. And no, we haven't talked yet."

"He hasn't called you?"

"No, but I think he's just giving us both time to think."

"Want me to talk to him?" Toni continued with the questions.

"No, please don't. This is our problem and we need to work it out. I still love him. He is my soulmate and I will love him forever. But he needed a wake-up call and I needed some space to sort out my thoughts and feelings."

"You sound like you are ready to come back home."

Molly paused. "You know, I think I might be. Laci asks every day when we are going home. I need to talk to Jay first, though."

"Will you do me a favor before you come home? Will you please call me?"

"I'll try to remember to do that," Molly agreed. She said goodbye and went to check on the girls. Jay should still be home so maybe she should try and call him before they woke up. Her stomach lurched as she dialed the number. What in the world would she say?

JAY SAT IN his office in the dark with the door shut. A tree had fallen on him, a squirrel monkey, mountain lion, bobcat, and macaw were dead on his watch, and now Rick was dead. Molly and the girls were gone. Lucas was nowhere to be found and Jolie and Kaycie were afraid to go anywhere in the zoo without Jay. They were sitting in the lounge right now waiting for him to come out. At least the day shift had made sure all the animals were put up and fed. His crew was fragmented and upset, barely worth the paychecks they would expect next week. Somehow he had to figure all of this out before he and Lopez lost their jobs.

Oates and the curators tried to explain away Rick's death as accidental, but there was no mistaking the stab wound in his back. The only accidental thing about Rick's death was that he had gone into the warehouse in the first place. Lopez had ordered the warehouse locked and prohibited anyone entering for any reason. Maybe the one who had been "nesting" in there would either be locked in or unable to get in, whatever good that would do. He or she could easily find another hiding place and continue the killing.

The big question was why? Why would anyone want to harm innocent animals? Was this person now graduating on to killing people? A chill ran up and down Jay's spine. Poor Rick. He had never hurt a fly, and now his widow was alone in her grief. The senseless killing had to stop. There was no other option.

IN THE LOUNGE, Jolie tearfully explained to Kaycie how she had given herself to Cade, believing him to be the man she had been looking for, and then how he had asked her to give up her job at the zoo. "I thought he knew me better than that," she sniffed.

"Men!" Kaycie exclaimed. "What did you tell him?"

"I told him that the zoo was my life and that I didn't want to do anything else. He wants me to take a job at the bank where he works." She looked at Kaycie and shook her head. "Can you imagine, K? Me at a bank? I just can't believe he would ask me to do that."

Kaycie took her hands in hers. "He's probably just concerned about you, Jo. Tim is worried about me. He asked me if I should think about finding another job, too."

"He did?" Maybe Kaycie was right. Maybe it was just that Cade was afraid something would happen to her if she stayed at the zoo. What he didn't realize was that she would rather die at the hands of a killer than die of boredom at a desk job.

"Yeah, and he knows that I would never want to work anywhere else. He is just worried about me. I'm sure that is all that Cade meant. He is just worried about you."

"You really think so?" Jolie hoped she was right.

"Yes, I really think so," Kaycie replied. "Now come on, let's clean up your face." She led Jolie into the restroom.

LUCAS CARRIED THE last box out to his truck and returned to the house he and Deana had shared to lock the back door. Then he placed the key in a flowerpot on the tiny porch. The "For Sale" sign in the front yard swayed in the wind as if taunting him. He never wanted to go inside that house again and hoped it would sell fast so he could forget it. Deana's family had stepped in and planned the funeral, which he would not attend. He couldn't look her family members in the eyes after what he had done. He felt fully responsible for her death. If he had been there, she and the baby would still be alive.

He drove toward the zoo. As he approached, he saw the bus parking lot completely full of school buses, which meant there would be hundreds of schoolchildren running around the zoo screaming at the top of their lungs, herded by frazzled teachers and parents who were doing intense self-analyses about their choices of vocation and parenthood. Snow cone cups and popcorn bags would litter the ground outside and even inside exhibit areas.

At the last minute he drove on past the employee gate, heading north toward the interstate. He had no idea where he was going, but he knew one thing. He would not be going to work. No way he could handle a zoo full of screaming kids, even if they would be gone in a couple of hours. Glancing at his gas gauge, he saw that he had about 150 miles to go before he needed to fill up. That should do just fine.

THERE WAS NO answer. Either Jay was ignoring her calls or he did not have his cell phone with him. She would not be able to tell the girls they were going home yet. Maybe Jay didn't want them to come home. Maybe he had decided he liked being single again. That would explain why he hadn't tried to call her himself. Molly fell onto the bed and cried herself to sleep, unaware that the girls were waking up from their naps and her mother would once again have to tend to them.

KAYCIE AND JOLIE spent the rest of the evening in the lounge waiting for Lucas to come in and for Jay to come out of his office. At one point they thought that maybe he had left the office while they were in the restroom, so after a discussion about who should knock on the door and risk being yelled at, Kaycie summoned the courage and rapped on the office door.

To her surprise, Jay opened the door. Even more surprising was his unkempt appearance. His hair was a mess, his eyes swollen, his face red and in need of a shave. His shirt had come untucked from his waistband as well. They had never seen him look so bad, even after finding out that Molly had left town.

"What is it?" Jay frowned as if he was irritated with them for disturbing him.

"Are you okay?" Kaycie asked. "We just wanted to make sure you—"

"I'm fine," he stated as he moved to close the door.

"Wait, Jay," Jolie interrupted. "Is there something we need to be doing?" She glanced at Kaycie, who was shaking her head. There was no way she would go out into the zoo at night without Jay or Lucas.

"No!" Jay cried unnecessarily loudly, making the girls both jump. "No," he repeated in a normal voice. "I want you to stay right here in the lounge until I figure out what to do. Promise me you will just stay in here, okay?" He looked at them with wild and reddened eyes.

Kaycie and Jolie glanced at each other. "Of course, Jay. We won't go anywhere until you say."

"Good." Jay shut the door without another word. It struck Kaycie that there were no lights on in his office before the door shut.

"He's sitting in the dark," she remarked as she walked over to her locker to get her bag. Opening the metal door, she retrieved her purse and pulled out a novel. "I have an extra if you want to read," she told Jolie, holding up another one.

"No thanks," Jolie replied. Kaycie tossed the book back in the locker and slammed the door. It echoed in the quiet room.

AS KAYCIE CURLED up on the lumpy old couch with her book, Jolie sank into an equally lumpy and old easy chair that someone had recently brought in and placed next to the couch. She pulled out her cell phone to see if there were any new messages. Sure enough, Cade had texted her. She hesitated before reading it, glancing at Kaycie to see if she was paying any attention, which she wasn't.

"I'm sorry." The message was simple, sent a couple of hours ago. She wondered if she should respond and how.

"Ignore him," Kaycie suggested, startling Jolie.

"Excuse me?" Was she talking to the characters in the novel or was she talking to her?

"If it's Cade, ignore him," Kaycie repeated. Good advice, but she wasn't sure she could do that. Kaycie must be psychic. Of course, she had peripheral vision and the expression on Jolie's face when she realized the message was from Cade had probably been a dead giveaway. She sighed and looked for a game on her phone. . .something that could take her mind off the man she was afraid she had fallen in love with. Kaycie said nothing else and Jolie was glad of it.

JOLIE AWOKE WITH a start. She glanced at Kaycie to see if she had noticed Jolie dozing off, but Kaycie's nose was in her book and probably in another world. Jay's office door had opened, which is probably what had awakened her. He maneuvered his crutches out of his office and almost smiled. "You guys ready to go home?"

"I am." Kaycie closed her book with a snap and began her usual chatter. "What a boring night! I'd rather clean three flamingo ponds than sit around here doing nothing all night!"

To Jolie's surprise, Jay cracked a wide grin. She noted that he didn't look quite as haggard as he had earlier. Maybe he had taken a nap as well. "I can arrange that," he said.

Kaycie laughed as she went to her locker. Jolie retrieved her cell phone from where it had fallen between the chair cushions. After they gathered their things and clocked out, Jay watched the women get into their cars and they in turn watched him get into his truck. It had been a long night.

JOLIE TURNED THE corner on her street and saw a car in her driveway. Fear paralyzed her for a second, making her think of driving past and heading to her parents' house. Who would be in her driveway this time of night? Then she recognized the lines of the classic Cutlass Supreme that belonged to Cade. He was persistent—she had to give him that.

She pulled her old Taurus into the driveway and parked next to him, all the while fighting with herself and her emotions. Had she overreacted to his insistence that she find another job? Was he really just concerned for her safety? Should I give him another chance?

He stood leaning against his car, watching her as she turned hers off and opened the door. She took her time gathering her things, still uncertain as to how she should act. Pushing the car door shut with her foot, she walked around the car toward him. He unfolded his arms and opened them with his hands outstretched in a sort of peace offering. She hesitated before falling into his arms, her face buried in his shoulder.

Cade nuzzled her neck, taking in her scent for a moment before swooping her up in his arms. She handed him her keys so he could unlock her front door. As he carried her back to her bedroom, she inhaled his scent deeply, trembling with anticipation. She couldn't have refused him if she had wanted to. God forgive me.

Chapter Sixteen

LUCAS AIMED HIS old truck east, hoping it would hold up to a long road trip because he intended to continue driving until he couldn't drive anymore. With the windows down, the stereo blasting mournful Alice in Chains music, and the speedometer holding steady at 75, his head began to clear. He let the tears flow, the wind in his face drying them quickly.

"God, where are you?" he shouted at the darkening heavens as he pounded his steering wheel. As if in answer to his cry, there was suddenly a flash of lightning and a deafening clap of thunder. Heavy raindrops pelted him in the face and left side of his body but he didn't bother to roll up his window. The driving rain felt healing.

He would never be able to erase from his memory the sight of his wife lying in her own blood on their marriage bed—stiff with death and its stench. As angry and hurt as he had been, he had never wanted it to end like this. Even as he had driven away that awful day after finding her with the other man, he had believed they would have a chance to work things out; he just needed time. But now their time was up. It was over. She had died alone and he had let it happen. No, he had been the cause of it.

The old truck hummed along at a slower 60 miles per hour, handling well in the pouring rain. He realized that he had been driving for two hours and had just crossed the Texas state line into Louisiana. He slowed down and exited the interstate, looping around until he could pull into the parking lot of a large casino. He had just decided what to do with his time. Maybe a little gambling and drinking would help him deal with the pain. He didn't care if he wasted every dime he had to his name. What good was money anyway? He had lost everything that was important to him. Even God seemed too distant to bother with him.

SEVERAL HUNDRED MILES away in Oklahoma, Molly tossed and turned, unable to sleep. After an hour she threw the covers off and got up. The girls were fast asleep, Laci on the other side of the bed and Liza safe in the portable crib. Molly walked over to the window where the moonlight streamed down onto the hardwood floor. Memories of dating Jay flooded her mind, when she would watch out this window for him barreling up the dirt driveway to pick her up.

It had been a whirlwind courtship that ended in a small church wedding. It seemed not so many years ago that she had pledged to be his wife—to love, honor, and obey—until death parted them. He had given her everything she needed and much more than she deserved. Being married to Jay had resulted in a happy life with two beautiful daughters, but now everything was broken.

Tears filled her eyes. Was he still the one after all these years? Did he even want her back? Why would he? She was the one who had broken their trust by leaving. She wished she could take it all back as she imagined him racing his pickup up the driveway to come and get her and the girls. If only she could wish it into reality. Maybe if she just wished hard enough. But the long dirt driveway remained calm and dust-free, the sounds of insects and frogs the only roar she heard.

Laci stirred in her sleep and mumbled, prompting Molly to return to bed so the child wouldn't wake up. It was her fault that the girls had trouble staying asleep at night. Laci had kicked the covers off, so Molly pulled them up over them both. Summer was coming to a close. There was just a hint of fall in the night temperatures lately, and the last thing she needed was for the girls to get sick.

Her thoughts turned to her husband again. She would try calling him again tomorrow. There was too much at stake to wait for him to call. Her girls needed their daddy back. So did their mommy.

AS EXHAUSTED AS he was, Jay couldn't go to sleep. He had left the back door unlocked in case Lucas decided to show up. Weird that he hadn't called to explain why he hadn't come to work. His truck was gone but his things were still in the guest room so he had to be planning to return. Well, Lucas was a big boy; he would let Jay know where he was when he was ready. Jay just hoped that nothing had happened to him. Who knew with all the weirdness going on lately?

He threw the bed covers off and went to the bathroom before heading into the den to his recliner. He was so tired of those stupid crutches he decided just to hobble on his cast the best he could. To his surprise, there was no pain. Did this mean he could ditch the crutches? There was a small pad on the bottom of his cast to protect it from the floor. He limped carefully to the den and then decided to go get a soda out of the refrigerator. He wondered what he might find on TV at 2:00 in the morning.

The kitchen was a mess. Jay surveyed the countertops and table and for the first time in his married life realized just what his wife had been doing all these years. She would cringe at this mess. Dirty dishes were piled in the sink and on the counters along with empty cereal boxes and opened cans of food. He and Lucas had not bothered to put away anything the last few days and it showed. He felt ashamed of himself, as if he were betraying his wife by messing up her space. This kitchen was not state of the art by any means, and it was small, but it was the hub of their family life and she took pride in keeping it clean and organized. He set his soda on the counter and started loading dirty dishes into the dishwasher.

To his amazement, after only half an hour of putting things away and wiping down counters and sinks, it looked almost as good as it had before Molly left. With that thought his throat constricted. How he missed her and the girls. He couldn't sleep because his wife's warm presence was not there next to him. He couldn't stand the absence of Laci's laughter and Liza's baby chatter. He even missed the crying and temper tantrums. Their noise meant there was life in the house. The silence had become deafening and almost unbearable.

He hobbled to his recliner with another soda and clicked the TV to life. Good, there was a marathon of "Law and Order" reruns. That would keep him occupied and maybe even put him to sleep. He had nothing but time on his hands. The screen lit up the dark room as the voices on the screen soothed him. He wouldn't remember what time it was when he finally fell asleep, or how many episodes he had watched. He welcomed the sweet nothingness of sleep.

AS SOON AS the girls were dressed and fed, Molly asked her mother to watch them for a few minutes so she could call Jay. She hadn't actually told her mother she was calling Jay because she didn't want the girls to hear. She just told her she needed to make some phone calls and wisely, her mother hadn't asked any questions. As Mrs. Martin engaged the girls in helping her start laundry, Molly headed back up the stairs and dialed her home phone number from her cell phone.

Just like before, the answering machine picked up. And just like before, she tried several more times before giving up. Was he just not answering the phone? She tried his cell phone, but his voicemail picked up. Again. Was he refusing to answer her calls? She didn't know that he was sleeping so soundly he didn't hear the phone ring, and that his cell phone was still in his pants from the night before. She decided to call his office later on. He would have to answer there.

JOLIE AWOKE TO the smell of bacon and eggs cooking. Confusion gave way to warm memories of the night that she had shared with Cade. He was cooking breakfast for her! She rolled out of bed, shards of guilt stabbing her heart. God was telling her that what she had done was wrong. Her rational mind told her that being intimate with the man she loved was totally acceptable. A Scripture popped into her mind: "I beseech you therefore, brethren, by the mercies of God, that ye present your bodies a living sacrifice, holy, acceptable unto God, which is your reasonable service." (Romans 12:1)

She closed her eyes, breathed a prayer for forgiveness, grabbed her bathrobe, and padded barefoot into the kitchen. She knew God would forgive her, but He expected her to change her ways and not do the same thing again. Would she be able to do that? Did she want to do that? Did she even have the right to ask for forgiveness if she had no intention of stopping? She wouldn't think about that now.

"Hey, Sweetheart! I hope you like bacon, scrambled eggs, and biscuits!"

She walked up behind Cade and put her arms around him as he handled the skillet. "Where did you get all this stuff? Did you go to the store?"

"I knew you were used to sleeping later because of your schedule, so I went to the grocery store earlier. I didn't want to wake you up."

"That's so sweet of you. I love a homecooked breakfast." Jolie squeezed him. "You found out how disorganized my kitchen is, though."

"I found everything just fine. There's coffee if you want it."

"Am I really awake or is this a dream?" Jolie shook her head as she glanced at the coffee maker.

"If we're still asleep I don't want to wake up," Cade chuckled as he tilted the skillet so that the scrambled eggs slid off onto a plate. He set the plate on the table where he had already put two place settings, complete with napkins and silverware.

Jolie poured herself a cup of coffee as she watched him. He pointed to her chair where she obediently sat down as he retrieved juice, jelly, and butter from the refrigerator. It was a breakfast like her mother would fix. Was this man perfect or what?

Chapter Seventeen

ELLIE WOKE JOLIE up the next morning singing at the top of her lungs some song she had learned from a kid's TV show. After three repeats she tried to pry open Jolie's eyelid with her chubby fingers.

"Mommy, wake up! I wanna watch Mickey, 'kay, Mommy?"

Jolie blinked her eyes open, feeling her eyelashes being pushed in by those little fingers. She grabbed those fingers before any damage was done.

"I'm awake, Sweetheart," she mumbled, forcing her eyes fully open. She wished Ellie was old enough to make coffee and bring it to her. Jolie pushed herself up and patted the bed next to her.

"Want to sit up here with me?"

"I wanna watch Mickey!" Ellie insisted, shaking her head. She toddled off to the living room. Jolie sighed and swung her legs off the side of the bed. She could have used a couple more hours of sleep, but that wouldn't happen when Ellie was home. As soon as her eyes were open, the kid was raring to go.

When Jolie came out of the bathroom, Ellie was there at the door handing her the television remote. "Mickey, Mommy!"

"Okay, okay," Jolie laughed. "Mickey it is."

After Ellie was settled on the couch watching her favorite cartoon, Jolie went to the kitchen to get the child some juice and peanut butter toast and herself some coffee. With a steaming mug in her hand and Ellie happily munching on toast, Jolie relaxed on the couch with her daughter to enjoy a morning in pajamas. It might even turn into a whole day. The only way it could have been any better was if Cade was right there with them.

That thought could become a reality if she agreed to move in with him. What would Ellie think about moving into Cade's house with Maddie and Mrs. Johnson? Would she be excited to have a playmate so readily available, or would she be upset about leaving their cozy little house, the only home she'd ever known besides her grandparents' house? And if she was okay with moving, would she later begin to exhibit behavior or sleep problems because of the stress?

Not only that, but with Mrs. Johnson there, her parents wouldn't need to keep Ellie as often. Jolie couldn't imagine having to break the news to her parents. Not only would they disapprove strongly of her living with a man she wasn't married to, they would not want Ellie's life disrupted. It would most certainly be a battle.

It was a tough decision to make, but there was no question that whatever Jolie decided would ultimately be based upon what was best for Ellie. There was a niggling feeling that she should pray about it, too, but she squelched it. Immediately I Thessalonians 5:19 popped into her head. "Quench not the Holy Spirit." She prayed for forgiveness again. She seemed to be doing that a lot lately. Guilt washed over her.

"Mommy, look!" Ellie screeched, her cheeks smeared with jam and toast crumbs. "It's Thomas!" She had just recently discovered the popular train engine.

"It sure is, honey." Jolie smiled, resisting the urge to wipe Ellie's face. She wasn't finished yet so it would be futile. Glad the couch is old.

Jolie got up to get a wet cloth and a refill for her coffee mug, leaving Ellie singing commercial jingles at the top of her lungs. As she entered the kitchen, her phone rang. Please don't ask me to come in to work today, she pleaded, hoping it wasn't Jay. As she picked up she saw that it was Cade. Her stomach did a double backflip good enough to qualify for the Olympics.

"Hello?" She hoped Ellie would stay occupied so they could talk.

"Hello, Gorgeous. What are you doing?"

"Still in my pajamas watching cartoons with Ellie. Are you at work?"

"Pajamas, huh? Baby dolls?"

"And spoil your imagination? No way." Jolie giggled.

"Party pooper." He chuckled and then paused. "Actually I am at work, but I thought I would take the afternoon off if you and Ellie would like to join me and Maddie at the Children's Science Museum."

Jolie had never taken Ellie there before because the admission was beyond her budget. She hated to decline because of that, but she couldn't be sure that Cade would offer to buy the tickets for all of them.

He sensed her hesitation. "You'll be our guests, complete with overpriced snacks and useless trinkets from the gift shop. You can't refuse. I'll even take you to dinner afterwards. If you don't say yes, I will be sentenced to spend another four boring hours stuck here in the bank wasting the most beautiful early fall day yet."

"How can I refuse, even though I feel like I am taking advantage of you if I accept? What a treat for Ellie!"

"So that's a yes? Great! I'll pick you up at 1:00. Ask your parents to come along. We can make it a family affair."

"Ellie and I will be ready." She hesitated. "But are you sure about my parents? Not that they can come, but I will ask them."

"Yes, I'm sure! I'll see you at 1:00."

Jolie couldn't wait to break the news to Ellie. She would be ecstatic, probably more about seeing Maddie again than going to the science museum.

"Ellie! Guess what!" she called as she headed back to the living room.

"What, Mommy?" Ellie asked, her innocent eyes wide with curiosity.

"Remember Mommy's friend Mr. Cade? He is coming to take us to the science museum! And Maddie is coming, too!"

Ellie clapped her sticky hands together in glee. "Yay! Hurry, Mommy, let's get dressedth!" Even the sticky hands that grabbed Jolie's couldn't spoil the high she felt right now.

Jolie put Ellie in the tub with bubble bath, which was a rare treat for the little girl but the best way to keep her happy and in one place while getting her clean. As she sat on the pink faux fur-covered toilet lid watching her daughter chatter and play, she dialed her mother's number. After a few rings her father answered.

"Dad? It's Jolie. What are you guys doing today?" She tried to contain her excitement.

"Same ol,' same ol,' Mr. McCray replied cheerfully. "How's my best girl?"

Your only girl. "We are doing fine," she said with emphasis on the *"we."* She knew that his only grandchild was really his favorite.

"How would you and Mom like to go with me and Ellie to the Children's Science Museum this afternoon? Cade is picking us up here at 1:00 and he said the museum and dinner will be his treat!"

"Really now?" Her father sounded doubtful. "And he wants Mama and me to come as well?"

"Yes, Daddy! Please get Mom and ask her for me. I'll wait." Ellie looked up at Jolie. She must have heard the conversation, but she hadn't caught on to the fact that Grampa might be coming with them. She turned her attention back to the two fistfuls of bubbles she was holding.

Her mother must have been right there in the room with her dad. "We're game," Mr. McCray said after a moment. "We'll be at your house before 1:00."

"Great! Tell Mother to wear walking shoes." Jolie set her phone on the counter and prepared for the battle of getting Ellie out of the bubbles. But this time all she had to say was that Grammy and Grampa were coming with them, and Ellie was out of the tub in a flash, willingly being wrapped up in the fluffy towel Jolie had retrieved from the cabinet. She was almost as excited as Ellie was.

LUCAS SAT IN his truck in the cemetery drive, watching the last of the funeral attendees scatter. It had been a well-attended graveside service. Deana had more family and friends than he realized. He had recognized her mother and her sister, finally visiting their daughter and sister now that she was dead.

He also recognized a few people from the church they had gotten married in; Deana had tried to get him to go to church with her, but he never had. Those people were awfully nice to see that she was buried properly. The church had probably planned the entire funeral; no one had contacted him, and he knew her family didn't care. At least he had enough insurance to cover the expenses. He would call and thank the pastor later.

After everyone was gone, one of the attendants walked up to the shiny silver flower-covered coffin and turned the crank which would lower it into the ground. Tears rolled down Lucas's unshaven face as he started his truck and made his escape. That part he couldn't bear to watch.

He needed to get in touch with Jay to see if he was still employed. If he was, it was time to find a place to live, time to get a grip and move on. I'll never forget you, though, Deana, he prayed. I will love you forever.

LAST NIGHT, HE had gone back to the zoo warehouse to update his kill book, as he called it. He needed to mark some items off and add some photos. When he reached the building and tried to unlock it, his key would not fit the lock. A chain had also been added to the double door handles with a lock he didn't have a key for.

"What the—" He yanked and jiggled the chain and doors. They didn't budge. He kicked the doors but the heavy metal didn't give at all and left him with possibly injured toes. Spewing forth a string of curses, he stomped off to find some bolt cutters. New locks wouldn't keep him out, especially with him needing his journal.

The thought suddenly occurred to him that someone may have found his hiding place and decided to lock him out of the warehouse. They might have even found the notebook. A new level of rage filled him, almost blinding him as he stumbled to a storage shed behind the rhino exhibit. It was locked as well. He should have the key, but in his emotional state he was unable to find it on the massive key ring which held a key to almost every door and gate at the zoo.

After kicking a dent in the door but still unable to get inside the shed, he stalked off to his hidden exit, a trail which led to a flap of fencing that zoo officials had not discovered yet. His car was parked on the other side of the fence. He heard a squirrel barking and there it was, right on the trail. With lightning speed he squeezed the air out of it with his foot, then grabbed it and choked the life out of it with his bare hands. Satisfied and feeling strangely vindicated, he tossed it behind him so that it landed on one of the visitor sidewalks. He didn't care who found it in the morning. Blood stained the sidewalk under the tiny animal, making its own trail down the slight hill.

AS JAY HOBBLED out to the mailbox, he was struck by how unkempt his front yard was. The knee-high grass was interspersed with even taller weeds, making the work he had done to provide a beautiful carpet of grass for his girls for naught. All the flowers that Molly had planted and taken care of had fried to a crisp under the Texas sun. It was a wonder the neighbors hadn't complained. Maybe they had and he didn't know it. He couldn't remember the last time he had checked his phone messages. He wondered if he would be able to start the old riding lawn mower and get his yard under control before he went to work.

The old John Deere mower was right where he left it under the carport in front of Molly's parking space. He checked the gas tank and the oil before turning the key to see if it would start. To his amazement the old lawn tractor roared to life, ready to reclaim his yard for him. He threw the mail onto his workbench and found his seat on the tractor.

The usually monotonous laps around the yard invigorated him. When he finished mowing the front yard, he puttered to the backyard and, like Pacman, ate the grass and weeds up in a matter of minutes. The smell of the fresh cut grass was like an herbal tonic to him. He inhaled deeply, appreciating what he usually took for granted.

After mowing, Jay found the end of the garden hose where Molly had left it in the flower bed and began watering her desperate flowers. Maybe some water would bring them back. It was worth a try. She would be pleasantly surprised when she came back, or at least he hoped so.

When. Not if. When. Why hadn't she tried to come back? He rolled up the hose and hung it on its rack by the faucet. It was time he took matters into his own hands and called her himself. Living without her and the girls was getting old. It was ridiculous. She was his wife and they were his daughters. They needed to come home.

He couldn't get back into the house fast enough. Banging his injured leg on the door jamb as he entered the kitchen forced a couple of words from him that Molly would not have approved of, but he managed to grab his cell phone from the counter and sit on a barstool to dial her number. Then he heard her phone ring. And ring. And ring. When her voicemail picked up, he hung up. She was obviously not as ready as he was.

AS MOLLY PASSED through the kitchen on the way to her mother's laundry room, she glanced at her cell phone where she had left it sitting on the counter. It showed a missed call. Her heart skipped a beat when she saw that Jay had called. She picked up the phone as if it would bring him closer somehow. She wanted to retreat to her bedroom and call him back. Now. But her mother was watching the girls while Molly transferred the wet laundry to the dryer. Calling him back would have to wait.

CADE, JOLIE, ELLIE, Maddie, and Jolie's parents stormed the Children's Science Museum with all the noise and energy the preschoolers could possibly bring. Maddie took up quickly with Mr. and Mrs. McCray as they were kept hopping between the two little girls' demands to come and see. Cade and Jolie hung back, holding hands while talking and watching their daughters enjoying themselves with Ellie's grandparents.

Jolie tried to imagine what her life would be like with Cade. Would her parents enjoy their new step-granddaughter? Would Maddie and Ellie get along as well as they were today? Would Cade continue to be the devoted lover and companion she craved? Or would moving in with him spoil everything? "Why buy the cow when you can get the milk for free?" her mother used to say to Jolie to try and convince her to avoid premarital sex, or fornication as she called it.

She cast a sidelong glance at her boyfriend—did I just think of him as my boyfriend?—as he pointed out an open, shallow water trough exhibit where the girls could touch a live turtle and manta ray. He was so handsome her heart swelled with pride as she realized that other women were looking at them with envy. She loved the crow's feet that deepened when he smiled at the girls. She loved the way his hair curled out at the nape of his neck. She loved the sideburns that extended even with his ear lobes and the way he combed his hair back around his ears. She loved his strong jaw and the mustache and beard he had begun growing. She loved his broad shoulders and the way his tailored shirts set them off to perfection, and she especially loved the way his muscles showed when he rolled up his sleeves. She also loved those strong but tender and gentle hands, but most of all she loved his eyes and the love for her and Ellie that she saw in them.

Jolie squeezed his hand, eliciting a curious gaze. She smiled and shook her head as she cast her eyes downward. He smiled and returned the squeeze, making her wish this day could last forever.

As Jolie watched the girls tentatively touching the animals in the tank, her cell phone rang. It was Lopez. Why on earth would he be calling her on her day off? She hoped no one had called in sick, but Jay was usually the one who would call to ask her to come in. Her stomach lurched. Instinctively she knew it was bad news.

"Hello?" she asked after excusing herself and stepping a few feet away from everyone.

"Jolie, it's Lopez. Where are you right now?"

"I'm at the Children's Science Museum with my parents, my boyfriend, and our kids. Something's wrong, isn't it?"

"Find a place to sit down, Jolie." She could hear the sadness in his voice.

She walked across the large room to an unoccupied bench and sat down, afraid to hear what was coming next.

"I'm sitting down."

Lopez was silent for a moment longer, filling Jolie with fear. She needed to hear what he had to say but at the same time she didn't want to. She listened as he cleared his throat.

KAYCIE HAD GONE in to work earlier than usual. She had gotten bored at her apartment and wanted a few minutes to read before everyone came in to clock out and then her own shift came in. She curled up on the lumpy old lounge sofa with her latest novel. She was deeply involved in its make-believe world when she was startled by someone coming out of the men's restroom behind her. As she turned to see who it was, she felt something heavy club her on the back of the head. The world turned black. Her last conscious thought was of her kids.

HE DRAGGED HER limp body off the couch and into the women's restroom. He was still holding her by the arms when her eyes fluttered open after a few minutes, sparking with recognition as she realized who he was. Removing a knife from his toolbelt, he held it over her so that she could see it and show him the fear that he craved. Her eyes widened and then narrowed with confusion and hurt. Before she could make the effort to speak, he swiftly sliced her throat and then dropped her to the cold tile floor. Rivulets of blood filled the grout lines between the one-inch tiles as she closed her eyes for the last time.

As he stood staring at the blood pulsing out of her neck, he felt strangely dissatisfied with the ease of killing Kaycie Harlan. He stepped over her body and washed his hands and knife in the sink. He could have made it last longer with a bit of torture, but there was the possibility of being caught, and he was pushing his luck by remaining in the restroom. Torture wasn't really his style anyway. He took one last look at his handiwork.

"You got what you deserved," he sneered as he stepped over Kaycie's body to exit the restroom. His heart pounded with the flood of adrenaline he had become addicted to. Would he be able to leave the lounge without anyone seeing him? No one was around, either inside or outside. It had been too easy. Way too easy. Not even fun this time. The redhead was next. She would be more fun.

JOLIE LOST CONSCIOUSNESS and slid off the museum bench, the battery and back cover separating from her phone as it hit the hard tile floor.

"Jolie!" Mrs. McCray screamed as Jolie crumpled to the floor. Museum employees came running as a crowd formed around Jolie.

Before her parents could get to her, Cade knelt by her side and pulled her head and shoulders onto his lap. He fanned her face with a museum brochure and urged her to wake up. Maddie soon appeared near them, picking up the pieces of Jolie's phone.

As soon as Ellie saw her mother lying on the floor, she began to cry. Mrs. McCray picked her up and stood back as Mr. McCray knelt next to his daughter and Cade.

Jolie's eyes fluttered open to see Cade's worried face looming over her. Tears escaped her eyes as she remembered the news she had heard.

"Thank you, Lord," Mrs. McCray breathed. Ellie had stopped crying and stuck her thumb in her mouth. Maddie clung to her daddy's side.

"Help me up," Jolie said.

Mr. McCray and Cade took her hands and helped her back onto the bench. "Easy there," Mr. McCray whispered as he settled her safely on the bench.

Jolie looked up into Cade's eyes and began to sob. "Kaycie's gone," she managed before breaking down. Cade sat down next to her and put his arms around her as she buried her face in his shirt. "Kaycie is dead!"

"Kaycie?" Mrs. McCray questioned. "Your friend Kaycie? The one you work with?"

Jolie nodded her head and continued to cry. Both little girls began to cry as well.

The museum manager asked Mr. McCray if he should cancel the ambulance that was coming. Jolie's father nodded and helped his wife gather up the girls while Cade helped Jolie to her feet.

They made quite a procession leaving the museum, Jolie unaware of anything that was happening. All she knew was her best friend was gone, her life cut short by a deranged killer. Poor Tim. Jolie wondered if he knew yet. After the girls were loaded into Jolie's parents' SUV and she was settled in Cade's car, she reached for her phone but it wasn't in her purse.

"Are you looking for your phone? Here, honey." Cade offered her his phone. "Yours was broken. I think your dad has it."

She took the phone gratefully but could not remember Tim's number so she just held it in her lap.

Jolie stared out of the window, shock and grief paralyzing her. Lopez had said that a keeper had found Kaycie's body in the ladies' restroom in the lounge. He hadn't given any details except that she had died of a knife wound, which was enough information to send Jolie's imagination into a tailspin. How much pain had Kaycie suffered before she died?

Did she know her attacker? What will the night shift do without her? What will I do without her? Havew her parents been notified? Would someone remember to call Tim? Poor Kaycie. Poor, poor Kaycie. Tears washed Jolie's face as she and Cade finally arrived at her house.

She realized that Ellie was not with her. "Where's Ellie?" she managed to choke out.

"She went with your parents. Do you want me to bring her back here?"

Jolie almost said yes before realizing that Ellie would be full of questions she would not be in a good mental place to answer. It was probably best for her to stay with her parents today. "Could you ask them if they could keep her today?"

"I'm sure they won't mind, but I will ask when I pick up Maddie."

Jolie laid her hand on Cade's arm. "Thank you for everything. I'm sorry for spoiling the outing for everyone."

"Don't be silly, honey. Kaycie's death is a tremendous blow."

Blunt, but true. Jolie looked at him. His response seemed a bit strange, but then, she was just getting to know him. She opened the car door before he could beat her to it, but then he went ahead of her to open her front door for her. He didn't offer to come in. She knew that he needed to get Maddie so as not to take advantage of her parents' kindness.

"Are you sure you will be okay?" he asked before turning to leave. "I can stay if you want."

"No, I'm fine," Jolie replied, sounding more sure than she felt.

"Please call me if you need me, Sweetheart." Cade kissed her lightly on the forehead. "I can be here in a flash."

She nodded and closed the front door. She parked herself on the couch, glad that all the window blinds were closed. She rarely opened them unless she was going to be home all day. She sat on the couch in the dimly lit living room all day, only moving to use the bathroom, until the sun set, leaving her in the same spot in the dark until she finally lay down, pulling a throw over her as she gave in to exhaustion.

Chapter Eighteen

JOLIE DIDN'T GO in to work the next day. Or the next. Or the next. Lopez had to pull keepers from the day shift to fill in for Kaycie and Jolie while Jay and Lucas worked through their days off. Using day keepers created a headache for Jay and Lucas because the day keepers didn't know the routine. Not only did they not know the night routine, they tended to question the guys about the way they did things.

Jay was at his wit's end. Lucas still occupied the guest bedroom in his home, and he wasn't a difficult guest—he cleaned up after himself and bought his own groceries—but just his presence in the house kept Jay from completely relaxing when he was home. When Jay came in from working in the yard or tinkering in the garage, Lucas would be settled in Jay's recliner watching TV, which irritated him to no end. First of all, no one sat in his recliner, and second, as the man of the house, he had first dibs on the TV and remote. That might seem petty and childish, but it was how he felt.

And, of course, when Lucas started to get out of the chair or hand over the remote, Jay did the polite thing by telling him to stay put, which irritated him even more. He wanted to be more assertive, but he just couldn't bring himself to be rude to the grieving man who was also his houseguest.

Most of all, Jay wanted his family back. Molly's calming, nurturing presence was the glue that held everything together, something he had not realized until now. He longed for her lilting voice and her soothing touch, and the sight of her in her cut-off jeans and pony tail as she tended to the girls. The house screamed her name when he woke up and continued to scream it every hour, every minute, every second he was there. The house needed her maybe more than he did. It seemed forlorn and dark in her absence. Molly and the girls were the light of his life, and also of their home.

He had been ready to ask them to come back home, but the events of the past few days at the zoo had changed everything. He couldn't even think of bringing his family back now that one of his crew had been murdered. Murder! On his watch! Who knew when it would happen again, and if it would be him or somebody else on his crew? Or maybe the killer would decide to attack one of their family members. Molly and the girls were safer where they were.

Molly's feelings were probably hurt that he hadn't asked them to come back, but he would just have to allow her to be hurt for now. Once all of this was over, and it had to be over soon, he would explain everything, hoping she would understand and bring the girls back home with her. He just hoped it wasn't too late by then.

Kaycie was gone. He could hardly wrap his mind around that. One of the day keepers had found her on the restroom floor lying in a massive pool of blood with her throat slit. The young girl had gone into hysterics and thrown up until she had nothing left to throw up. She would have to live with that image the rest of her life, something Kaycie would never have wanted.

The sight of her leaving the lounge in a body bag was something he would never forget. Of course, the zoo had closed early, keepers scurrying around getting visitors out as fast as they could so that they could get Kaycie's body out without anyone seeing it. Unfortunately, the news media had been alerted—by a visitor probably—so they were outside the gates clamoring to get in as zoo officials barred the gates. No one was prepared for such an emergency; they had been trained for animal escapes and natural disasters, but never for a zoo employee murder. The whole thing was surreal.

Jay was thankful that Oates had taken it upon himself to be the spokesperson to the media so that neither Jay nor Lopez had to answer any questions. Still, it fell to Jay to notify the next of kin.

The hardest thing he had ever done in his life was tell her parents. He decided it would be best to drive out to their house and tell them in person. They lived in the Azalea District, which wasn't far from the zoo. That part of town boasted beautiful old homes and displayed beautiful blooming azalea bushes during the month of April each year. Their home was one of the homes featured during the annual Azalea Trails each year. But money and high society does not shield one from the grief of losing a loved one.

Kaycie's mother crumpled upon hearing the news of her daughter's death, while her father grimly thanked Jay and shut the door so they could grieve in private. Leaving their beautiful home and neighborhood, Jay released the emotion that had been building up since the discovery of Kaycie's body. Tears fell, not only for Kaycie, but for his marriage as well.

MOLLY WAS BEGINNING to believe that Jay did not want her or the girls back. Had he wanted this separation all along? Had it been a relief for him when she finally decided to take the girls and leave? If so, that would explain the moodiness and irritability of the few weeks before she had made her final decision. She had attributed it to the pain of his broken leg and the medication he had been taking, and had only meant to give him, the girls, and herself a break. She had never meant this separation to last forever, but maybe that is what he intended.

The realization sent her spiraling into despair. She could hardly eat and when it came time to give the girls their baths and get them into bed, she could barely make her limbs work. She felt as if she weighed a ton and was trying to move through gelatin. Thankfully, Laci was old enough to get her own pajamas and get in and out of the tub by herself, but Liza was another matter altogether. Molly thought she would never get them bathed, their stories read, and them tucked in for the night.

Please don't fuss tonight, Molly prayed as she set Liza in the crib. Liza was so tired from playing with her grandmother and Laci all day that she flopped down, stuck her thumb in her mouth, cuddled her blanket, and fell asleep within five minutes.

Molly tucked Laci in and lay down beside her as she usually did until Laci went to sleep. But instead of getting up to change into her nightgown and do her nightly routine, she went to sleep on top of the covers fully dressed. Her last thought before falling asleep was that she would have to start looking for work.

JOLIE COULD NOT get out of bed. She had finally moved from the couch to the bed, but she did not have the energy or desire to change clothes or shower. She finally summoned the energy to remove her clothes, but she left them on the floor and crawled under the sheets in her underwear.

Her mother got worried about her when she didn't come to pick up Ellie, which was not unusual if Jolie was especially tired, but she usually called to tell her mother when she would be there. Mrs. McCray hadn't heard anything from her, and she wouldn't answer her phone, so she asked Jolie's father to go and check on her. Ellie kept asking when Mommy would be back, and they could not give her an answer.

Mr. McCray had to break into the back door to get into the house. It was so quiet he almost panicked but he refused to think the worst. He made his way through the house, noticing nothing out of place.

A loud meow startled him. Jolie's cat slipped around his legs, meowing with an urgency unlike her. A glance at the bowls on the floor showed that she had neither food nor water. From the odor he could also tell that her litter box needed cleaning. First things first.

The bedroom door was open. Jolie's tousled red hair tumbled over her face, her thin arms and legs sticking out from under the sheets. As she slept on her stomach, he could see the slight rise and fall of her back as she breathed. Thank you, Lord, he prayed. She was alive at least.

He almost woke her but then decided against it. He left the room to call his wife to let her know that Jolie was okay.

"Does she need something to eat?" was Mrs. McCray's first question. *Always fixing things with food, Jolie's father thought. But food couldn't fix this.*

"She's still asleep. I think I will just sit here and wait for her to wake up. I'll let you know if she needs anything."

"All right, honey," his wife agreed. "Just don't keep me in the dark, okay? Let me know how she is when she wakes up."

"I will."

"Promise me?"

"Yes, I promise. You just take care of that baby girl." He moved some clothes off of the old easy chair in the corner. The chair, which had been one of their castaways, would provide a reasonably comfortable place for him to sit and wait, even if it was going to be hours. He needed to make sure she was going to be all right.

He sat there for a while, hoping she would wake up and at least know he was there. He wondered how long she had been sleeping. His mind began to wander back to the days of his only daughter's childhood and the times he took her fishing with him or let her "help" him fix things around the house.

Jolie had been an inquisitive, spunky little girl, born with a head of flaming red hair which set her apart from the other babies in the hospital nursery. Neither her mother nor he had that hair, but after some research they had found a great uncle on Jeanie's side with the same flaming red curls. She had come by it honestly.

One of his favorite memories was watching her run, those red curls flying behind her like flames on a race car. As she reached her teens her hair lightened into a strawberry blonde color.

There was never any shortage of boys around, but Jolie had ignored them until the day she met Sean at the grocery store. She had fallen head over heels in love and stopped listening to all reason, especially if it came from her parents. At least he had done the honorable thing and married her. But the marriage was doomed from the start, something Jolie apparently had to learn for herself. The McCrays believed the Scripture that promised that "all things work together for good to those who love the Lord." Ellie was certainly part of that good.

A plaintive meow from Jolie's cat interrupted his thoughts. "Okay, kitty," he muttered as he rose from the chair to feed and water the animal. Then he would tackle that nasty litter box. Even the noise he made opening and closing cabinets and talking to the cat didn't wake Jolie.

LUCAS ARRIVED AT work to find Jay in the lounge talking with Lopez. He nodded to them both, not wanting to interrupt their conversation. Lopez motioned for Jay to follow him into the office, and then he shut the door.

Lucas put his lunch in his locker and gathered his equipment. He decided to go on and start the evening routine without Jay. They would both have to do double duty with Kaycie and Jolie gone.

Outside, he jumped in the zoo truck and headed for the commissary to pick up animal diets. He could at least get the diets dropped off in case some of the day keepers wanted to feed their animals before they left.

As he pulled up to the cheetah exhibit, he noticed a young mother with a little boy who was probably about four years old. He was pointing at the cheetahs and chattering excitedly. The female cheetah had given birth to twins a few months earlier, and they had just been put out on exhibit for the public to view. Lucas killed the truck and got out with the bags of cheetah diet, a grayish-brown mixture of no-name meat product.

"Look, Cameron, a zookeeper," the young mother said as Lucas came closer.

"Where? Where, Mommy?" the little boy asked, even more excited. His head covered in loose blonde curls, he clutched a stuffed animal cheetah from the zoo gift shop.

"Hey, Son." Lucas stepped closer to them. The little boy's eyes widened. He backed up against his mother, a little afraid of the stranger, even if he was a zookeeper. "How are you, Ma'am?" Lucas asked his mother politely. She reminded him of Deana for some reason. Maybe it was a glimpse of what his future could have been if Deana and the baby had lived. No doubt she would have taken the child on numerous educational trips, the zoo being one of them.

"Fine, thank you. Cameron, say hello to the nice man." The little boy's gaze shifted to the ground as he clutched his toy and remained silent. "I guess he is a little shy. He loves cheetahs—he has been asking to come and see them for weeks, ever since we saw the story of their birth on the news. We have been waiting for them to go on exhibit."

She blushed and looked down. Lucas noticed her looking at his left hand. She's looking at my wedding ring.

"It's no big deal," he replied, feeling a bit uncomfortable. She was cute, and she had this hopeful expression on her face that he often recognized when meeting women, but she wasn't Deana. And he wasn't ready to even consider a replacement—he might never be ready. He turned his attention to the little boy.

"Want to help me put their food out?" It wasn't normally done for the public, but it would be something this little one would never forget, and no one else was around, so crowding would not be a problem.

Cameron glanced up at his mom behind him. "Wouldn't that be fun, Cameron?" she asked him.

The little boy nodded and turned to Lucas, still not sure about the big zookeeper man.

"Okay, give your toy to your mom and follow me." Lucas handed the little boy one of the bags of meat after his mother took his toy. "Don't put your hands in your mouth until we wash them, okay?" he told the boy with a meaningful glance at mom. "It would taste really yucky to us, but the cheetahs love it."

"Okay." The boy obediently followed him through the door into the holding area. Mom followed, gripping the boy's shoulder with one hand and his toy with the other. She hesitated as she realized they would be going into a building alone with Lucas.

"It's okay," Lucas assured her, sensing her hesitation. "You're safe, I promise." She nodded.

After unlocking the door, Lucas led them into a narrow passage, pausing a moment to unlock a second gate made of chain link. Beyond that gate, there was a narrow concrete area with a wall on one side, and a wall of chain link allowing a view of the holding areas on the other. Lucas went to the end of the passage and pulled a lever which brought a steel container swinging out of the cage. He opened one of his bags of meat and dumped it into the bowl and then pulled the lever, swinging it back into the cage.

Then he moved to the next area. "Want to do this one?" Cameron glanced at his mother and then nodded to Lucas, who helped him empty his bag into the steel bowl. There was one holding area left, and he let the boy do that one as well.

"Now watch this!" Lucas then pulled another lever which lifted the heavy steel gates at the back of each caged area, opening the area up for the cheetahs to enter. Sure enough, in a few seconds, the cheetahs trotted inside, delighting the young boy.

He clapped gleefully. "Come on, come on!" he shouted. "Time to eat!" He began to run back and forth, watching them eat from each bowl.

"Don't get too close," Lucas warned, watching to make sure he didn't try to put his hand through the bars. His mother followed closely, ready to stop him if he tried to reach in.

The cheetahs ignored them until they finished eating, but then they eyed the visitors warily. It was time to leave the area and let them settle in for the night.

"All right, Cameron, say goodnight. It's time for the cheetahs to go to bed now," Lucas announced.

"Where do they sleep, Mr. Zookeeper?"

Lucas chuckled as he followed the boy and his mother out of the area and locked the gate. "Did you see those shelves in the corners? They usually sleep there."

Cameron nodded as if he fully understood.

Once they were back outside, the mother turned to Lucas in gratitude. "Thank you so much, Mr.—"

"Just Lucas. It was my pleasure." That hopeful look again. Bending down to talk to Cameron face-to-face, he asked, "Will you come back to see me?"

"Can we, Mommy?"

"I'm sure we can, Sweetie. Thanks again, Lucas." She extended her hand. "By the way, I'm Jill."

Lucas nodded and shook her hand quickly, averting his eyes. Bending to the boy's eye level, he patted him on the shoulder.

"Thanks for your help today, Buddy."

Then he turned and headed away to finish delivering diets. He suddenly missed Deana.

FRUSTRATION. HIS DISCUSSION with Lopez about what the police and zoo officials were doing to find the murderer did not satisfy him at all. It seemed to Jay that the machinations of the law were way too slow. His crew depended upon them to protect them, but his superiors did not seem very concerned. Lopez's answers seemed well-rehearsed. He had obviously been coached on what to say in response to questions, even Jay's.

Jay decided to take matters into his own hands and do some investigation on his own, starting with unlocking the warehouse tonight. Maybe the killer would try the door again. He radioed Lucas to meet him in his office. He would need help with his plan.

JOLIE'S PHONE RANG, startling Mr. McCray as he dozed in the chair in Jolie's bedroom. He jumped up to answer it before it woke Jolie, but it was too late. Her eyes opened just as he dug her cell phone out of her jeans pocket. He put on his daddy smile and winked at her.

"Hello?" There was a short pause. "Yes, it is. This is Bill McCray, Jolie's father. Who is this?"

JOLIE PUSHED UP against the headboard and rubbed her eyes, keeping the sheet over her bosom. Her mouth felt like cotton, and her breath had to be awful. She tried to smooth her wild hair down a little.

"It's Cade." Mr. McCray placed his hand over the speaker. "Do you want to talk to him?"

Jolie nodded, so her father handed her the phone and retreated from the room to give her some privacy.

As he shut the door, Jolie replied hoarsely. "Hello?"

"Hey, Sweetheart. I just wanted to check on you. Are you okay?"

Jolie hesitated, remembering suddenly why she was in bed. The realization of her loss slammed her again. Her stomach lurched. The pain in her chest returned with crushing force.

"Jolie?" Cade's voice held concern.

"Can you come over?"

He could barely hear her. "I'll be right there."

Weak and thirsty, Jolie put the phone down and swung her legs off the bed. She was amazed at how thin they looked. How long had she been asleep? Her stomach turned in on itself, it was so empty, but there was no way she could eat anything.

She stood up, albeit wobbly, to grab her robe and go to the kitchen. As she reached her bedroom door, it opened in, almost hitting her. Her dad caught her before she fell.

"What are you doing, Pumpkin?" He put his arm around her, steadied her, and turned her back toward the bed.

"No, I need to go to the kitchen, Daddy," Jolie pleaded. "I'm thirsty."

"Let me bring you something to drink then."

She resisted him. "Okay, but I want to go to the living room and sit down. I've been in bed too long." Her voice was weak but determined.

McCray didn't argue, but instead helped her to the living room couch, sat her down, and covered her lap with a throw. Then he went to get her a glass of water.

Jolie waited on the couch, staring at nothing, feeling nothing but numbness, until he returned.

"Here you go, honey." He handed her the glass of water, which she downed all at once, surprising herself. She had been so dry.

"Whoa, don't make yourself sick," her father chuckled. "Need some more?"

She managed to smile and nod. He went to the kitchen for more water and brought it back to her along with a microwaved cup of soup. She wrinkled her nose as he set it down on the coffee table in front of her.

"You need to eat something, honey. Just try a bit." He sat down next to her on the couch.

She held the cup with shaky hands, sipping the liquid from the soup. Then she used the spoon he had brought to eat most of the noodles. When she was finished she set the cup down and finished the rest of the water.

"Thanks, Daddy," she said, leaning into him.

"You're welcome, honey." He wrapped his arms around her and kissed the top of her head.

"Do you think you could get Mom to bring Ellie home? I bet she is wondering what is going on."

"I would imagine she is. I'll call Mama now. She wanted to know when you woke up anyway." He gathered up the dishes and headed to the kitchen to use Jolie's cordless phone.

As he returned to the living room, there came a knock on the door. "Surely that isn't Mama already."

"Maybe it's Cade." Jolie had noticeably more life in her voice.

Mr. McCray opened the door to indeed find Cade standing there on the other side of the screen door holding a small but bright bouquet of flowers. Cade greeted him politely and entered the house, walking straight over to the couch where Jolie was sitting with a weak smile on her wan face. Cade leaned over and kissed her on the cheek.

"I hope you like daisies." He set the bouquet on the coffee table.

"I love daisies," she answered as he sat down on the couch next to her. "Thank you for coming." She laid her tousled head on his shoulder. His arm went around her as he bent his head down to hers.

"I'll be out on the porch watching for Mama," Mr. McCray said, shutting the door behind him.

With Mr. McCray out of the room, Cade reached up to lift Jolie's chin with his finger while stroking her cheek. "Are you okay?"

He had never looked more beautiful to her. His hair fell over his forehead, his beard had grown in more, and his smoldering eyes melted her. She nodded.

"Now I am," she whispered, inviting him to kiss her by closing her eyes and lifting her face toward his.

His kiss was a welcome tonic for her wounded soul, filling her with warmth and security even though grief threatened to overpower her again.

"I'm sorry about Kaycie. But now I really must insist that you and Ellie move in with me. I'm worried about you." Cade took both of her hands in his and gazed into her eyes.

"Cade, please, I can only deal with one thing at a time," Jolie countered. She sat up. Why would he bring this up now? "I can't uproot Ellie and deal with packing and moving right now. I need time."

He refused to accept her answer. "But something might happen to you if you stay here," he insisted.

Tears spilled over and rolled down her face. "I can't deal with this right now." She scooted away from him on the couch.

He placed his hands on her upper arms, keeping her from moving far. "I'm sorry, Jolie. Forget I brought it up." He pulled her closer, putting both arms around her. Then he set her back enough so that he could kiss the tears from her face. "Don't cry any more, Sweetheart."

Just then the screen door opened wide and Ellie bounded into the room. "Mommy!"

Jolie and Cade separated, Jolie wiping her face with the sleeve of her robe. She fixed a smile on her face as her little girl scrambled into her lap. "I missed you, Mommy!"

"I missed you, too, Baby Girl. Give me a hug." Jolie held her daughter tightly, not wanting to let go, but Ellie wiggled out of her grasp to chatter about what she had been doing at Grammy's.

Mr. McCray filled his wife in on Jolie's condition, and when Jeanie was satisfied, she went over to the back of the couch where Jolie and Cade were sitting and kissed Jolie on top of the head.

"Hi, Cade," she said politely. He nodded in acknowledgement. "Ellie and I had a real good time, but she misses her mama," she told Jolie.

"Thank you for bringing her home," Jolie told her mother.

"Are you hungry? Is there anything you need me to do around here? Laundry? Is the cat okay?" As usual her mother needed to do her mothering.

"I cleaned up the kitchen and litterbox and fed the cat," Mr. McCray announced. Was there a little pride in his voice?

Jolie looked at him in surprise. "Thanks, Daddy." It was unlike him to do anything remotely domestic.

All eyes on him, Mr. McCray shrugged his massive shoulders. "I had to do something while I was waiting for you to wake up."

His wife patted him on the back. "Good job, honey. Have you eaten, Jolie?"

"Daddy fixed me some soup. I'm fine, Mama. Would everyone please relax and stop hovering? I'm sad, not handicapped. Now please sit down."

They spent the rest of the morning listening to Ellie's chatter, her mother starting laundry while Jolie showered and dressed, and her father and Cade talking about Cade's classic car.

Chapter Nineteen

AFTER EVERYONE LEFT, and after Jolie insisted that Ellie stay home with her, she fed her daughter the meal of chicken, vegetables, and brown rice that her mother had prepared before they had been ushered out of Jolie's house. Cade had gone a few minutes later when he was satisfied that Jolie was in good enough shape to be left alone. Jolie was glad she felt well enough to take care of her daughter, but once she had bathed Ellie and put her to bed, she was also relieved to be able to return to her own bed. How could she still be so tired after all that sleep?

Jolie awakened the next morning to the sound of Ellie talking to the cat. She got up, and this morning it was a few minutes before the memory of Kaycie's death hit her. She almost felt guilty that she hadn't thought of Kaycie right away. She needed to call Kaycie's parents to express her condolences and find out when services would be. She might even need to help them get Kaycie's things from the zoo. But first, Ellie.

. .

"Ellie, what are you doing?" she called from her bedroom.

"Kitty, kitty!" Ellie shrieked happily. She trotted into the bedroom holding the poor cat around its neck. That cat has the patience of Job, Jolie mused.

Jolie quickly rescued her from Ellie's grasp and put her down. The stressed-out cat darted under Jolie's bed.

"Kitty!" Ellie called, falling to her knees to look under the bed.

"Leave the poor kitty alone, Sweetie. You didn't eat any of her food, did you?"

"No," Ellie said while nodding her head. That helped.

"So you did eat some of her cat food?" Jolie pressed, looking for signs of food on her face.

"No cat food!"

Jolie had never heard of anyone dying from eating cat food, so hopefully Ellie would be all right if she had. She reached down to pick up her little girl.

"Umph," she groaned as she shifted Ellie to her small hip. "You're growing, young lady."

"Growing," Ellie repeated.

Jolie carried her into the kitchen to feed her breakfast, and once she had set the cereal on the table and Ellie was eating, she picked up her phone to call Kaycie's mother. What would she say? She took a deep breath. She could not back out. She had to do this. She was Kaycie's best friend. Kaycie's parents would expect her to call. Kaycie would expect her to call. She pressed the call button.

It was a few rings before someone answered, and before Jolie convinced herself to hang up. Ellie was eating happily and chattering to herself and the cat which was still hiding, so maybe Jolie would have a few minutes to talk to the person who answered. It was Kaycie's father, John Harlan.

"Hello," came his voice, calm and steady. The grief he was surely experiencing was well controlled. She would have expected nothing less from the astute and wealthy businessman. According to Kaycie, he had never been one to express emotion, particularly towards his daughter.

"Mr. Harlan?" Jolie asked. He had always intimidated her with his piercing eyes and all-business manner, but this time she would not allow him to make her feel inferior. She would honor him as Kaycie's father, and extend love to him as if he were her own.

"This is Harlan." No emotion, no hint of the sorrow he must have been experiencing.

"This is Jolie Sowell. I work with, I mean, worked with Kaycie at the zoo. We were best friends," she managed to say in spite of her fluttering stomach.

"Yes, I remember. How are you, Jolie?" There was no sign that anything out of the ordinary had happened. How did he do that?

"I'm heartbroken," Jolie admitted. "As I am sure you and Mrs. Harlan are." She hesitated. He said nothing.

"I called to offer my deepest condolences to you and your family."

"Thank you." Jolie detected a slight tremor in his voice.

"I also want to offer you my assistance if you need it. I will be glad to help you get Kaycie's things from her locker at the zoo, and to assist with the services."

He was silent. Had she stepped over the line of etiquette? Had she offended him? She waited patiently, resisting the urge to break the silence with chatter. At last he spoke.

"That is most kind of you, my dear. If you could gather Kaycie's things from her locker and bring them to the house, we would be most grateful." He breathed deeply before continuing. "We have not made arrangements yet. We have been waiting for autopsy results."

There was a break in his voice. His words stunned Jolie. She had not even considered that there would be an autopsy. Tears spilled down her cheeks as she struggled to keep her composure, both for his sake and for Ellie's.

After a moment he spoke again. "Mrs. Harlan and I would be honored to have you take part in Kaycie's memorial service. We will be in touch."

Without a goodbye, he hung up the phone, leaving Jolie staring at her phone. It was done. She swallowed hard, set down the phone, and wiped her eyes before Ellie noticed.

"Finish your cereal, Sweet Pea."

Ellie grinned brightly at her mother and obediently dipped her spoon into her bowl of Cheerios. She imagined Kaycie's parents watching Kaycie as a little girl. How their hearts must be broken. She couldn't imagine losing Ellie. She couldn't imagine how anyone could ever get over losing a child. She bent and kissed the curly reddish-blonde head of her child.

"Quit, Mommy!" With her mouth full of cereal, Ellie waved her hand in the air as if to brush Jolie away.

"I love you, Ellie Bug."

Ellie beamed. "I love you, too, Mommy!" Kaycie's parents would never hear those words again from their daughter.

TONI SETTLED HERSELF on the couch with a cup of coffee after Kent left for work. Things had been going so well between them that she was almost afraid that something bad might happen to change things. She had stopped pining for a child and staying in suspense every month waiting to see if her period came. She had decided to accept whatever their fate was to be. If they were meant to have a child, it would happen. If not, then it was not meant to be. Her change of attitude had taken the pressure off their marriage, causing them both to relax and enjoy each other's company again instead of wondering what day of the month it was and worrying if they were trying hard enough.

Toni felt as if Kent had fallen in love with her all over again, and she felt the same way about him. He looked at her with the same gaze that she remembered from their dating days. She would be working in the kitchen and suddenly find him looking at her from the doorway, bringing the old butterflies back to her stomach. He kissed her tenderly when he left for work instead of just leaving without saying anything other than reminding her to pick up milk or something. And then he would call her during the day, just to hear her voice, he said.

And the nights, oh the nights. Toni blushed, recalling the night before. It was as if they had just married and were discovering each other. They couldn't seem to get enough of each other, almost like their honeymoon years ago.

Toni flicked on the TV for the local morning news. She jerked her cup, burning her mouth as she heard the words: "A night keeper was found murdered in a Taylor City Zoo restroom."

Jay Latimer was a night keeper. Toni set her cup down, grabbed her cell phone from the coffee table, and searched for Molly's number.

"Molly!" Toni exclaimed as Molly answered the phone. "It's Toni. Is Jay okay?"

TONI WASN'T ONE to mince words and often spoke before thinking. This time it was Molly whose heart stopped.

"What do you mean? Why do you ask?" Molly asked, trying to ignore the alarm bells going off in her head. The girls were finishing their breakfast. Molly's mother was seated at the table with them. She looked up at Molly curiously.

"I just heard on the news that a night keeper was murdered! Have you talked to Jay? Is he okay?"

Molly's cell phone clattered to the counter, startling her mother and girls.

"Molly! What's wrong?" her mother asked, jumping to her feet.

"Mommy?" Laci whimpered.

Molly sat down in one of the kitchen chairs and stared at her mother, who grabbed the phone which thankfully had survived the fall.

"Hello?" she demanded. "Who is this? What is going on?" There was a pause as Molly's mother listened. Then she blurted, "Don't you think you should have done some checking before calling my daughter?" With that, she hung up and turned to Molly. "I'll watch the girls. You go make some calls. I'm sure everything is fine." Turning to Laci, she said, "Everything is fine, Sweetie. Finish your breakfast." She patted her granddaughter's arm. Laci obediently resumed eating her toast.

Molly's eyes were wide with unshed tears. She refused to give in to fear or panic as she found the strength to stand. "You're right, Mom. Thanks. Girls, finish your breakfast. I'll be back in a minute." She took

234

her cell phone and headed to her bedroom to call her husband. There had to be a mistake.

JAY'S CELL PHONE rang, waking him from a deep sleep. He had taken a sleeping pill he had found in the medicine cabinet, hoping it would help him sleep, and it had worked. But he had also remembered to put his cell phone on the nightstand in the off chance that Molly tried to call him. Forcing himself awake, he blinked several times, trying to read the display without his reading glasses. Did it say "Molly"?

"Hello?" he croaked.

"Jay?" came his wife's voice. Was he dreaming? He tried to shake off the pill's effects.

"Molly? Is it you?"

"Yes, honey. Thank God. I thought something had happened to you."

"Why would you think that?"

"Toni called and told me that a night keeper had been murdered. I was so afraid it was you." Molly's voice broke.

The unpleasant memory flooded his consciousness. Sleep had made him forget for a while. "No, it was Kaycie. Some psycho killed Kaycie." His voice broke. It was so good to hear Molly's voice. He wished her arms were around him now. He needed her more than ever.

"No! Weren't she and Jolie best friends? Poor Jolie."

"We all miss her." He paused. "And I miss you and the girls. I miss you more than you know."

"We miss you, too." There was an awkward pause.

Did she want him to ask her to come home? "I want you to come home, but I need you to stay there until we find the killer. You understand, don't you?"

When there was no answer, he continued. "I can't risk something happening to you or the girls. We don't know if this killer will try to hurt someone else, and I have to make sure you are safe."

"What about you? You aren't safe! How do I know that something won't happen to you?" Jay could hear panic rising in her voice.

"I'll be careful, I promise. Please promise me you'll stay there with the girls until I ask you to come back. Please promise me." He closed his eyes, wishing with all his heart that he was doing that now—asking her to come back.

"I promise." Her voice was barely audible.

He choked back the tears that threatened to overtake him. "Tell the girls that I love them and miss them. I want you back here. I want you back here so bad, but I can't—." He stopped to regain his composure. "I love you, baby. I love you."

"I love you, too." Her voice caught in her throat. "Be careful. I'll be waiting for your call. I love you."

Jay pressed the red button on the phone and rolled over, still clutching it as if it would keep Molly and the girls closer. He gave in to the best sleep he'd had in weeks.

MOLLY WASHED HER face before going back downstairs. Although she was sad about Kaycie, she felt light on her feet as she drifted down the stairs to the kitchen. With a song in her heart, she greeted her mother and the girls. The love of her life was not only alive, he still loved her and the girls, and he wanted them back. Please God, keep him safe, she prayed silently before tending to the girls. The hours and days would be much easier now that she knew he wanted them back. She had to believe that he would be all right, and that they would all be back home together soon.

After settling the girls in the den with a cartoon video, Molly helped her mother clean up the kitchen. She could still keep an eye on them from the kitchen, but for the moment Liza was content to sit right next to Laci, her thumb stuck in her mouth as she watched for cues from Laci to laugh at the appropriate times.

Molly was wiping the table when her cell phone rang again. Was Jay calling her again so soon? Glancing at the screen she saw that it was Toni again. "Hello?"

"Hi, Molly. It's Toni again. Hey, I wanted to apologize for upsetting you so badly earlier. Jay is okay. I called the zoo."

"Yes, I know. I talked to Jay myself. It was Kaycie who was killed. So sad. And it's okay. I know you didn't mean it."

"Please apologize to your mother for me. I know that I upset her as well."

"I will." Molly waited, turning away from the questions in her mother's face.

AT THE ZOO, Lopez heard his name called on his two-way radio. He picked it up from his belt and pressed the button. "This is Lopez."

"Code Five, alligators," came the reply. Code Five? Never in his fifteen years at the zoo had he ever had to respond to a Code Five. He dropped the pen he had been using to sign employee evaluations, his heart racing. Outside his office, he broke into a run toward the alligator exhibit. There was no time to look for a zoo vehicle.

The few visitors he passed stared at him quizzically but thank goodness no one followed him. He arrived at the alligator exhibit to find several keepers standing in a group on the boardwalk over the edge of the exhibit trying to look nonchalant. A quick glance revealed nothing amiss.

"What's the emergency?" Lopez growled at them, out of breath. This had better be something serious.

One of the keeper supervisors nodded down below the boardwalk where the swampy water met the shore beneath the boardwalk. There was something pale and bright in the reeds.

"What is this, an early Halloween prank?" Lopez grumbled, throwing one leg over the railing. "Where are the gators?" he demanded.

"On the other side," another keeper replied.

"All of them?" He didn't trust these jokers.

"I counted five," the keeper answered.

"Come on, you're going with me," Lopez told him. With great reluctance the other keeper swung his leg over and they both hopped down onto the mushy ground next to the pond. "You guys keep an eye on those gators," he ordered.

Several visitors passed by but they didn't stop to investigate. Lopez peered into the reeds where the pale object rested. It looked like one of those disembodied hands from a Halloween party store. He pushed it with the toe of his boot, expecting it to bounce back like rubber latex, but it didn't. The outer layer flaked off, revealing muscle and bone beneath. The keeper who had followed him turned away to vomit.

Lopez fought the bile that rose in his own throat and grabbed his radio from his belt to call for an early zoo closing. The announcement came seconds later, zookeepers scrambling to get everyone out of the zoo. Back on the boardwalk, Lopez and the keepers who had discovered the decaying human hand blocked it from view, hoping the alligators would not return to this side of the pond.

Lopez wracked his brain trying to figure out where that hand might have come from, and whose it was. Nothing. How could someone have disappeared—or at least lost a body part—without his knowledge?

The police arrived on the scene just as the last visitors were leaving. Reimbursement for tickets or replacement tickets were promised to unhappy visitors. Lopez dreaded Oates finding out about this. More negative publicity. When was it all going to stop?

IT HAD BEEN a long, lazy day for Jolie and Ellie. After breakfast, Ellie had helped Jolie clean house and do laundry, which took twice as long as it ordinarily would have, but Jolie enjoyed Ellie's fresh and fun approach to doing the chores that Jolie usually dreaded. They had stopped to enjoy a lunch of peanut butter and jelly sandwiches and milk. After a short nap they resumed cleaning, had more of Jolie's mother's chicken, rice, and vegetables for dinner before watching a program on Animal Planet and getting Ellie's bath.

After tucking Ellie in, Jolie settled into her comfortable couch and flipped on the news while she finished folding the laundry. The first story of the night was the grisly discovery of a human hand on zoo grounds. As the reporter interviewed Lopez, who was visibly shaken by the find, Jolie began to tremble. First Rick, then Kaycie. . .now who?

Not to mention all the animals that had died. Who would be next? Maybe Cade was right. Maybe she should quit.

As if in answer to that thought, her cell phone chimed. She had a text message. She moved to get it, her body feeling numb, like moving in slow motion. It was Cade.

"Missing u."

She closed her eyes, wanting his arms around her now. She dialed his number as quickly as she could.

"Hey, Doll." She could hear a smile in his greeting.

"Cade, there's been another murder," she blurted.

"At the zoo?" he asked, concern in his voice.

"Keepers found a severed hand in the alligator exhibit. They think the killer threw a body in the pond." Jolie couldn't believe how calm she sounded. She felt like she was on the edge of hysterics. Thank goodness Ellie was asleep in the other room.

"I'm coming over. Will you be okay until I get there?'

She had to be okay. What choice did she have? She just hoped the killer didn't know where she lived. "I think so." But she wasn't so sure.

Trembling, she wrapped herself in a throw and watched the door until Cade got there. Even though she was expecting him, the headlights of his car through the window still startled her so much that she was crying by the time he knocked on the door. She collapsed into his arms as soon as he came through the door.

They spent the night on the couch, him sitting at one end with his legs stretched out, her lying with her back against him. She didn't sleep well, but at least each time she woke she could feel his arms around her and hear his even breathing. She felt much safer than if she had been alone in the house.

The next morning, she awoke abruptly to find Cade gone. Peeking out the window, she saw that his car was not in the driveway. Ellie came into the room, rubbing her eyes, and crying a little.

"Mommy, I couldn't find you."

"I'm here, baby," Jolie said, gathering her little girl up in her arms. Why would Cade leave without letting her know? Then she spotted a note under a doll that Ellie had left on the coffee table. She reached for it as Ellie cuddled on her shoulder. Ellie grabbed the doll as Jolie read the note.

"Had to go to work, couldn't bear to wake you. Will call to check on you. There's fresh coffee. XOXO"

Any anger or irritation she had felt vanished. She hugged Ellie close. He was just trying to be a gentleman. She considered going to work if she still had a job, which she assumed she did because no one had called to tell her differently. But after the news of another killing, she wouldn't be going in. She decided to check with Kaycie's family about services. They had promised to let her know, but she hadn't heard a thing yet. She hoped she hadn't missed the funeral.

This time Mrs. Harlan answered, her voice tremulous. "Hello?"

"Mrs. Harlan?" She had only spoken with Kaycie's mother a couple of times. Most of what she knew about the lady had come from Kaycie, and their relationship had been strained, to say the least. Mrs. Harlan disapproved of Kaycie's divorce, her job, and her choice to live in an apartment instead of living in the large family house with them. What good had all that done? Now Kaycie was gone.

"Yes, to whom am I speaking?" Mrs. Harlan asked with her usual formality.

"This is Jolie, Mrs. Harlan. I hadn't heard from you or Mr. Harlan and I wanted to find out about Kaycie's service."

"Kaycie's memorial service will be a private affair, family only."

Jolie swallowed. She would not be allowed to pay her last respects to her best friend? "Kaycie was right about you all along." With that, she hung up. Kaycie would have been proud of her for standing up to her mother. But Jolie had lost in the end. She had burned the bridge that might have repaired itself with some careful tending. She had repaid unkindness with unkindness when God's Word said plainly to repay evil with good. She felt even worse.

Jolie dressed Ellie in play clothes and drove them both to her parents' house. She had eaten a little breakfast, but she was shaking so much that Mrs. McCray noticed. "Jolie, are you all right?"

Jolie burst into tears right there in the living room in front of her mother, her father, and Ellie, and then Ellie began to cry. Mrs. McCray gave her husband a meaningful look, picked up the toddler, and swept her from the room with promises of cookies and a story. Mr. McCray put his arm around his daughter and sat down with her on the sofa. He pulled a tissue from the box on the side table and handed it to her.

"All right, out with it," he said.

"Kaycie's parents aren't allowing any friends to attend Kaycie's service. They said it is for family only," Jolie sniffed. Somehow she felt like a teenager again.

"That is a family prerogative and not uncommon in families of their status."

"I told her that Kaycie was right about her. She will never speak to me again."

Instead of scolding her as she expected, he drew her against his broad chest and stroked her hair as he used to do when she was younger. The tears began to flow again. He allowed her to weep for a few more minutes before he placed his hands on her upper arms and set her back a bit so he could look at her face.

"I think you need some time away. Do you have any vacation time?"

She nodded. Since she was single she never took a vacation because there was nothing she wanted to do alone, or just with her and Ellie.

"Good. I'm going to call Jay Latimer and request a leave of absence for you. I want you to take the Explorer and go somewhere far away from here. Mama and I will take care of Ellie."

"I can't leave just like that," Jolie protested.

"Sure you can. If you need money, we will help. Stay right here while I go talk to Mama and call your boss." With that, Mr. McCray rose and went to the kitchen, leaving Jolie alone with her thoughts. Maybe it would be good to get away. She loved the mountains of Colorado, and time alone might be exactly what she needed to clear her mind. Plus she could get out of the way of that horrible killer. She felt better when her father returned.

"Here, catch," he warned as he tossed some keys at her. "You're good to go."

Chapter Twenty

TO JOLIE'S COMPLETE surprise and dismay, Cade hit the roof when he found out she was leaving. She would have understood if he had been upset because he was going to miss her, or if he was upset because he wanted to go with her but couldn't take off work, but his anger seemed unreasonable and misplaced. He drove over during his lunch hour to check on her and found her in her bedroom packing clothes into a small wheeled suitcase.

"Where do you think you are going? And why was your front door unlocked?" His beautiful brow was drawn together in anger, and was it fear she saw in those snapping eyes? She had always heard that anger was a form of fear, so maybe it was a moot point. But why such an intense emotional reaction? Did he not trust her?

"My parents think I need a vacation and they offered to take care of Ellie, so I thought I would drive west, maybe to the mountains," she ventured, afraid to tell him exactly what her plans were. This was the first time she had ever felt afraid to tell him the truth. "Jay approved it, and I have the vacation time built up. And I guess I forgot to lock the door."

"Why would you leave the safety of this place where people love you and can take care of you? Why would you go out alone somewhere?" She had the feeling he was talking down to her as if she were a brainless child. "And what were you thinking, leaving your door unlocked when there is a killer about?"

The safety of this place? Anger kindled inside her, came to a boil, and bubbled out. "How do you know what I need? Why do you think I need taking care of? What do you know about me anyway?"

His eyes widened in surprise. He grabbed her arm, a little too tightly for her comfort. She yanked it away and stared at him. Where was the tender and self-controlled Cade she had grown to love? Was this a part of him she just hadn't met yet? She wasn't sure she liked this Cade at all.

"What are you afraid of, anyway, Cade? Don't you trust me?" She rubbed her arm where he had grabbed it and then turned away, not wanting him to see the tears that threatened. She had lost too much all at once. Was she about to lose him, too? This was feeling too much like her arguments with Sean over his infidelity. Her stomach roiled, threatening to empty its contents.

She jumped as she felt Cade's arms come around her from behind. She felt his warm breath on her neck and then his lips, his hair tickling her neck as he kissed her. He turned her around gently to look at her.

"I do trust you. It's just that I don't want to lose you, and I don't like the thought of you traveling alone and so far away." The Cade she knew and loved was back, but still...

"But you have no right to—."

"I realize that." He interrupted her before she could finish. "Just promise me that you will be extra careful, okay?"

She nodded, a lump forming in her throat. He kissed her on the forehead, and then his lips claimed hers, making her forget about the argument or anything else except the feelings he stirred deep within her. She clung to him, memorizing his scent and the feel of his mouth on hers, his body against hers, and the feel of his hair intertwined in her fingers. She would miss him, probably ache for him, but she was determined to do this. Her father was right. She needed space and time to think.

He left a few hot minutes later to return to work, his lunch hour over. Jolie resumed her packing. That had been their first fight. Fighting was bound to happen in a relationship, but she had hoped theirs would be immune to it.

She debated with herself on what to bring on her trip until finally she just started grabbing things from her closet and chest of drawers. It didn't matter anyway. She knew the nights would be chilly in the mountains, so she selected her favorite hoodie and threw it in the bag, too. She couldn't wait to get out of the heat of the Texas summer and the situation at the zoo.

JAY ARRIVED AT work early, trying to figure out how to fulfill the duties of the second shift with only himself and one other person. He needed Jolie desperately right now, but he didn't have the heart to insist that she show up when her parents were begging him to allow her some time off. If he hadn't been the supervisor, he would have taken time off himself.

Lopez had given him the go-ahead to interview applicants to try and find a replacement for Kaycie, so he rifled through his file of applications, pulling out a few candidates. Most people who applied for a job at the zoo were young, often college graduates who wanted experience before going on to something else. It seemed he was constantly training new workers who would stay a few months and then go on to bigger zoos. However, there were a few here and there who sounded promising, so he selected them from the file and prepared to make some phone calls and set up some interviews.

He would be surprised if anyone he called still wanted to work there after the news media had gotten hold of the murder stories. What surprised him more, though, was that no one he knew of had quit working at the zoo because of the recent events. He dialed the number on the first application in the stack, somebody named Cade Bishop.

JOLIE LOADED THE packed suitcase into the back of the SUV and slammed the hatch shut. She did a mental checklist of everything she had done to prepare for a long absence. Feed and water the cat and change the litter box: check. Arrange for her parents to pick up the mail: check. Turn off the air: check. Turn off the water: check. Leave the kitchen light on: check. Her parents had a key to the house in case they needed to get something else for Ellie, and also so they could check on the cat. She had packed all of Ellie's clothes, favorite toys, and medicines and given them to her mother when she dropped her off that morning. She couldn't think of anything else that she needed to do.

It had hurt a little to kiss her baby goodbye this time, knowing that it would be several days before she would see her again. Ellie had taken the news well, but then she had no concept of days or weeks, one day or a few days. Jolie would miss her baby girl, but she hoped Ellie wouldn't miss her too much and make life miserable for her parents. As soon as she found a place to stop for dinner, she would call and check in.

Jolie walked back up to the porch and checked the front door one more time to make sure it was locked. After making sure she had her cell phone, she climbed into the car, tossed her purse into the backseat, turned the ignition, and took a deep breath. She had punched her trip into the GPS, so all she had to do was follow the picture and the voice instructions. She plugged in her phone, placed it on its magnetic holder on the dash, put the SUV in reverse, and backed out of her driveway.

She was on her way. Destination: Colorado. Lord, please give me a safe trip, she prayed. And watch over my baby girl while I'm gone.

The feeling of freedom as she hit the open highway was exhilarating. She could drive as long as she wanted to, stop as many times as she wanted, shop if she wanted, or stay in a hotel wherever she wanted. She could eat wherever and whatever she wanted without worrying about anyone else. She had a little money in her pocket, her daddy's credit card, and the open road ahead. She couldn't remember the last time she had felt this free. She turned up the radio as some old Lynyrd Skynyrd song came on, then she rolled down the windows and sang along as her hair blew in the wind.

About six hours later and only one stop to use the restroom and purchase a bottled water, Jolie wheeled into Amarillo. A few minutes later, there it was, the Big Texan, as gaudy and flashy as she remembered. She pulled in the drive, parked, and readied her taste buds for a steak. Her parents had stopped here a couple of times during their few family vacations, but the memories made there would last Jolie her entire lifetime.

Outside the restaurant, a little girl sat perched on the back of a real live Longhorn steer, with a cowboy talking to her in exaggerated Texan while her parents watched and took pictures. He placed a pink cowboy hat on her head and lifted her down to the ground. Jolie had done the very same thing as a little girl. Maybe she could bring her daughter here someday, and maybe Cade's.

"Howdy, ma'am," the cowboy greeted her as she walked by him to enter the restaurant.

Jolie smiled. A giant rocking chair greeted her as she entered, one big enough for Paul Bunyan. She recalled her father giving her a boost as she climbed up into it and posed for a photo. She wondered if her mother still had that photo and made a mental note to ask when she returned home. Ellie would get a kick out of it.

She was seated in a booth with a window by a perky young hostess dressed in a short denim skirt, cowboy boots, western shirt, and cowboy hat. She barely had time to pick up the menu when her server stopped at her table looking like a cowpoke from a corny elementary school play. He knew it, too, judging by the sheepish look on his face.

"Something to drink? Iced tea? Draft beer?"

"Diet Coke, please," she replied, needing the caffeine since she planned to drive a few hours more before she found a place to stay.

"I'll be right back. Will someone be joining you?"

"No, it's just me."

She chose a 12-ounce rib-eye steak with a loaded baked potato. When her salad arrived, practically drowning in ranch dressing, she dug in with gusto. It had been a long, long time since she'd had a good steak dinner.

As she enjoyed her meal, her attention was drawn to a platform in the center of the restaurant where a strapping college-aged man was about to accept the Big Texan challenge. If he could eat a 72-ounce steak with potato, salad, and roll in one hour, the meal would be free. The hostess sat him down at a table set on the platform so that everyone in the restaurant could watch. Probably a football player, he looked as if he might be able to do it. A raucous group in a corner of the restaurant cheered him on.

He dug in with zeal, but as time went on, he slowed down as each bite became more difficult. The cheering section grew more boisterous as their cheers turned into jeers. Jolie found herself feeling a little sorry for him. She lingered over her own dinner, not wanting to leave until his hour was up. Would he win, or would the steak?

As the clock ticked on, 30 minutes rolled into 45, and then slowly to 55. He was not going to give up easily. Continuing to take bites, a groan escaped. Still, he did not stop. 56, 57, 58, 59. As he stuffed the last bite into his mouth, the restaurant manager grabbed the young man's hand that clutched the fork and raised his arm in victory. His rowdy group of friends roared, and then, one by one, every diner in the place stood up clapping, including Jolie.

The victor grinned, holding his stomach in discomfort. His eyes swept the room and caught Jolie's. He lifted his glass to her, and everyone in the restaurant turned to see who he was toasting. She glanced around, and after realizing it was her, she turned six shades of red, as her mother would say. Not knowing what else to do, she nodded her head and continued to clap for the newest Big Texan champion.

Eventually the noise died down and everyone resumed their meals. She finished hers and waited for the check. She would have to stop at the huge gift shop on the way out and buy something for Ellie—maybe a giant stuffed steer or a Big Texan doll. As she placed her napkin and silverware on her plate, she caught someone out of the corner of her eye walking up to where she was seated. Thinking it was her server, she prepared to ask for the check, but when she looked up to speak to him, she realized it was the young steak champion. He wasn't in the restroom throwing up?

He smiled down at her as she looked up at him with her eyebrows raised in curiosity.

"How are you doin', Miss?" His big eyes, the color of a tropical sea, were fringed with the longest lashes she had ever seen. This guy was not only a big eater, but a real charmer as well.

"Fine, thank you." Jolie arranged her fork, knife, and napkin on the plate. "And you?"

"Wonderful. I just earned a free steak. I saw you watching me. One of my buddies wants me to ask you something." He gave a nod over his shoulder where she could see his friends watching them with expectant grins on their faces. No doubt they had a bet going.

She rolled her eyes. "Okay. . ." she agreed with some trepidation.

"My buddy Joe wants to know if you're from around here because if you are he is going to move down here."

"Oh really? And which one is Joe?" She decided to play this game for a bit. It couldn't hurt, and the attention was flattering.

"He's the one with the orange camo cap."

He pointed to a nice-looking kid who looked fresh out of high school with his skinny neck and smooth face. She returned her gaze to the steak champion. "Tell him no, I'm not, but thanks for asking." She suddenly realized that talking to these guys might be a bad idea. The last thing she needed was for them to follow her down the highway. She pushed her plate to the center of the table and glanced around for her server, hoping the guy would get the message and go on back to his friends.

Instead, he slid into the seat opposite her in the booth. His friends hooped and hollered from across the dining room. "My name is Jake," he said. He paused, as if waiting for her to tell him hers. Not in a million years would she tell him her name. After a few seconds of silence, he continued. "We're going out for drinks. Would you like to join us?"

Was he kidding? She was years older than these guys. Not once in her entire life had any guy asked her to go out for drinks until she had met Cade. Now here was a whole group of them. Seriously. Of course she knew that they were only looking for a good time, but it was flattering that they had singled her out. On the other hand, it was also scary.

"Jake," she said as nicely as she could, "I am really flattered. Really I am. But I just stopped in for dinner, and I really have to be on my way." She again scanned the large dining room for her server. Where is my waiter? I need my check.

Jake was not so easily deterred. "Come on, just one drink. You can ride with us to the nightclub downtown and we will bring you back here."

Did she have "stupid" written on her forehead? She shook her head. "No thanks." She frowned.

"You'll have a really good time." He just wouldn't quit.

A knot of panic formed in her belly and began rising toward her throat. Here she was, alone at night far from her family and friends with a group of redneck boys trying to make her go clubbing with them. She took in a deep breath. They were harmless. At least she hoped they were harmless. They had downed a few beers during dinner.

"No, thank you," Jolie repeated, a little more loudly this time. Her server was coming this way. She stared him down and raised her hand to get his attention. It worked. He hurried over to her table.

"Is there something I can get you?" he asked, glancing at Jake.

"My check, please."

"Just add hers to mine," Jake told the server, who nodded as he picked up Jolie's plate.

Jolie frowned. No way was that going to happen. "That won't be necessary," she told the server.

Jake shook his head and gave the server a stern look. The server looked at Jolie again.

"No," she told Jake, frowning. Then looking back up at her server, she stated, "I want my check."

"I'll be right back." The server hesitated, as if not sure he should leave her alone, but then he headed toward the back.

Jake remained seated. "You know you want to."

He was not going to give it up. Her heart beat even faster. She was going to have to be rude.

"Look," she said, leaning over the table toward him. "I have tried to be nice, but you aren't getting it. I do not want to go anywhere with you or your friends. End of story. Please move along."

His eyes narrowed. He glanced over at his friends, but they had lost interest in what he was doing and were talking and laughing among themselves. He put both hands on the table, looking as if he wanted to say something, but he decided against it and slid out of the booth.

"Have a nice trip." He tipped his cowboy hat towards her and winked.

She stared at him, unwilling to give him any encouragement at all. He sauntered off to rejoin his friends.

Jolie thanked her server, left a generous tip, picked up her ticket, and went to pay for the meal. She had planned to visit the gift shop but all she wanted to do after that encounter was get out of the place as fast as she could. Afraid they would try to follow her, she hurried to her car, started it up, and left the parking lot. It was only eight o'clock, so maybe she could drive an hour or two more before she stopped for the night.

THERE WERE NO leads. Oates was breathing down Lopez's neck, wanting answers now. With school back in session, it was normal for visitor numbers to fall, but they had fallen drastically since the discovery of the severed hand in the alligator exhibit. The police investigators had come up with absolutely nothing except for the hiding place in the warehouse, which Lopez and Jay Latimer had shown to them.

Fingerprint dusting had turned up nothing, and there were no footprints anywhere that couldn't be attributed to visitors or zoo workers. No equipment was out of place, no keys missing. Police had met with curators and supervisors to tell them what to look for, but so far there was nothing. The zoo was mentioned daily in almost every local television news broadcast, which was turning Oates into a red-faced, blubbering, apoplectic mess. In his frustration he increased pressure on Lopez and Jay. Both men had resigned themselves to the possibility of being fired, while at the same time knowing that Oates depended upon them too much to fire them. It would be foolish to have to train new managers while the investigation was going on, and Oates knew it.

In the meantime, all Lopez could do was endure the ranting and raving and hope something broke soon. He tried not to pass the madness on to Jay; he knew Jay was under enough pressure trying to run the second shift with only two people while at the same time looking for a replacement for Kaycie.

Not only was Jay shorthanded, but at least three more supervisors had come to Lopez telling him that several keepers were putting in their notice to quit. The random killings were understandably making the keepers jittery, so many were applying for jobs elsewhere. Lopez himself had several requests for letters of reference in his inbox. If the killer wasn't found soon, the zoo would not have enough keepers to keep all the exhibits open.

Lopez tossed his mail onto his desk and sat down. A few visitors passed through the breezeway off the main offices. It was a beautiful early fall day, not too hot. Maybe there would be more visitors today. He needed something to distract him from his worries, and interacting with visitors would be good for that.

HE TRIED THE door to the warehouse just in case. To his surprise, the Master Lock was gone. Glancing around to see if anyone was near, he slipped in, shutting the large barn door behind him. Finding his usual pathway clear, he crept softly through the maze of boxes, equipment, and assorted junk to where his hiding place had been. There it was, undisturbed. No one had found it. Or maybe it was a trap. He scanned above him, checking for cameras that might have been installed since his last visit. He saw nothing except the usual exposed steel beams and hanging warehouse lamps.

He unzipped the heavy khaki coveralls he had been wearing to look like a maintenance worker. It was way too warm for the thick tan coveralls. He wiped the sweat from his face and neck after slipping his arms from the sleeves. Everything looked the same, nothing moved or missing. No one had found his spot. He plopped down on the beanbag and reached into the seam for his journal. It was in its usual place. Opening it to the page with the dog-eared corner, he marked out three names with the pencil he kept in the notebook's binding. Three names remained.

After he crossed out the last name, he would be able to leave town. His work would be done here. He could start over somewhere else with a clean slate, find a good job and live a normal life, all this behind him. All that had been eating at him for years would finally be over. The torment would stop. He could finally be happy.

JOLIE PUSHED HERSELF until her eyes refused to stay open any longer. She had reached Texline, a small town on the Texas-New Mexico state line. It was well past midnight. There had to be a room left in the only hotel in town. She rolled into the parking lot of the Texline Inn. There was a well-lit entrance and lobby, so she pulled in under the portico.

Getting out of the car, she realized how stiff she was. She bent over and stretched a couple of times before locking the car and going in. Please let there be a room available, she prayed. She couldn't imagine having to get back in the car and continue driving.

A young woman behind the counter stared at a TV screen showing an old "Golden Girls" episode. Jolie stopped at the counter.

"Can I help you?" The young woman didn't even look away from the TV screen.

"Do you have any rooms left?" Jolie asked, fatigue threatening to overtake her.

"Um hm." The clerk popped a bubble in the gum she was smacking. She placed a form on the counter. "Double or king?"

"Either is fine." Jolie took the pen offered, filled out the form, and signed it as the woman picked a key from the board behind her. Computers must not have made it to Texline yet, or at least not to this hotel.

"Fifty-five dollars plus tax. Check-out at 11:00." She turned her attention back to the TV.

"Is there a continental breakfast?" Probably not, but it didn't hurt to ask.

"Nope, but there's a restaurant across the street that serves breakfast." The woman took three twenty-dollar bills from Jolie. "Room's around the back, number 117." She slid a key across the counter to Jolie.

"Thanks," Jolie replied, too tired to wait for her change. She walked out, got back into the tired and dusty SUV, and drove it around the building. At least there was enough light, but she still felt a little uneasy as she parked, even though her parking space was directly in front of room 117. She grabbed her purse and her suitcase as quickly as she could and then unlocked the room and entered even faster, slamming the door behind her. Traveling alone might be romantic, but it could also be dangerous.

No deadbolt, just a door lock with a chain. Flipping on the lights, she pulled the nearest chair toward the door and put its back under the doorknob. Glancing around, she found the room to be cleaner than she expected. Granted, the furniture was old and a little battered, but the bedspread, curtains, lamps, and artwork looked almost new. Even the carpet was thick and newer.

She set her bag on the luggage stand and went over to check the mattress seams as her mother had taught her. Better to be safe than sorry. All she needed was a crop of bedbug souvenirs. The mattress was clean and also new. Thank goodness for remodeling.

In the tiny but pretty bathroom, Jolie brushed her teeth and her hair, and then washed her face. She slipped out of her clothes and fell into the bed in her underwear, not bothering to fish her pajamas out of her bag. Tomorrow she would see the mountains. Her last thought before falling asleep was how much she already missed her baby girl.

Chapter Twenty-One

THE NEXT DAY dawned bright and clear as Jolie rose early from a long night of tossing and turning. She heard every noise—each car that drove past, every car door that opened and shut, every motel door that opened and shut, muffled conversations on the sidewalk or in the next room—she never reached the deep sleep that would have brought rest.

She fixed a pot of coffee to brew as she took a shower. The hot water invigorated her a bit, and as she sipped her coffee, anticipation filled her with excitement. She would get to see the mountains today; perhaps the tallest ones would still have snow on their peaks. The sad thing was, she had no one to share it with.

She pulled on some jeans and a long-sleeved tee and then ran a brush through her curly hair. The further north she drove, the better it did, even though it needed a shampoo. She didn't bother with makeup either, but after finishing her coffee she did brush her teeth before gathering her bag and purse and heading to her car.

The smell of homecooked bacon and eggs got her stomach's attention as she loaded her suitcase into the car. Her empty tummy rumbled, reminding her that she needed to get some breakfast before hitting the road. Bacon, eggs, and biscuits were her first choice, but a convenience store would be quicker and she needed to fill up the car, so she decided to go for a honeybun instead. There would be time for a hearty breakfast later, once she got to her destination.

JAY WOKE UP early. Nine a.m. was early for him after getting home around 12:15 and staying up a couple of hours before turning in. These days he just couldn't sleep. In addition to the absence of his wife next to him in bed, he and everyone he worked with were bundles of raw nerves, wondering when and where the killer would strike next. Lopez and the other curators had instructed employees to work in pairs and never leave anyone alone for any reason. Jay had the added burden of trying to cover the entire zoo at night with only two men who had to stick together instead of splitting up to cover two areas at once.

He still needed to hire someone to replace Kaycie. The Cade Bishop he had tried to contact had never answered his calls, so he had only been able to interview one person and that one was a young woman in her last year of college who was only able to work certain days of the week and had no experience with animals other than her pet parakeet. Her replies to his questions also indicated a lack of maturity and preparation for the interview. She even called him by his first name. He had to keep looking, but it was difficult to find time to make the calls and schedule the interviews without leaving Lucas alone.

Jay got up and after a quick visit to the bathroom headed toward the kitchen, hoping there was coffee left. He was not doing a very good job of keeping the kitchen stocked or the laundry done, and the house was beginning to show signs of neglect. He desperately needed a day off, and not just for housecleaning and shopping. His nerves were beginning to show their ragged edges as well. Lucas had still not found another place to live, and his presence in the house was wearing on Jay. As much as he didn't want to, Jay was going to have to say something to him about finding another place, and since they were the only two workers on their shift, the strain would be felt at work as well.

It doesn't matter, Jay told himself. If he continued to suppress his feelings, an unpleasant confrontation was inevitable and would mess up their work relationship anyway.

The door to the guest room was closed, so he figured Lucas was still sleeping. Jay continued to the kitchen to fix coffee. There was barely enough left in the canister for one pot. He would have to go to the store today. Opening the refrigerator, he reached for the milk carton, only to find it empty. He crumpled it in one hand and tossed it into the overflowing garbage can. The milk carton bounced off the heaping pile of trash and landed on the floor.

Great. No cereal this morning. He could have sworn there was half a gallon left yesterday. If the guy was going to drink all the milk, the least he could do was replace it or leave a note. He was starting to sound like a woman. Suddenly he understood what he called his wife's nagging. She was right. All those little things don't get done by themselves. He was gaining new respect for his wife and everything she did around the house.

He would make that trip to the store, but Lucas was going to pitch in if he was to continue to stay there. They would have that discussion before work today.

LUCAS, ON THE other hand, was so wrapped up in his own torment that he could not see beyond the day he was in. Along with the grief of losing Deana, he grappled with guilt for not being there when she needed him. Add to that the grief of losing Kaycie. He was barely able to get back and forth to work, and it mattered little to him whether he stayed at Jay's or slept in his truck.

He stayed up into the wee hours of the morning, usually tossing back at least a pint of whiskey before dragging himself to bed and then sleeping until one or two in the afternoon. On some level he knew he was a mess and that he should be pitching in, but he was unable to do anything about it. He had washed his work clothes only once since he began his stay at Jay's. He just kept wearing them over and over. The only clarity he experienced was during his work routine. He continued to be efficient and dependable as far as work was concerned—how he didn't know.

If Jay hadn't needed him so badly, he probably would have quit and left town. He couldn't do that to Jay, though, not when they were so shorthanded. If nothing else, Lucas was a loyal employee, and it would have been against his nature to leave Jay in a bind. He didn't realize that Jay was having second thoughts about him being there as he slept the morning away.

IT FELL TO TIM White to clean out Kaycie Harlan's apartment and go to the zoo to ask for the personal contents of her locker. Neither her parents nor her sister or brother could bring themselves to do it, or at least that is what they told him.

He was still angry about the way he had learned of her death. Since he was only the boyfriend and not the husband, he had not been the next of kin contacted, and because her children were minors, the authorities had called Kaycie's parents first. He had learned of her death by watching the evening news the night after she had failed to answer his calls and text messages. She was notorious for leaving her cell phone in her bag and forgetting to check her messages, so he hadn't pursued it.

The news had hit him like a sledgehammer. Just that morning before leaving for work, he had pressed his last kiss against her forehead as she slept.

Jay had graciously opened Kaycie's locker and left Tim alone as he proceeded with the difficult task of going through her belongings.

There were the usual things: a couple of those romance novels she loved to read, a hooded fleece jacket, a zippered makeup bag, a trucker hat with the logo of her parents' company, and one lone hoop earring. What he hadn't been prepared for was the collage of photos that she had taped inside the locker door. The two of them at a Texas Rangers game, the two of them at his company Christmas party, one photo of him with her and Jolie, and several others.

He removed each one, carefully removing the tape from the back, and then inserted them into the paperback novels to keep them from getting bent in the bag he was carrying. Anything that looked like zoo equipment he left in the locker—gloves, flashlights, water hose nozzles. If they had belonged to her, Jay could give them to someone else. He closed the locker quietly when he had finished, and then removed the remaining photos from the front of the door. Her smiling face alongside his brought tears to his eyes.

It was at that moment when Jay came out of his office to see if Tim needed anything else. Tim wiped his eyes with the back of his hand.

"Thank you for allowing me to do this," Tim said, his voice hoarse with emotion.

"No problem at all," Jay replied. "Let us know if we can do anything else."

Cleaning out her apartment was something else entirely. Tim took off work on a Friday and spent the whole weekend going through her things, emptying her closets and drawers and packing all of her personal possessions until nothing remained except furniture, appliances, and kitchen items. It was the hardest thing he had ever had to do.

Especially difficult was the discovery of the dress she had worn on their first date. For her to wear a dress was totally out of character, yet she had chosen this dress to impress him. As he pulled the red silk dress out of her closet, he sank to the floor, crushing the dress to his face. He could still smell the perfume that lingered on it. She must have never had it cleaned. Hot tears darkened the crimson fabric.

Kaycie had been so beautiful that night. He would never forget the way she looked as she opened the door to greet him. It was one of those rare occasions when she went all out with hair and makeup instead of her usual ponytail and jeans. She would have fit in well with her parents' lifestyle of charity events and board meetings if she would have wished to do so. Her natural elegance betrayed her upbringing.

But as elegant as she had appeared that night, she couldn't hide her playful, adventurous spirit. They had dinner at a trendy restaurant and then played miniature golf before going out to the city park where she handed him her heels and waded in the water of the lake before collapsing on the grassy shore to watch the sunset with him. The dress still bore signs of the evening where several of the pointed handkerchief ends of its hem had dipped into lake water and mud. Faint grass stains had soiled the back of the dress where she had plopped onto the grass.

So full of life, she had brought joy and excitement into his lonely one. Now that her short bright light had gone out, he wondered what he would do without her. He would keep this dress as a reminder of what they had shared, and what he had lost.

THE NEW MEXICO highway stretched seemingly forever before Jolie as she drove northwest. The scrubby, sagebrush-spotted land was beginning to rise and fall with small Rocky Mountain foothills as wild pronghorn antelope appeared, grazing among free-ranging cattle. Jolie took advantage of small towns spread miles apart, offering relief to travelers and giving her an opportunity to stretch her legs, use the restroom, and get a snack. These quick stops also helped her to stay alert.

"How far is Raton Pass from here?" she asked the clerk of one convenience store as she paid for sparkling water and peanut butter crackers.

"Oh, probably a couple of hours," the lady replied kindly. "Drive careful," she called as Jolie thanked her and left.

Jolie could see the faint purple shadow of a mountain range on the horizon. A thrill of excitement revved her heartbeat. She was almost there! But then the realization that she had absolutely no one to share it with hit her. She willed the sadness away, choosing to enjoy the opportunity she had been given.

Raton Pass was a winding wonderland of towering mountainsides and cliffs. Signs warning of falling rock dotted the highway, with rocks and boulders at the roadside lending proof. As much as Jolie wanted to view the scenery, she paid careful attention to the road as drivers more accustomed to mountain driving zoomed around her. Occasionally she would glimpse part of a home hidden in the trees, which made her wonder what living so deep in the mountains would be like. Private drives to these homes cut into the sides of mountains made her imagine that winters would be quite a challenge for those people.

She soon arrived in the mountain town of Trinidad where a quaint visitor's center beckoned her to stop. As she read about Trinidad in the visitor's center, she found out about a little bed and breakfast outside of town that seemed to be a perfect place to settle in for some regrouping. She had the attendant call and make her a reservation.

The dirt and gravel road she was told to take wound through the mountains, ascending high over the town. When Jolie reached the charming little inn and got out of her car, she noticed immediately the thinner air and the effort it took to lift her bag out of her car and roll it into the building. It would take a few days to adjust to the increase in altitude. Her nose almost hurt as she inhaled the crisp, clear air.

A white-haired heavy-set woman in her 70's greeted Jolie from behind a counter set at the entrance to a cozy living area on the left. A large dining room sat to the right of the foyer. Jolie approached the counter.

"Good afternoon, dear. You must be Jolie Sowell." She peered over glasses perched on her nose and attached to a beaded necklace.

"Yes, ma'am. I'm finally here."

"All the way from Texas. You must be exhausted. Welcome. I'm Winnie Hill, and I'm so pleased you have chosen The Winnie." She smiled and extended her hand.

"Pleased to meet you, Ms. Hill." Jolie shook the woman's hand lightly.

"Please call me Winnie. Everyone does. I will need you to sign this form, and then I will show you to your room."

Jolie obliged as Winnie came around the counter with a key. "Just follow me, dear."

She led Jolie up a flight of stairs which had Jolie breathless by the time she reached the top. Without missing a beat or turning around, Winnie remarked, "You'll get used to the altitude in a couple of days. Your body has to make more red blood cells to supply enough oxygen in this thinner air."

"Here we are," she announced after they had walked down a long hallway past several doors. This place was larger than it appeared from the drive. "There is only one other room occupied at the moment, a delightful retired couple from the Midwest. Please feel free to join us for dinner at 8:00 in the downstairs dining room. You'll find tonight's menu on the information card on your nightstand. Please dial "0" if you need anything."

Jolie had followed her into a large bedchamber complete with a four-poster Victorian-style bed and a formal seating area, along with a small table and chairs next to floor-to-ceiling windows overlooking a mountain lake. This would be perfect.

"Do you have any questions before I leave you to settle in?"

Jolie scanned the room again and managed a tired smile. "No, ma'am. This looks wonderful. Thank you."

Winnie smiled and shut the door, leaving Jolie alone. Jolie walked over to the large window where the curtains had been drawn to let in the light and impressive view. To Jolie's delight, one side of the window was a French door which led out onto a small terrace overlooking a beautifully landscaped backyard which extended downhill to the lake. A flock of Canadian geese waddled at the shore, looking for someone to give them a piece of bread. Scattered on the shore of the clear blue water which lapped gently at the rocks surrounding the lake were rustic log benches inviting visitors to sit down and relax. The air was cooler and drier than the air in Texas, and there was a slight northerly breeze which would probably cool things down quite a bit at night.

Returning inside, Jolie lifted her suitcase to the bed and began to unpack her things. She set her toiletries in the tiny but tastefully decorated bathroom and then placed her clothes in the antique dresser which sat opposite the bed. She reached into her purse for her cell phone and climbed into the high bed, sinking into the softness of a down comforter and piles of pillows. She could just possibly stay here forever.

She wondered if Cade had tried to call her. She had been so tired last night after the encounter with Jake the redneck in Amarillo that she had just gone straight to bed. Cade was probably wondering why she hadn't checked in yet. Dinner was in half an hour, but she wasn't really that hungry. She decided to call Cade instead.

His voice always made her heart beat faster. "Hello?"

"Hi, Cade, it's Jolie."

"Hey, Darlin,' where are you tonight?"

"I found a nice place in Trinidad, Colorado. I thought I would call and check in." She paused. "I miss you."

"I miss you, too, Sweetheart. How was your trip?"

"It was long. What are you doing? Are you busy?"

"Just sitting here in my den waiting for you to call," he said, endearing himself even more. "Maddie is helping Mrs. Johnson with the dishes and then we are going to play Chutes and Ladders. Just another typical night in the Bishop household."

"I wish I could be there," Jolie said with a wistful note in her voice. She imagined her and Ellie sitting at the table playing Chutes and Ladders with Cade and Maddie in his cozy home while Mrs. Johnson supplied them with steaming cups of hot chocolate.

"I wish you could too." His voice lowered almost to a whisper.

Jolie ached for the feel of his arms around her.

"How long will you be away?"

Jolie could hear Maddie in the background. "Daddy!"

"I'm not sure," Jolie replied. "It all depends on. . ." She stopped herself, suddenly feeling uneasy talking about her job for some reason. "I will let you know," she said instead.

"Maddie is getting impatient. I promised to play the game with her," Cade said. "It was really good to hear from you."

"It was good to hear your voice as well." More than he knew.

"May I call you while you're away?"

"Yes, but sometimes I don't have reception in the mountains. I will call you back, though."

"All right, love. Good night, and stay safe."

"Good night, Cade," Jolie laid her phone down on the nightstand. The feeling of uneasiness she had experienced earlier had not gone away. It must be that she was alone in a strange place far away from home for the first time in her life.

Jolie quickly changed into her pajamas and slid between the luxurious sheets of the antique mahogany bed. She pulled the covers up to her chin and hugged a pillow to her breast. A tear fell from her eye, surprising her. She missed Cade, and she missed Ellie. She also missed Kaycie terribly. It was Kaycie she wanted to talk to this very minute. That one little tear was soon followed by many more. She ended up crying herself to sleep.

Chapter Twenty-Two

WHEN JOLIE OPENED her eyes the next morning, for a moment she was disoriented. Then she remembered where she was. The gauzy white fabric draped over the canopy of the four-poster bed made her feel like a princess. Sunlight flooded the room from the windows. Off in the distance, a mist hung suspended among the trees and midway up the mountains. She threw off the warm covers and swung her feet to the thick antique oriental rug before tiptoeing over to the window. The hardwood floor under the rug was cold but she didn't mind. She opened the French door leading onto the terrace and stepped outside.

The air was crisp and cool, probably in the upper 40's, but the bright sunlight warmed her skin as she leaned against the rail with her arms crossed. In the morning quiet she could hear the unmistakable sound of water tumbling over rocks somewhere below. Birds called to each other in greeting. She would definitely go exploring down there after breakfast.

Reluctantly she returned to her room to get ready for breakfast. She could already smell it cooking downstairs. Her stomach rumbled, complaining about her skipping dinner the night before. She showered quickly and pulled out a clean shirt to wear with the same jeans she had been wearing for three days. It took only about a half hour to apply minimal makeup, pull her unruly hair back into a ponytail, and dress in a simple long-sleeve tee, jeans, and the only pair of shoes she had brought, which was a pair of comfortable mules with a one-inch heel. They wouldn't be the best choice for hiking through the woods, but they were all she had.

Gathering her nerve, she descended the stairs, half hoping that the other couple would be there so she wouldn't be alone with Winnie, and half hoping they wouldn't so she could avoid awkward small talk. Her fears abated when she walked into the dining room where an older couple sat reading a newspaper and sipping from delicate tea cups. As soon as she entered, the man, who reminded her very much of her father, stood up to greet her.

"Good morning, young lady. You must be Jolie." He extended his hand. "I'm Darren Roberts and this is my wife Sandra."

"Hello," Jolie said, shaking his hand and then his wife's. "I'm Jolie Sowell. Pleased to meet you."

"Please join us." Darren pulled a chair out from under the lace-covered table for her. She sat down and allowed him to push her up to the table.

"Winnie tells us that you are from Texas." Sandra remarked kindly. Winnie must have filled them in on everything she knew about her, Jolie mused. She was glad she hadn't told her much.

"Yes, East Texas," Jolie replied. "And you?"

"Northern Arkansas." Sandra patted her husband's hand. "Born and raised."

"Home of the Razorbacks," Darren added, smiling at his wife.

"He's a huge fan of the Razorbacks," Sandra explained. "Our son played for them, and now he's one of their coaches."

"How about you? Are you a football fan?" Darren asked Jolie.

"Not really. But my dad loves the Dallas Cowboys, so I watch them sometimes, especially if they are winning."

"No favorite college teams?" Darren prodded.

Jolie shook her head. "But that's cool that your son is coaching his favorite team. Are y'all on vacation?" she asked, changing the subject. She reached for the coffee carafe and poured herself a cup. Then she added heavy cream from a tiny pitcher and stirred with the silver spoon next to her china plate.

"Actually our life is a vacation," Sandra said, winking at her husband. "We sold our home a year ago and have been living the RV life ever since. We just park the Airstream wherever or whenever it strikes our fancy."

"We've been here for a week," Darren added.

"That sounds like an interesting life." Josie wondered what it might be like to not have a permanent home to return to.

"Can't beat it if you like to see new places and meet new people."

"When he retired, we sold everything we had and bought our Airstream, something we had dreamed of for years and years," Sandra added. "We've never looked back. God has been really good to us."

They continued to chat about their mobile lifestyle, telling about the various places and people they had met in their travels, which was fine with Jolie because it kept her from having to talk about herself. Her mind wandered to other things, such as how much she was missing Ellie and Cade, and even her parents. She would call and check on Ellie this morning after breakfast.

Winnie brought in a steaming bowl of scrambled eggs and a plate of crispy bacon and set them on the table, sending Jolie's saliva glands into overtime. She was starving.

"I'll be right back," Winnie promised as she rushed out the door again.

"Looks wonderful," Jolie remarked. "I didn't realize how hungry I was."

"We have enjoyed her breakfast every day for a week, and haven't had a bad one yet," Darren informed her. Sandra nodded in agreement.

"So you are staying in the house instead of your Airstream?"

"Every once in a while, we like to stay in a regular building and stretch our legs a bit." Darren chuckled.

"It does get cramped in the trailer at times. It's nice to get a break and enjoy a regular bedroom and bathroom." Sandra winked at her husband.

Winnie returned in a flash, carrying a tray of homemade biscuits and a carton of milk, which she set on the table. Juices and coffee were already on the table, along with an assortment of jams and jellies, some real butter, creamer, and salt and pepper.

"Are you guys hungry?" Winnie plopped her ample self at the head of the table.

"Yes!" All three guests chimed in unison and then laughed.

Jolie hesitated, deciding she would wait until someone else began before she helped herself. To her delight and surprise, Winnie reached out with her hands, prompting Darren to reach out to grasp hers and his wife's. Jolie, in turn, grasped Sandra's and Winnie's and they all bowed their heads for the prayer that Winnie offered, asking God's blessing on the meal. Jolie felt at home.

AFTER A SATISFYING breakfast, Jolie went back upstairs to call her mother. Even with the time zone difference of an hour, her parents should be up by now. She settled on the bed, her stomach feeling uncomfortably full. If she ate like that every day, she would soon be buying bigger clothes.

"Hey, Daddy!" she said as her father answered the phone.

"Well, hey, Sugar, we were hoping you would call."

"Why? Is something wrong with Ellie?" Jolie's heart jumped to her throat.

"No, no, you know we would have called you if Ellie needed you. We were just wondering how you were doing, where you decided to stay. . .that kind of thing."

She could hear the morning news show in the background. "So how is Ellie? Is she wearing you guys out?"

"Your mother was pretty tired last night when she went to bed, but we knew she would be. We're having lots of fun with Ellie. Having her here reminds us of when you were little." She could count on her dad to be honest.

"Should I come back early?" She knew that her father enjoyed having his granddaughter there, but he wasn't the one chasing Ellie down, dressing her, feeding her, bathing her, and putting her down for her nap and bedtime. Caring for a toddler was demanding.

"No, we don't want you to come back early. You need a break, and you need to stay away until they catch that killer. We will manage here with Ellie." His tone grew stern.

"May I speak to Mom, please?" She would be able to tell by the sound of her mother's voice whether it was time to come home or not.

"Sure, just a minute." Jolie heard him set the phone down and then she heard his footsteps and the sound of his voice calling for her. "Mama, phone! It's Jolie!"

Then there were muffled footsteps and voices, but Jolie could make out Ellie's voice asking to speak to Mommy. More muffled sounds and her daughter's voice came through loud and clear.

"Mommy?"

"Hi, Sweetheart!" Longing filled Jolie's heart. She had never been away from her little girl this long.

"What have you been doing? Are you having fun with Grammy?"

"Yes." Ellie became shy. Jolie could barely hear her.

"Mommy misses you," she told her.

"Miss you, too."

"Be good for Grammy and Grampa, okay? I'll be home soon. I love you very much."

"Love you very much," Ellie repeated, tugging at Jolie's heartstrings.

There was a pause, and then Jolie heard her mother's voice. Ellie had handed the phone to her grandmother.

"Jolie, is everything okay? Where are you?"

"Everything is fine, Mom. I just wanted to call and check on you all. I'm staying at a bed and breakfast in Trinidad, Colorado. How are you doing with Ellie?"

"We are doing just fine, aren't we, Ellie?" Jolie pictured Ellie's curls bobbing in agreement. "She has been really good."

"You're not getting too tired, are you?"

"I'm tired at the end of the day, of course, but I'm fine this morning. She takes a lot of energy, I'll have to admit. But you don't worry about a thing. We will be all right. You just rest and enjoy your stay, okay, honey?"

Jolie believed what her mother was telling her. She sounded upbeat, causing Jolie to feel much better about the situation.

"Okay, Mom, but will you tell me when you have had enough and need me home?"

"Of course, honey."

"All right, I am going to go now. Please give Daddy and Ellie a hug for me. I love you," Jolie said before hanging up. Satisfied that everything at home was going okay, she decided to explore the outdoor grounds of the house where she was staying.

LUCAS STIRRED AND woke up. According to the digital clock on the nightstand, it was still early, only 10:00 a.m. He wondered if Jay was still asleep. He got out of bed without bothering to dress and walked down the hall in his boxers. Jay's bedroom door was still closed. After a quick visit to the bathroom, he went through the den into the kitchen to fix some coffee.

There wasn't enough coffee in the container to fix a whole pot, so he emptied what was there into the basket after lining it with a piece of a paper towel because there were no filters. Then he filled the carafe with his best estimate of the amount of water that was needed. After switching the coffee pot on, he opened the cabinet doors to find something to eat. He picked up each cereal box, only to find that each one was empty or almost empty. Perhaps he could have eggs and toast instead.

What few slices of bread were left turned out to be science experiment material, so he tossed the package into the overflowing garbage can. It wobbled on the top of the trash and then fell to the floor. He sighed and grunted as he picked it up placed it on top again, smashing the contents down into the can. Somebody needed to take out the trash soon.

He wondered if there were any eggs to scramble, but soon discovered that the egg carton in the refrigerator had only one egg in it. The milk carton was empty, and there was no juice, no canned biscuits, nothing. He slammed the refrigerator door shut, turned around to get his coffee, and almost lost control of his bodily functions. Jay was standing right behind him, scowling.

"Nothing to eat?" he asked, glaring at Lucas.

"Not much," Lucas replied after recovering from the shock of Jay appearing in front of him. What was his problem?

"There was enough coffee to make a pot?" Jay stood in the middle of the kitchen in his pajama pants, no shirt or shoes. Lucas noted how thin he had gotten. He still had that cast on his leg, too.

"Not really. I just used what was left and guessed how much water it needed. I don't know what it will taste like."

Jay glanced at the trash can and the litter around it and growled, "Ever thought about taking out the trash?"

"Me?" Lucas pointed to himself.

JAY STARED AT him, standing there in his boxers, barefoot, needing a haircut and shave. He was in sad shape, and he had lost weight since Deana died. His lack of care for himself was obvious. But Jay's impatience with him overrode any sympathy he might have felt. The guy needed to get a grip.

"Nah, the other guy who is staying here." Jay's voice dripped with sarcasm. "Yes, you. The container is in the garage and needs to be taken to the curb on Thursdays before six a.m. Trash bags are under the sink. As long as you are staying here, that will be your job."

"Okay, boss." Lucas's eyebrows rose as he gazed at the floor.

The coffee pot finished its cycle, and from first glance the four cups it made looked very weak, fueling Jay's temper even more.

"Did you ever think about going to the grocery store?" Jay asked as Lucas poured coffee into the last clean cup. "Or washing dishes?"

Lucas stared at him, bristling. "Hey, dude, if you have something to say, say it. I'm guessing you're ready for me to leave?"

Jay considered the question for a moment and then took a deep breath. "Lucas, I really don't mind you staying here while Molly and the girls are away, but there are a few things I need you to do."

"Spell it out, Boss. I didn't know anything was bothering you."

"Okay." Jay pulled a chair from the kitchen table and motioned for Lucas to sit down, and then he sat down at the table himself. "This is what I need you to do."

Lucas seated himself and took a sip of coffee. He made a face; obviously it did not meet his standards.

"I need you to take out the trash and pull the bin to the curb on Wednesday nights when you get in. I need you to buy your share of groceries. I need you to pick up after yourself and do your own laundry. And I need you to shower every day and keep your hair cut and your face shaven." He stared directly into Lucas's eyes. "I also need you to keep your bedroom and bathroom clean."

Lucas seemed to consider Jay's demands for a minute or two before responding. Jay waited, ready for a fist fight if necessary, or at the very least have to kick Lucas out. But Lucas was repentant.

"I apologize for not doing my share, Boss. All you had to do was say so. I will do all those things you mentioned and more. As soon as I get dressed, I will go to the grocery store."

"It's all right, Lucas. I know that you have been dealing with your own problems. I should have said something sooner. So before I let it eat at me anymore, I am telling you now. I would really appreciate your help around here."

"You got it."

"One other thing. Could you please put on some pants before you come out of your bedroom?"

Lucas's face reddened. "Sure thing. Sorry again, Boss."

Jay stood up and slapped him lightly on the shoulder. "You're a good guy. Thanks for your cooperation. Now I think I will go back to bed for a while."

Lucas nodded.

AFTER JAY LEFT the room, Lucas got up, poured the weak coffee down the drain, and placed all the dirty dishes in the dishwasher. He found some detergent in an upper cabinet after looking under the sink, so he poured some into the dispenser and started the dishwasher. Then he took a dishrag, added some water and soap, and wiped down every flat surface in the kitchen. When he left, the kitchen was as clean as he knew how to get it, except for the floor. He would clean it when he returned from the grocery store. He would show Jay that he was not a moocher. In the fog of his grief, he hadn't realized that he wasn't pulling his weight. He would remedy that at once. The last thing he wanted was for his boss to be unhappy with him.

JOLIE HAD WALKED the perimeter of Winnie's property. She was sitting on a log bench watching the geese when her cell phone rang. It was Cade.

"Hey, Doll, what are you doing?" His voice stirred something deep inside her. She longed for his arms around her.

"Cade! It's good to hear your voice. I'm just enjoying nature. Are you on your lunch break?" It was only 10:30 Mountain Time.

"About to be. I wanted to call you before I went to lunch."

"I'm glad you did," she admitted. "I'm sitting on a mountain lake shore, watching geese waddle around. It is actually quite cool. I'm wearing a sweater. How is work going?" It seemed like a married couple's conversation.

"I'd rather be there with you. Have you heard from the zoo at all?"

That was an odd question. Maybe Cade had talked to Tim or Jay.

"No, I haven't, but I am kind of worried about Jay and Lucas."

"Why is that?"

Jolie could hear people talking in the background. He must still be at his desk in the bank lobby area, which wasn't very private.

"Well, Kaycie was killed, and I'm worried that they might be next," she explained, the familiar lump forming in her throat. She decided to change the subject and talk about Ellie and Maddie instead. "Did Maddie enjoy game night?"

"She got sleepy in the middle of our first game, so Mrs. Johnson had to put her to bed. I wish Ellie could have been there to play with her. She would probably have stayed up longer. Is Ellie staying with your parents?"

Jolie was suddenly overcome by a feeling of uneasiness. She didn't feel comfortable talking about Ellie. She certainly didn't want him to take Ellie from her parents without her being there to go with them, even if it was for a playdate with Maddie.

"Yes, she is staying with my parents, but I left strict instructions that she was to have no playdates until I get back. Sorry, I can be kind of a mama bear sometimes." Why do I feel the need to apologize?

"I wouldn't dream of taking Ellie without you coming along," Cade assured her. "I was just curious."

"Oh. Sorry, I guess I am being overprotective, but I don't want to give my parents anything else to worry about."

"Of course not," Cade agreed. "I have to get some lunch. I will call you later if that's okay."

"Please do, Cade." Jolie paused. "I miss you." It was true. She ached to the core of her being for the touch of his hands, the feel of his arms around her, his kiss.

"I miss you, too, and--I love you," Cade declared, surprising her. He hadn't said that yet. Why would he say those words over the phone? She hesitated.

"I love you, too," Jolie replied, hanging up after hearing the click of his phone. Was she sure? If she really did love him, why did she suddenly feel so unsettled?

She dismissed her feelings as a ridiculous lack of confidence in herself as she rose and began the walk back up to the house. When would she be able to trust a man again? Her room was probably clean by now, and she would certainly enjoy some time just simply watching television. Besides, clouds were gathering and there was the sound of distant thunder. Curling up in her room during a mountain thunderstorm sounded like heaven. She walked a little faster.

AFTER A SHOWER and shave, Lucas headed to the grocery store and spent almost a hundred dollars replenishing supplies for the Latimer household. He not only bought things to replace what he had taken, he bought what he thought they might need in the next few days. When he returned to the house, he brought everything in and put it away before emptying the trash and sweeping and mopping the kitchen floor.

By then it was time to get dressed for work. Jay had already left, probably to get his paperwork done before their shift began so he could join Lucas in the animal areas. Lucas was also aware that Jay was trying to set up interviews for Kaycie's position. They would all be glad when Jolie came back and another person was hired and trained. Having only two people on the second shift was difficult, and it also placed a burden on the other shifts because they had to take up the slack.

Jay greeted him as if nothing had happened at home. Lucas could hardly wait for him to get home and discover the kitchen fully stocked and clean. Jay was right; it was the least he could do for free room and board. He would have to start looking for another place to live, and soon. When Jay's family returned, he would be back to sleeping in his truck if he didn't have something else lined up.

They were running the last of the deer into the hoof stock barn when Lucas heard an unusual sound in the corner of the room where the hay was kept. It almost sounded like a baby's cry. Jay was out in the yard shooing the deer in, and as the last one came through, Lucas shut and locked the gate and then went to investigate the sound he had heard.

As Lucas entered the room, he flipped on the lights and paused to listen. In a couple of minutes he heard it again. The cry was coming from behind the stack of hay bales on the right side of the barn. He walked over and pulled some hay bales away from the wall, revealing a fawn so tiny and helpless that it must have been born just an hour or two before. Strange that he hadn't been aware of any doe pregnancy. He wondered if Jay knew. Something was wrong, though. The fawn's head rested on the concrete floor, and it didn't raise as Lucas got closer.

Then he noticed a deep red puddle forming under its head. The sound—the cry—was becoming weaker and more faint. Was that blood? As he moved closer and bent to investigate, he felt the impact of something heavy smashing his skull. Everything went black as Lucas fell unconscious beside the dying fawn, missing the attacker raising a piece of rebar for the final blow.

JAY TROD BRISKLY to the hoof stock barn, relieved that it had only taken a few minutes to get all the animals run in. The whitetail deer were usually the most stubborn and the last to go inside. Maybe they enjoyed being out in the meadow more than the rest. Checking the locked gate, he walked inside where he expected to find Lucas putting more hay into the stalls for the night.

Lucas was nowhere to be seen. Had he already finished with the hay and gone on to the next area? He knew better than that. No one was supposed to be working alone now. Maybe he was getting more hay from the back. As he rounded the corner to check, he heard something or someone bolt from the room through another door. His heart pounded with a rush of adrenaline. If he'd had a gun he would have pulled it.

"Lucas?" He noticed the hay bales pulled away from the wall, and then he noticed a man's boots from behind the bales.

"Lucas!" He shoved the bales aside with the strength adrenaline gave him and knelt next to Lucas's body, seeking a pulse in his neck. Blood pumped from a gash in the back of his head.

Jay detected a pulse, though it was faint. He peeled off his shirt and wrapped it around Lucas's head in an effort to stop the bleeding. He didn't notice the dead fawn in the corner. As soon as he had the bleeding somewhat under control, he grabbed his radio to call for help, but then realized there was no one to call. Pulling his cell phone out of his pocket, he dialed 911 and waited for the operator to respond.

LUCAS'S ATTACKER ESCAPED into the thick woods behind the hoof stock yard. He didn't get to finish the job, but one day soon, he would.

One day very soon.

Chapter Twenty-Three

JAY MET THE ambulance, police, and fire truck at the gate in the mule and led the ambulance and police down to the barn where Lucas lay, still unconscious. At least Jay's shirt had stopped the bleeding. As he led the first responders into the barn, he absently hoped that his dirty shirt wouldn't do more harm than good. There was no telling what kind of bacteria he had picked up on that shirt while going about the zoo cleaning and moving through exhibit areas. At the very least maybe Lucas wouldn't bleed to death.

The EMTs hurried to Lucas's side, one taking his vitals and the other checking the head wound. "Did you know there is a dead animal here as well?" one of them asked him.

"No, no, I didn't." Jay looked over to where the EMT was pointing. He shook his head in disbelief. Not another one.

Two police officers scanned the area quickly. As one returned to the car to make a report, the other stood near, waiting to see if Lucas would be able to speak.

Lucas moaned and stirred. "Easy there, mister," one of EMTs said.

They helped Lucas sit up. He winced, emitting a groan as he moved. "What happened?" he managed, clutching his head.

"Seems you took a pretty good blow to the head," the EMT replied. "Did you see who did it?"

Lucas glanced up at him, wincing as he did so. "Somebody hit me?"

"Pretty hard. I'd say you are lucky to wake up," the other EMT remarked. "You'll probably need stitches."

"Aw, man," Lucas groaned.

"Better do as they say," Jay advised. "Zoo rules."

"If you're able I'd like to ask you a few questions." The police officer intervened as one EMT opened the back doors of the ambulance to get the gurney.

"Can it wait?" Jay asked. "You can see he's in quite a bit of pain."

"It won't take long. I'll need to ask you some questions as well."

Lucas seemed to try his best to answer all the questions the police officer asked about why he was there and what he had seen. When the officer was satisfied, he nodded and Lucas and the gurney were loaded into the ambulance.

The police officer proceeded to ask Jay questions about Lucas and his duties in the barn, where the fawn came from, and others that made Jay wonder what in the world they had to do with anything. But he cooperated as best he could and tried to remain patient. When the officer was finally finished, Jay excused himself and went to call Lopez. Jay was the only employee on zoo grounds for the rest of the night and Lopez would want to know what happened. Since zoo policy required at least two workers be present at all times, Lopez might want to come in himself and finish the shift.

He did. "I'll be right there," he told Jay. He didn't sound happy, either.

Jay only had to wait ten minutes before Lopez stormed into the lounge, flinging the door open.

"I want to hear the whole story," he demanded as Jay came out of his office. He stood aside as Lopez strode into the office and sat down. Jay sat down at his desk facing his boss.

"Let's hear it, Latimer." The muscles in Lopez's jaw flexed as his eyes bore into Jay's. Jay had the feeling that Lopez considered this incident his fault, but he refused to be intimated by Lopez's attitude as he launched into the story.

"Damnation!" Lopez stood up and walked over to the window where darkness obscured everything outside. "Nobody saw who it was?"

"Whoever it is sneaked up behind him and hit him with a blunt object so hard it knocked him unconscious. Lucas never knew what hit him. I was out in the yard getting the rest of the deer in and when I came in and didn't see him I called for him. He didn't answer so I started looking for him and that is when I found him unconscious and bleeding. You can't believe that all this was my fault."

"No one said it was your fault," Lopez retorted. "Were fingerprints taken?"

"I don't know. I'm sure they were, but no weapon was found. I suppose they could have taken fingerprints from the gates. I didn't see anyone do it, though."

"Do you realize that you could be a suspect in this?"

Was he kidding? Anger welled up inside Jay. He bit his tongue in an attempt to stop the words that were bubbling up, but they came out anyway against his better judgment. There were just some things he couldn't let alone.

"I just talked with the police!" he erupted, rising from his chair. "If I was a suspect, they would have arrested me and taken me to jail! You are just as good a suspect as I am, Mr. Curator!"

Lopez whirled around to face him, his eyes narrowed. "I suggest you carefully weigh your words before you speak them, Mr. Latimer. You may regret those."

"So you're firing me now?" Jay asked, trembling with anger. This is what Lopez thought all along, that he was the killer? There was absolutely nothing to support an accusation like that.

"Keep me posted on anything that you find out, or anything else that happens on your shift," Lopez ordered before making a swift exit.

Jay stood at his desk looking down at his calendar until Lopez had left the lounge. He had no idea if he was supposed to stay through his shift or go ahead and leave since there was no one else working. There was no way he was going to venture out into the zoo tonight alone and with no weapon. It took him a while to cool off after the visit with Lopez, but when he finally did, he decided to go through his file of applicants again to see if he had missed any good prospects for Kaycie's position. So far no one had been up to his standards, but he had to have some help, and he had to have it soon. But who in their right mind would take a position on the night shift with all these unsolved attacks?

AS JOLIE SAT on the terrace sipping her first cup of coffee in the chilly morning air, she went to the Taylor City News app on her phone to see if there was any breakthrough in the search for Kaycie's killer. What she saw caused her to drop the coffee mug onto the deck, its contents splashing the bottom of the robe and slippers provided by the bed and breakfast.

Lucas had been attacked and another animal killed. Lucas had been taken to the hospital, and Jay was alone on the night shift. Jolie felt she had no choice but to get back to Texas and back to the zoo where she was needed. Lucas was in the hospital and she didn't know how long he would have to stay, or if he would even be able to come back to work. A lump formed in her throat as she dressed.

WINNIE TRIED HER best to talk Jolie into staying longer, but Jolie was adamant. She had to leave now. As she loaded her bag into her parents' SUV, Darren and Sandra Roberts walked out of the house, stopping when they saw Jolie.

"Leaving without saying goodbye?" Sandra asked.

"And without breakfast?" Darren added.

Although she was in a hurry, Jolie couldn't be rude, so she closed the liftgate and turned to greet them. "Good morning! Yes, I need to head back. My boss needs me. I was hoping to see you before I left, though," Jolie said, telling a little white lie. She actually hadn't thought of the sweet older couple at all since hearing the news about Lucas.

"We are sorry to see you go, Jolie. We were hoping for some more conversation around the breakfast table. Can't you just stay a little longer and have breakfast?" Sandra glanced at her husband, who nodded in agreement.

"I really can't. I would love to, but I have to be back in East Texas tonight and I need to be on the road."

Sandra started to protest, but Darren put his arm around his wife and patted her shoulder. "Of course you do, and we wouldn't want to delay you. Have a safe trip home. We enjoyed your company." He extended his hand.

Jolie suddenly realized how similar these two were to her own parents. She ignored the extended hand and surprised Darren by giving him a hug instead. Then she hugged Sandra. "Thank you for the wonderful company. You take care, too, promise me?"

They both nodded and watched Jolie as she climbed into her vehicle and started the engine. As she took off down the gravel road, she could see them waving in the rearview mirror. Such sweet people. She wished them all the best in their retired traveling life.

JAY HEADED TO the hospital to check on Lucas who was being released at the very moment Jay entered the emergency room. Lucas looked great except for the bandage around his head and the dried blood on his zoo shirt. He was signing papers and didn't see Jay walk up.

"Ready to go?" Jay walked up to his side at the counter.

"Hey, Boss." Lucas grinned. "Here to pick me up?"

Jay rolled his eyes. "No, I heard there was a beautiful blonde waiting for me here, but I guess I'll have to settle for you."

"She's not here, remember? You sent her off to Oklahoma," Lucas deadpanned.

Jay raised his eyebrows in surprise. He was right. "Come on, buddy, let's go home."

An orderly brought up a wheelchair and told Lucas with a no-nonsense look to sit in it. "I have to wheel you out, Sir. It's policy."

Lucas had been given a release by the doctor to return to work, but only if he promised to take it easy for a few days: no heavy lifting, no running, no unnecessary exertion, and lots of pain reliever.

At home, Jay went over the doctor's orders with Lucas, both agreeing to abide by them so he could heal as fast as possible.

"Maybe we should get married," Jay remarked. "I'm beginning to feel like a wife."

Lucas laughed. "Without benefits, though."

Jay's look made him lose the grin.

JAY WAS CALLED to a mid-morning meeting at the zoo the next morning, and Lucas had to ride with him because his truck had been left there, so they both went early. Lucas relaxed in the lounge with a wildlife magazine as Jay attended the meeting in the conference room adjacent to Lopez's office. Oates, Lopez and two other curators, two police officers, and a detective were also in attendance.

Jay prepared himself to be arrested as a suspect. He greeted everyone and shook their hands before seating himself next to the curators at the conference table.

"Is this everyone?" Oates asked Lopez.

Lopez nodded.

Oates stood up, straightened his jacket, and looked everyone in the eye before speaking. "Gentlemen, as you know, there has been a rash of animal killings and murders here at Timber City Zoo, and I intend to get to the bottom of it before we lose anything or anybody else." He paused and cleared his throat. "I have invited the police chief and his partner, as well as a private detective, to help us come up with a solution. Officer

Mallory, I will turn the meeting over to you now." Oates seated himself and wiped his brow.

Mallory stood. "We have gathered evidence from each crime scene and believe we have enough to catch the perpetrator. We believe that one person is responsible for every death, animal and human. We have also discovered a hiding place and believe that the killer is using that as a sort of headquarters to plan his attacks. A journal containing pictures, cut-outs, and words and phrases has also been found. We believe this journal is where the killer has chronicled his conquests, so to speak, and what is alarming is that there are several more attacks to go, if that is the case."

Jay grew impatient. All that was common knowledge. What progress had they made? However, to avoid invoking the ire of his bosses, he forced himself to wait until the chief finished.

The police chief then described each crime scene in detail, both animal and human, as well as the attempted crimes. Jay shifted in his chair and tried to listen as Mallory rehashed everything that had happened over the last few months. Jay felt as if he were living a bad dream. Two friends were gone, one had almost been killed, his shift was crippled, his family was gone, and his leg would never be the same. He needed someone to take action, not sit around and talk, but then again, everyone needed to know the facts.

At least they hadn't accused him of the crimes. Mallory began to outline some of the things the police had been doing to find the perpetrator, but they had not actually sent anyone into the zoo to sit and wait for him, which to Jay seemed the logical thing to do. They could try to trace fingerprints and examine the nest in the warehouse, but they would catch no one until someone was willing to take the time to sit and wait for the killer to show up.

Oates and Lopez seemed satisfied with the police chief's presentation. Jay was not.

"May I ask a question?" he asked before Oates had a chance to dismiss the meeting.

"Why, certainly," Oates replied, surprised.

"Did anyone take DNA samples from any of the crime scenes to see if they matched each other or matched any on record?"

"Of course they did," Lopez said. "Right?"

Police Chief Mallory stared at Jay as if he was offended. "I cannot tell you what the investigators are doing; however, I can assure you and everyone here that everything possible is being ruled out using the latest technology at our disposal."

"I am completely confident that our police department is doing everything they can to solve these crimes, Mr. Latimer," Oates said, giving Jay a look that forbade him to say another word. "Thank you, Chief Mallory, and everyone else for attending this meeting. I trust that you will keep us apprised of any new developments in the case." Oates stood, signaling the end of meeting.

As everyone stood up to leave, Jay decided that he could probably do a better job if he took matters into his own hands, but he needed a plan. As he headed toward the door, he heard Oates's voice. "Mr. Latimer, meet me in my office in ten minutes, please."

Now he'd done it. Oates was going to let him have it for challenging the police chief and making Oates look bad. He hurried to the lounge to get more coffee and then went back up the hill to the zoo offices. Oates's office was empty; he could tell because the large picture window overlooking zoo grounds also allowed a full view of his desk and chair. He hadn't gotten back from the meeting yet, so Jay stood at the fence overlooking the giraffe yard and sipped his coffee.

Fall was in the air. The leaves on the trees were beginning to turn colors, which meant leaves would soon be falling and filling up every creek and moat in the zoo. Though day keepers worked on keeping all the waterways clean, it was still a job for the night shift because drains would stop up with decaying leaves, making it impossible to drain moats and ponds, meaning that someone had to get wet to clear the blockage so draining could occur.

Weekday visitor numbers would decrease as fall progressed, although weekend visitors would come by the droves because of the cooler weather. Still, the cooler weather took the edge off tempers and made for happier keepers and more contented animals. Jay loved the fall when he had to wear a jacket at night against the slight chill but could still wear short sleeves during the day.

He watched a young mother pushing one tot in a huge stroller while one a little older held on to the handle of the stroller. The tot in the stroller was bundled up in a hoodie and blanket while her big sister wore a long-sleeve tee shirt over leggings. Both children sported mops of curly blonde hair like their mother, whose blonde curls were tamed somewhat under a stylish cap. Homesickness washed over him as they reminded again how much he missed his wife and girls. He wanted them home so badly. The loneliness was starting to get to him.

Oates came out of the conference room onto the terrace and spotted Jay at the fence. After he motioned for Jay to come along, Jay followed him into his office where he pretended to listen to Oates's ranting and raving about zoo image and his responsibility to represent them and respect those who were investigating the crime and so on, ad nauseum. His mind began to formulate a plan for the night. By the time he left Oates's office with a perfunctory thank you for the constructive criticism and a promise to improve his behavior, he had a plan to catch the killer before he struck again.

JAY AND LUCAS started their shift early so they could get the work done before implementing Jay's plan. As soon as the zoo closed and the animals were hustled in for the night, food bowls picked up and washed, and a baby anteater tended to, Jay and Lucas headed to the warehouse to check the nest where the journal had been found to see if the killer had come back.

Jay carefully opened the door of the warehouse so that if someone was in there they wouldn't hear anything. He signaled Lucas to follow him as he followed the path he had found a few weeks ago winding through the boxes and junk to the back of the warehouse. As they neared the nest, there was the unmistakable sound of a voice.

Jay stopped and put a hand up toward Lucas to stop him as well. Then he crept forward until he could hear the voice clearly. Someone was talking on a phone by the way the conversation was going. The voice sounded strangely familiar as well. As quietly as he could, Jay inched forward to try and get a glimpse of the person without being seen. Lucas moved around some boxes in another direction until he had a clear view of the back of the person talking. Lucas motioned for Jay to come to where he was standing.

It was a good thing that the guy was talking on the phone. It made him less likely to hear any noise that Jay and Lucas might inadvertently make. Jay joined Lucas and peered through the boxes to see the person talking. He was lounging in a beanbag with his back to them. Jay did a double take.

It can't be. He moved to the right a bit to get a better view of the guy's face. He knew that voice, and he knew that face. It belonged to Cory Bennett, the young man he had fired years ago after finding him in the ladies restroom dallying with a young married keeper. This guy had been volatile, but he had never pegged him as a killer. And who was he talking to?

Lucas glanced at Jay as if asking, what now? Jay put up his index finger. They needed to keep still to see if they could tell who was on the other end of the line.

"You're on your way home so soon? Have you missed me?"

A girlfriend, Jay supposed, wondering who it could be. He needed to listen some more. Lucas glanced at him and then focused his attention on Cory.

"I've got big plans for us tomorrow, Sweetheart. Has Ellie ever been to a horse ranch?"

Ellie? Wasn't that Jolie's daughter's name? Weird.

"Come on, Jolie, you can sleep in and then we will go out for brunch and take the girls out to a horse ranch south of town. I know the rancher."

Lucas and Jay stared at each other, dumbfounded. Jolie? Did he really say Jolie? His heart racing and his mind filling with anger, Jay nodded to Lucas, prompting him to stay where he was while Jay moved more to the right.

"Got to go, honey, I'll call you later." Cory must have heard something. He scrambled out of the beanbag awkwardly, pocketed his phone, and whirled around. "What the--?" Jay had stepped out in front of him.

"So it's you," Jay said, moving toward him. "What were you doing talking to Jolie Sowell?"

"I don't know what you're talking about." Cory's eyes darted around seeking an escape route.

"Oh, I believe you do." Jay moved even closer. Cory suddenly jumped over the beanbag, attempting to run in the other direction, but Lucas stepped in his way, grabbing his arm. Cory wriggled out of Lucas's grasp and ran toward the front of the warehouse, throwing boxes and assorted junk behind him to slow the guys down. When they reached the door, he had disappeared into the zoo.

"Call the police," Jay ordered Lucas as he went to get some guns out of Lopez's office. "I'll be right back."

CADE'S SUDDEN END to their conversation confused and perplexed Jolie. What was it this time? She was exhausted from driving all those hours to get home, but she wanted to stop by the zoo and talk to Jay and Lucas before going home. After checking with the hospital and learning that he had been released, she wanted to see for herself that Lucas was all right; she felt guilty that she had not been there the night he was attacked, although she didn't know what she would have done. She may have even been attacked herself. She decided against calling her parents because they would try to talk her out of going to the zoo.

It was around 11:00 p.m. when she rolled into the employee parking lot. It would feel good to get out and walk around. Jay and Lucas's trucks sat parked side by side. She parked next to them and carefully checked her surroundings before she got out of the car and hurried into the lounge to pick up a radio so she could call them.

It was just like it had always been—tables and chairs, lumpy couch and chair, kitchen area, snack machines, and the door to Jay's office. But the walls had witnessed Kaycie's attack and murder, and it would take Jolie a long time to be comfortable again in that lounge, if that were even possible. The door to the ladies' restroom gave her the creeps. She shrugged off thoughts of what had gone on in there when Kaycie was murdered and quickly grabbed a radio from its charger on the countertop.

"Jolie to Jay or Lucas, come in."

"This is Jay."

"Lucas here."

"What is your location?" Jolie exited the lounge, ready to head in their direction.

"Jolie, are you here in the zoo?" Alarm filtered through Jay's voice.

"Yes, I just made it back."

"You have to leave right now. The killer is loose in the zoo."

"Where are you?" Jolie insisted. *What does he mean, loose in the zoo?*

"Just go," Lucas interjected. "You're in danger."

Hearing a noise behind her, she whirled around, expecting to see a deranged killer. She did, all right, but it was one of the leopards, snarling and in position to pounce. She screamed and dropped the radio.

AS SOON AS Jay had returned to where he had left Lucas outside the warehouse, he gave him a 12-gauge shotgun. He carried a 416 rifle himself. They were taking no chances. They could run into Cory or any animal he may have released into the zoo.

"I'll take the front, you take the back, and we'll meet in the middle. Make sure you have your radio turned up. If you see him, hold him, but don't hesitate to shoot to kill if necessary. Good luck, man," Jay said, turning to head off toward the entrance.

"Yeah, good luck," Lucas replied, turning toward the back entrance.

Jay hoped Jolie had obeyed his order to leave. They didn't need to worry about her right now. As he trudged toward the main entrance, Jay's eyes swept back and forth with the aid of his flashlight, his body tense and alert for any movement or sound.

The sound of breaking twigs and rustling leaves to his left alerted him to lift his weapon. As he turned, he aimed the rifle, but instead of Cory, an African hunting dog strolled out of the underbrush, snarling and ready to jump him. Just as it leapt, Jay pulled the trigger, dropping it out of the air and killing it instantly. His heart racing, his skin pouring sweat, he picked up his radio. "Code Nine, Lucas. Animals loose in the zoo. Code Nine."

He heard a shot ring out across the zoo grounds. Lucas already knew.

Chapter Twenty-Four

STIFLING ANOTHER SCREAM, Jolie stood as still as she could, hoping the leopard would decide she wasn't worth it. Hadn't it been fed today?

"Suni? Is that you?" Jolie peered into the darkness, trying to distinguish which of the two leopards this one was. It continued toward her slowly with a low growl that vibrated throughout her body. Surely it would know her voice.

"No?" She felt strangely giddy. This was it, she just knew it. "Mara?" she choked, trying the other name. It seemed nothing would stop the leopard from moving closer. Jolie swallowed, trying not to panic. Don't move, she told herself. God, if this is it, please make it quick, she prayed.

Just then a shot rang out, sending Jolie crumpling to her knees. For a split second, she wondered if she had been hit by a bullet, but when she looked up, the leopard was lying on its side, blood pouring out of a gaping gunshot wound. A scream escaped her, sounding as if it had come from someone else. Sobbing, she wondered if she was the next target or if someone had just saved her life.

A soothing voice broke through her racing thoughts. "Jolie, Jolie, it's okay. It's me, Cade."

She opened her eyes in astonishment. What is he doing here? As he helped her stand to her feet, she stared at him. "Where did you come from? Did you see that leopard? Did you kill it?"

"No, I didn't kill it, but I saw it about to attack you. I was just about to do something when somebody shot it. It's okay, honey, it won't hurt you now."

As he drew her close she realized that he was dressed in khaki coveralls, something she had never seen him wear before. She still didn't know why he was at the zoo. She hadn't told anyone that she was stopping by the zoo on the way home. How did he get in? Was she just tired from the long drive? Was she dreaming? Is that why this was making no sense? And how did a leopard get loose? Where were Jay and Lucas?

He stroked her hair and began to kiss her neck. "I've missed you so much, Sweetheart." *Really? Now? After a leopard almost attacked her?*

"I've missed you, too, Cade," Jolie managed, but then she grew cold with the realization that something was not right. The hair on the back of her neck stood up as she tried to pull away.

As her mind struggled to make sense of everything, Cade suddenly stiffened and whirled her around in his arms until her back was pressed hard against him. His free arm raised a pistol. What in the world? So he had shot the leopard! She struggled but his arm held her against him. "Don't make me hurt you," *he growled.*

"Bennett! Let her go!" came a voice from the darkness. Jay stepped out of the bushes into the light of a security lamp. To Jolie's horror, he had a gun pointed at them. Bennett? Who's Bennett?

"Back off, Latimer, or I'll shoot Jolie. Then I'll kill you as well, you self-righteous pig."

It was Cade's voice, but it wasn't the Cade that Jolie knew. Had he been deceiving her all this time? Her heart shattered into a million pieces as her knees grew weak. You can't fall apart now. Stay strong, she told herself as she felt the cold barrel of his pistol against her temple. She fought the tears that threatened as she anger consumed her. She had been prepared to spend her life with this man, and not only was this devastating to her, but Ellie would be crushed as well. How dare he?

"You won't shoot anyone, Cory Bennett. Your problem is with me, not Jolie. Let her go."

Jolie cringed as Jay leveled the rifle at them.

"I'm not concerned with this little tramp. She means nothing to me. I have no problem knocking her off to see you suffer."

"You liar!" Jolie screamed, twisting around and grabbing the arm holding the pistol. She kicked him between the legs as hard as she could, praying the gun wouldn't go off. He dropped it as he fell to the ground, writhing in pain while clutching himself.

Lucas lurched from the bushes beside her, grabbed the pistol and pulled her away just as the other leopard appeared and pounced upon Cade, sinking its teeth into his neck. Jolie screamed, hiding her face in Lucas's shoulder as Jay carefully aimed his rifle at the leopard and fired.

The leopard dropped as it died instantly, leaving Cade lying in a large pool of his own blood. Lucas turned on instinct, inadvertently allowing Jolie a glimpse of the carnage that had been her hope for her future, her hope for a stable family life for Ellie. She tore from his arms, wanting to see for herself that it was really Cade who had threatened to kill her.

Before Lucas could stop her, she was on her knees at Cade's side. As he twitched and gasped his last breath, she smoothed his hair back, avoiding the gaping mass of torn flesh and bone that had been his beautiful tanned neck. Sobbing, she knelt in his blood, refusing to acknowledge what had just transpired, unable to absorb the fact that his stranger was not the man she had believed he was, the man she had fallen in love with.

"WE HAVE TO seek shelter." Jay motioned for Lucas to get her out of there. "There may be more animals loose."

"Come on, Jolie, we have to go." Lucas gently pulled her to her feet, half carrying her away from Cade's body. Jay glanced around them as he led them quickly to the nearest safe area. He unlocked the door to Lopez's office and ushered Lucas and Jolie in quickly before bolting the door shut and posting himself by the window. He reached for his cell phone to call for help.

JOLIE HAD STOPPED crying, but Lucas stayed close in case she became wobbly. The look of hurt in her eyes was unbearable. If that guy had not died, Lucas would have finished him off himself.

Jolie pulled away from Lucas, extended her hands and arms and saw that she was covered, practically dripping, in Cade's blood. Lucas sensed the panic that threatened to overtake her. His low gravelly voice penetrated her horror.

The Keeper

"Jolie, Jolie, look at me, look at me." He placed his large hands on each side of her face and forced her to face him, his eyes peering into hers. She focused her gaze on his eyes and nodded.

"Everything is going to be okay, Jolie." His face grew fuzzy around the edges, and then all white as she lost consciousness and would have crumpled onto the floor if Lucas had not been there to catch her.

"Is she hurt?" Jay glanced up from his phone in alarm.

"No, I think she is just overwhelmed is all," Lucas cradled her head as he sank to the floor with her.

"I've got the rifle team on the way, as well as the police and ambulance." Jay headed to the small sink and counter on one side of Lopez's office. "I'll get a wet cloth."

"Good idea, thanks." As Lucas caught himself stroking Jolie's hair, he realized how striking she was, something he had never really considered before. The delicate facial features--the small nose that turned up slightly, long lashes on eyes framed with well-shaped arching eyebrows, and a full-lipped heart-shaped mouth. How had he missed this natural beauty of hers?

He knew how. He had been completely and utterly in love with his wife. Looking at another woman had never even crossed his mind. But the loneliness of the last few weeks had him noticing Jolie for the first time. He couldn't stop himself from glancing down the length of her petite frame with her curvy hips, small waist, and skinny jeans clinging to shapely legs. She was beautiful.

"Here we go." Jay startled him, coming back so quickly with a damp paper towel. She stirred as Lucas dabbed her forehead and cheeks with it.

HER EYES OPENED to behold the faces of her coworkers looming over her. Then she remembered. Tears welled up in her eyes and spilled over. She pushed herself up from Lucas's lap.

"Easy," he cautioned.

"You okay?" Jay asked. "You've had quite a shock."

"Is Cade dead?" Her voice broke.

"Cade?" Jay was puzzled. "That was Cory Bennett. He used to work here years ago, and I had to fire him. Apparently, he has been waiting all these years to get back at me."

"Cade Bishop. My boyfriend. He was the killer all along." She fought the bile that rose in her throat. She had loved him and believed he loved her. She had allowed him around her baby girl. Her hand flew to her mouth to stop the nausea.

"Whoever he is, he is the killer. Or was. Thank God all that is over now." Jay knelt beside Jolie and Lucas and took Jolie's hands in his. "I'm so sorry you got involved with him."

The sound of sirens alerted them as flashlight beams appeared in the window. "The rifle team is here." Jay opened the door and called to them to come inside.

As Jay discussed with the team what had happened and went over a plan to secure the zoo, Lucas stayed with Jolie until she felt stronger. Her sadness gave way to anger. Suddenly she couldn't wait to get cleaned up and out of the blood-soaked clothing she still wore. Lopez's office had been outfitted with a bathroom which included a shower as well, and he kept uniform samples in his closet as time neared for new uniforms. Maybe there were still some in there from the last uniform order.

"Lucas, could you look for a uniform sample that I could wear?"

"On it."

As she used the shower, Lucas gathered some sample shirts and pants that looked like her size and waited for her to finish. She allowed the hottest water she could stand to wash the filth down the drain, and then used one of the hotel soap samples she had found in a cabinet to scrub herself clean. After a few minutes she felt more like herself, if that was even possible. When she stepped out of the shower, she tried her best to avoid looking at the bloody clothing piled in a heap on the floor. She would leave it there in case it was needed for evidence. She dried off the best she could with the only towel she had found in the cabinet, a hand towel. At least it was clean.

As she opened the door just enough to stick her arm through, Lucas was there as promised and handed her several items of clothing. After trying on a couple of shirts and pairs of pants, she settled on some that were only slightly oversized. She buttoned the shirt, tied up the tails around her waist, and rolled up the sleeves. Then she fastened the pants, using her own belt to tighten them, and then rolled up the cuffs. She had no underwear or socks and shoes, so she smoothed her wet hair back and tiptoed out of the bathroom in bare feet.

Lucas stared as she entered the office. Jay had gone with the rifle team, so they were alone. Jolie noticed his face turning red. She flushed in embarrassment, realizing what a sight she must be. Despite all she had just been through, her stomach gave a little flutter. Has he always been this handsome?

IT WAS ALMOST Thanksgiving. Jolie let Ellie and Maddie pick out small pumpkins and colorful gourds for her mother's holiday table display as she shopped for ingredients for her famous cheese potatoes.

She tried to include Maddie in as many activities as possible because her mother did not want her and her father was now dead. Mrs. Johnson had wanted to adopt Maddie, but Cade's parents insisted upon keeping her. Now she stayed with her grieving grandparents who did very little with her except send her to daycare.

It wasn't Maddie's fault that Cade or Cory or whoever he really was had turned out to be a murderer. It turned out that his real name was Cade Bishop, after all. No one really knew why he had used the name Cory Bennett when he worked at the zoo. His parents believed it was because he didn't want to be associated with the Bishop family of Timber City, well-known for their wealth and philanthropic interests. A change of name had given him anonymity and a chance to prove himself on his own merit.

Maddie had become a somber child since losing her father and live-in nanny and moving in with his parents. Jolie felt sorry for her and invited her to go places with her and Ellie as often as she could. She also included Mrs. Johnson whenever possible. They had all become close friends. Mrs. Johnson had come along with them to the grocery store, also shopping for Thanksgiving. She expected her son and his wife and children to come for a long weekend visit.

"M'Johnson!" Maddie squealed as her former nanny came into view with her shopping cart full of groceries.

"There you are!" The older lady approached them, kissing Maddie's outstretched fingers.

"We have punkins!" Ellie exclaimed, holding out a small one. Both girls were standing in the middle of Jolie's shopping cart with pumpkins and gourds piled all around them.

"Just look at all those pumpkins!" Mrs. Johnson turned to Jolie. "Thank you for inviting me along, Jolie. I certainly enjoyed it, but I must be getting home."

"We loved having you, Mrs. Johnson. Didn't we, girls?"

"Yes!" they chimed in unison.

"Let's say goodbye," Jolie prompted.

Mrs. Johnson bent and kissed each little girl on the tops of their heads. "Be good girls, promise me. I hope to see you again very soon. Happy Thanksgiving!"

"Happy Thanksgiving!" the girls repeated as they watched her push her cart toward checkout.

Jolie checked her cart one more time to make sure she had gotten everything before having the girls sit down so she could head to checkout as well. She needed to take Maddie home so she and Ellie could get home and start getting ready for the holiday. There was laundry, housecleaning, cooking, and baking to do, but Jolie looked forward to it. She had a lot to be thankful for this year.

JAY DOZED IN the recliner as a college football game droned on television. His team was losing. He started as something plopped onto his chest. Opening his eyes a slit, he beheld his beautiful four-year-old daughter's face crinkled into a perplexed frown.

"What is it, honey?" he asked, his hands recognizing Laci's favorite doll as it rested on his chest with its hair and dress all in a tangle.

"I can't get it off!" Laci cried, her little hands in fists on her hips.

"Laci, Daddy's trying to rest," came his wife's voice, sounding like music to his starved ears. He glanced over Laci's blonde head to gaze upon the most beautiful woman he had ever seen as she stood in the doorway to the kitchen with a dish towel in her hands. He caught her eye and she blushed in response, reading the message in his eyes.

"No big deal. This crisis Daddy can fix." He picked up the doll and wiggled the dress until it slipped off. Laci clapped with glee and grabbed it from her father.

"Say thank you," Molly prompted as her daughter took off running down the hall to her room.

"Thanks, Daddy." Laci returned with a skip and puckered her lips for a kiss. Jay obliged and smacked her playfully on her bottom as she turned away. She giggled and broke into a run.

"Where's Liza?" Jay asked as Molly came closer. He pulled her down into his lap and lavished kisses all over her face and neck.

"She fell asleep watching your football game, poor thing." Jay lifted his head to glance at the couch where his baby daughter slept against the cushions with her thumb in her mouth. To him she looked like a little angel. "She never did like those teams," he said with a wry grin.

Molly wriggled from his lap and adjusted Liza so she could sleep more comfortably. The little girl stirred and sighed but did not wake up. Jay reached for Molly and pulled her back onto his lap.

"Tell me you'll never leave me again," he ordered as he kissed her neck playfully. "Tell me."

"Okay, okay, I won't ever leave you again!" Molly laughed, his newly grown beard tickling her chin.

"Never? Say never!" His kisses came faster and faster.

"Never!" Then becoming serious, she caught his face with both of her hands and gazed into his deep brown eyes, her fingers gently caressing the weather-worn lines which gave him character and took her breath away. "Never. I love you, Jay Latimer, and I will never leave you again, neither I nor the girls. We missed you too much."

Reaching up, he grasped her fingers and brought them to his lips. "I thought I would never be able to do this again." His voice had grown husky with emotion. "I thought I had lost you." Her forehead pressed to his for a moment, then his lips claimed hers. There were not enough nights left in his lifetime to show her how much she meant to him, but he would try with what he had.

"COME SIT WITH me, Toni," Kent said, patting the sofa next to him. "Don't you want to watch 'Dancing with the Stars?'"

Toni closed the blinds and turned toward Kent. She just had to check one more time to make sure that both Jay's and Molly's cars were in the driveway. She had been so happy to see Molly and the girls return home that she checked almost every day and night to make sure all was well. Jay was off tonight and he was home where he should be. She and Molly had enjoyed long visits since their return home. Toni had not realized how much she had been missing her best friend.

"Everything okay out there, Mrs. Kravitz?" Kent teased. He often called her that because she was always looking out of her window at the neighbors like Samantha and Darrin's neighbor in the old TV sitcom "Bewitched."

Toni grinned. She went over to where Kent was sitting and settled down in the crook of his arm, resting her hand on her growing tummy. She had recently discovered that by some miracle she was pregnant. After all this time, they were finally going to be parents.

Kent put his arm around his wife and kissed her cheek as he turned up the volume on the television. It was time to dance.

"SEE YOU TOMORROW, Tim," Lucas called to his new roommate as he grabbed his keys and headed out the door to go to work. Kaycie's boyfriend rolled out from under the classic Mustang he was restoring and waved with a greasy rag in his hand.

"Have a good one, Lucas."

They were sharing an older rent house a few blocks from the house that Lucas had owned with Deana. At first it had bothered him to drive in that area of town, but he had gotten used to it. Most of the memories he had of their life together were fond ones, and he chose to focus on them. He would never regret loving her the way he did, and he would honor her memory in his heart forever, in spite of the way she had betrayed him. Perhaps he had not met her needs the way he should have. He would never know, but he would not allow himself to harbor ill feelings against her.

Especially now that he and Jolie had begun to see each other. Jolie was still pretty fragile after Cade's betrayal and finding out that she had been chosen as his ultimate prize. According to the experts who had studied his journal, he had intended to kill everyone else and save her for the last. Fortunately for all of them except Kaycie and Rick and the homeless person whose body had been thrown in the alligator pond, his plans had gone awry.

Lucas handled her tenderly and carefully, allowing her to decide how close she wanted to get to him and how much of her life and heart she wanted to share. Sometimes when he called her she talked openly and for a long time; other times she was more guarded and politely excused herself after a short conversation.

They had gone out to dinner once, but she remained so guarded and uncomfortable that he had taken her home early and said goodnight without attempting to kiss her. Afterwards he second-guessed himself, wondering if she thought he was a loser for not trying harder. To his relief, she never indicated anything of the kind. After a few more dates, she had become much more relaxed with him and even welcomed his first tentative kisses. Now they could not seem to get enough kissing.

He looked forward to Thanksgiving. She had invited him to dinner at her parents' house, something he took as a sign of her acceptance and willingness to pursue a relationship. She wanted her parents to get to know him. That had to be a good thing.

ON THANKSGIVING DAY, Lucas arrived at her house a bit early. He stood on her front porch, admiring the decorative touches she had added which revealed even more about her. Several pots of bright yellow chrysanthemums interspersed with pumpkins of various sizes were arranged attractively on each side of the door. A three-foot tall scarecrow grinned crookedly over the words, "Happy Fall, Y'all." A bird feeder hung from the porch eaves opposite some wind chimes that tinkled happily in the breeze.

Jolie swung open the door, washing him in the heavenly aroma of freshly baked pies. She appeared slightly disheveled and a bit stressed out but beautiful in a simple Henley tee and jeans, her feet bare with red-tipped toes. Flour dusted the full apron she wore over her clothes.

"Lucas! Come in!" She stepped back to allow his large frame through the door. "My kitchen's a bit messy, but I need to finish the potatoes, so come on in if you think you're brave enough." She laughed as she led him through the living room to the small kitchen strewn with pots and pans and utensils. He smiled as he watched her being domestic. It was a side of her he hadn't seen yet.

"How good are you at chopping onions?" She cocked her head at him while purposely batting her eyelashes.

He grinned and moved behind her as she stood over the boiling pot of potatoes, close enough to take in the scent of her freshly washed reddish-blonde hair, which to him was more intoxicating than any of the delicious smells in her kitchen. Slipping his muscular arms around her waist, he bent his head and planted a kiss on the top of her head. She put the lid back on the pot, closed her eyes, and leaned back against him.

"Can you repeat the question?" he murmured huskily after his lips had traveled down to her neck. She smelled like flowers.

She turned around to face him and slid her arms around his neck. "What question?" she asked as she stood on tiptoe and lightly touched his well-shaped mouth with her lips.

A throaty chuckle escaped his lips as they covered her mouth. Heat began to spread throughout her body as the kiss deepened, increasing their desire to be closer. Just as he pulled her body closer, the lid on the potatoes popped up, demanding her attention as water bubbled over onto the stove burner, sounding a loud hiss.

She pushed herself away and Lucas backed up so she could tend to the potatoes. It wouldn't do for her famous cheese potatoes to burn. Even worse would be having to explain how it happened. As she lifted the lid and lowered the heat, Lucas straightened himself and took a deep breath.

How was he able to feel so strongly about another woman so soon after the loss of his wife? How could he be sure his feelings were real, and not just loneliness? How could he be sure that Jolie was not just rebounding from the betrayal of her last relationship? He noticed a bundle of green onions lying on a cutting board and picked them up.

"Are these the ones you need chopped?" His voice sounded steadier than he felt.

"Uh huh," she replied. "There's a knife over there." Her face was flushed, her lips full and red from kissing. To keep himself from grabbing her, Lucas turned his attention to the onions as he washed them in the sink.

"I'll show you how to chop onions." He grinned at her.

"Oh yeah? Are you an onion-chopping champ or something?" Jolie teased.

"You better believe it. I actually have an onion-chopping trophy from 2014." He winked.

Just then a sleepy little girl wandered into the kitchen rubbing her eyes and looking for her mother.

"Mommy?"

"Hey, Sweetheart, did you have a good nap?" Jolie wiped her hands on a dish towel and walked around the counter to pick up her daughter. Ellie rubbed her eyes and nodded.

Lucas couldn't help but remember with a pang how much he and Deana had wanted the child she was carrying. He realized that he would be reminded of her often, and that he would be sad for a long time, but the live woman and child in front of him now were the ones who mattered. They were the ones he could devote his life to now. That thought startled him a bit, but as he pondered spending his life with someone else, it seemed right to him that it would be Jolie. Peace washed over him for the first time in months. For the first time in a long time he felt as if he had purpose.

"Can you say hello to Mr. Lucas?" Jolie was saying.

"Hello, Mista Rukas," Ellie complied, eliciting a smile from Lucas. She was a cute little thing, probably the spitting image of Jolie at that age. He would have to ask to see pictures when he became more comfortable with her parents.

"LET'S GET YOU a snack, and then you can play until it is time to go to Grammy's." As Jolie got juice and peanut butter crackers for Ellie, she watched Lucas out of the corner of her eye. He had thrown a dish towel over one shoulder as he chopped the bunch of green onions into perfect little cylinders for her potato dish. He looked so natural standing there in her kitchen that it occurred to her how nice it would be for him to make that a habit. Being with him was the most natural thing in the world. She couldn't remember feeling so settled. It was something new.

Could it be that she was falling in love again, so soon after Cade? Or had her relationship with Cade been built only upon her physical attraction to his movie-star looks and his ability to charm her with his expensive clothes and flashy car? She had never felt as safe as she did with Lucas, and he was just as physically attractive, just in a more rugged, outdoorsy sort of way. God, is this where you want me to be? Is this who you want me to be with? Please help me not make the same mistakes I made with Sean and Cade. Please show me the way.

As she situated Ellie in her booster chair with a snack, she glanced up to find Lucas staring at her. His eyes crinkled as he smiled, and then he sent her stomach flip-flopping as he winked at her. Maybe it was too soon to think about settling down with him, but she was definitely going to explore the possibility. Lord willing, this Thanksgiving would begin a new chapter in her life. She returned his gaze with a smile, surprising him as a happy tear slid silently down her face.

Jolie's Soon-to-be-World-Famous Cheese Potatoes

3 pounds red potatoes, skins on

1 bunch green onions

1 lb. soft cheese product

1 pint sour cream

1 stick margarine

Cut potatoes into chunks and boil until tender. Drain and pour into 9-inch by 13-inch casserole dish. Chop/mince green onions. Combine sour cream and melted margarine. Mix in green onions, and pour mixture over potatoes. Top with thick slices of cheese. Bake at 350 degrees until cheese is melted. Enjoy!

APRIL NUNN COKER

When April read the novel Harriet the Spy by Louise Fitzhugh as an elementary school student, she felt such a strong kinship to the book's main character that she decided she wanted to become a writer.

By age 10. April was writing short stories for her friends. By age 12, she was keeping a personal diary, and by the time she was a senior in high school, she had become editor of her high school newspaper.

But her intentions to become a journalist were derailed when she felt the calling to become a schoolteacher. Many years later she retired from teaching high school English and science and running alternative school programs and now lives her dream of writing from her home in East Texas where she resides with her husband Jimmy.

April also enjoys traveling, shopping at thrift stores, and spending time with her three grandchildren.